OUTLAWS
OF
TIME

The Song of Glory and Ghost

N. D. WILSON

OUTLAWS OF TIME

The SONG of GLORY and GHOST

Illustrations by
FORREST DICKISON

KATHERINE TEGEN BOOKS
An Imprint of HarperCollins Publishers

Katherine Tegen Books is an imprint of HarperCollins Publishers.

The Outlaws of Time: The Song of Glory and Ghost
Text copyright © 2017 by N. D. Wilson
Illustration copyright ©2017 by Forrest Dickison
Library of Congress Control Number: 2016957989
ISBN 978-0-06-232729-1

Typography by Carla Weise
17 18 19 20 21 CG/LSCH 10 9 8 7 6 5 4 3 2 1
❖
First Edition

For cousins . . .
Darby, Selah, Curran, Jack, Eden, Emma,
Faith, Julia, Cooper, Adam, Sam, Finn, Livy,
Ruby, Ryder, Nava, Max, Adeline, Rory, Lucia,
Seamus, and Marisol

In memory of one who loves them all . . .
Diane Linn Garaway

JUDE'S JOURNAL #7—THIRD ENTRY OF MAY 2013

We are stuck in a time ditch. Wandering down a time stream with no way of jumping out of it to hunt the Vulture. Our current year is some version of 2013, and we are moving through it like normal humans at the standard pace of one day per day. If Peter Eagle is going to become Father Tiempo, sooner would be a lot better than later. Wherever and whenever the Vulture is now, he isn't knitting sweaters for the poor or selling cookies. He wants the world. He's attacking the world somewhere, and Sam is desperate to stop him. But like I said, we're stuck. Once or twice, Peter has moved himself and us through a little bit of time, hopping a few years back or forward, but only with great effort, many attempts, and frequent failure. He says that his older self will probably send someone to train him, but that sounds more like wishing than believing. Those days we spent complaining together in the heat of SADDYR seem like another lifetime now. I guess they are. We were hiding with Sam then. Waiting to move. Now we wander in our bus like nomads, pretending to be hunters. But our prey can move from time to time. He can journey the outer darkness between times. Sam's chances are not good . . . if chance has anything to do with it.

After Sam shot off one of the Vulture's seven watches and rescued Millie, we were all confident that the arch-outlaw could be defeated. Sam's mind seemed clear for once, his purpose certain. But how quickly that vanished. Did we even weaken the Vulture? I'm not sure we did. We stole a girl from him. We ruined one plan in one time, but many others are possible. He was patient through repeated years, and Sam wrecked that patience. He's furious, no doubt. And I'm not sure he'll ever bother with patience again. With every day that passes, I get a stronger and stronger feeling that we are moving deeper into a trap that is being constructed all around us—above and beneath, before and behind. As long as Sam is alive, he will be feared as the boy who was destined to thwart El Buitre. Even if the Vulture conquers the entire world, he still will not rest easy until Sam is ground to powder.

I am certain that the Vulture has a plan, and that it will be bloody, cruel, and effective. Just as I am certain that our plan is clumsy, slow, and hardly a plan at all. We know that six of the Vulture's time gardens remain. Six places where he can enter and

exit time as he did in San Francisco. Our grand plan
is to find one of the six, but we've had no clues to
go on, and the more Sam guesses and leads us in the
wrong direction, the more frustrated Glory becomes
and the more bored my Ranch Brothers become and
the more distant Peter becomes, wandering off on
his own without a word.

Glory has the hourglass Old Peter (Father Tiempo)
gave her. It has powers. She wants Peter to help her
learn to use it. But that just makes things worse for
Peter. I know he tries to explore time on his own,
but he hasn't even attempted to move us all since
that night the first time garden was destroyed.

The only bright spot in our days of wandering
is Sam's sister, Millie. She has appointed herself
mother of our small tribe, and she does the job well.
Whenever Sam and Glory argue, or Peter teeters on
the edge of rage, she simply begins to sing, and for
a time, things calm down.

I miss SADDYR's library of comics, so I've begun
drawing my own. Short ones. Not nearly good
enough to show the others. All of our accommodations
are rough. 2013 is unkind to a group of orphaned kids
in a crowded van, camping and cooking their way up
California. We look like thieves, and sometimes we

act like thieves (if we're hungry enough). But the police haven't nabbed any of us yet.

This morning, Flip the Lip changed the name of our tribe. We are Ranch Brothers no more. He said we are the Lost Boys, like in Peter Pan. Millie is Wendy and Peter is Peter. But our Peter is the opposite of Peter Pan. Our Peter is desperate to grow up. And soon.

JUDE'S JOURNAL #8—FIRST ENTRY OF AUGUST 2013

The Lost Boys are no longer bored. Horrible things have begun to happen in this 2013—things that never happened in this year before. Every week it seems like there's some new and unexpected disaster in the newspapers and on televisions in gas stations. Fires killed tens of thousands on one side of Chicago while a lake tsunami attacked the other. In the west, three dams blew in the same week. The news called it terrorism. They called it man-made, but then came the earthquakes. Volcanoes. Forest fires. Now people everywhere are beginning to talk about curses. Judgment. The end. In Oregon, we found whole towns left empty. I don't know where they thought they could hide, but I don't blame them for trying. Some towns were choked with smoke. Others were choked with the smell of millions of dead fish floating in poisoned lakes.

We didn't even have to try to steal our gasoline. And we didn't need to camp. Oregon was the first time we moved into abandoned houses. We're in Washington now, and compared to what we left, it still feels more normal.

All of us are sure the destruction is the Vulture's doing, but there is fierce disagreement about what we should do. Sam is sure the Vulture has at least been passing through our time stream because his broken watch chain keeps moving by itself—but Sam is the only one who has seen it. He insists we're in the correct time, and he thinks there must be a time garden in Seattle connected to a roost in one of the tallest buildings. But Glory disagrees completely. She thinks all the destruction and tragedies we've seen and heard about are the downstream consequences of the Vulture's actions and that all of this is a ripple effect from the recent past. Glory thinks he has been planting the bombs and poisons and diseases before us, in previous moments, so she wants Peter to move us all backward until we find normal ground again and hunt the

Vulture by going to one of the places where we now know he will strike and setting up an ambush. It makes some sense. She's constantly carrying her hourglass these days, because it reacts when time has been altered nearby. More than once, I've seen her snatch it from her pocket and wait, as it trembles slightly in her hand. But it never trembles for long.

The rest of us Lost Boys have looked to Peter for advice. Sam is supposed to be a hero, but he isn't really our leader. We want Peter to tell us what to do and where to go, but he stays quiet. My sleeping bag has been close to his the last several nights. When he thinks we're asleep, he either rises and slips away, or he sits up and writes pencil notes on small cards—writing, waiting, erasing, rewriting, waiting, erasing. I know he must be trying to reach his older self. I hope he isn't going mad. He's taken to wearing his red headband at all times, and his worry has aged him. Even if his time-traveling abilities haven't grown, his temper has, and he's looking more like the boy who will become Father Tiempo every day. There's a fiery strength in his eyes, even if it's hiding behind a whole lot of worry and confusion. I've been trying to draw him, but I still can't get the eyes right.

JUDE'S JOURNAL #12—FIFTH ENTRY OF AUGUST 2013

We are near the center of the trap now. Everyone can feel it. We've spent days in Seattle and the city seems normal—none of the Vulture's destruction has yet reached it. But Glory's hourglass is almost always trembling, and I spend every second waiting for the world to explode around us. All day, we wander the streets, driving in whatever direction Sam's broken watch might be pointing. At night, when Sam finally collapses, he ties his left hand up before he sleeps. The snakes are nervous. Speck buzzes at anything, but Cindy will strike. I've seen the watch rise up out of Sam's pocket while he snores, tugging at the broken gold chain he has paper-clipped to his belt loop, straining for the Vulture.

The Vulture's blow will fall. Soon.

YOU CAN'T FIND ME FROM A DREAM.

NO, BUT THEY CAN.

NOW WAKE, MIRACLE. IT'S TIME YOU MET YOUR DEATH...

PERMANENTLY.

DON'T COME NEAR ME!

!

SAM!

WAKE UP! PLEASE!

SAM!

WE HAVE TO GO!!

OW!

BAM!

PROLOGUE

GLORY SPALDING STOOD IN THE MIDDLE OF THE HIGH HILLtop street and listened to the city's Sunday noises. She was wearing tattered pale jeans tucked into short boots and a loose flannel shirt with the sleeves rolled up as high as she could make them go. A small battered binocular case was belted onto her right hip, but there were no binoculars inside. The case held pencils, a knife, a small rolled-up notebook, and an hourglass with open ends, all on a perpetually sandy bottom.

Seattle was spread out in the summer sun before Glory—towers and buildings, rows of houses, tree-covered hills, factories and streets, and where the city met the water, piers and cranes and freighters. Distant cars flowed quickly on wide, walled-in roads, too far away to hear.

But tens of thousands of voices washed up the hill in a wave from the huge football stadium between Glory and the water. The sound broke around Glory like foam and was gone. But she knew the noise-wash would return, just as soon as the crowd was again disappointed or amazed.

The day was warm, and Glory's dark ponytail was hot on the back of her neck. She pulled her hair free, gathered it up, and folded it over, binding it into a loose bundle on top of her head.

Shifting her focus away from the stadium, she turned to face the short, blocky white bus parked at the curb. It had a stubby doggish nose that reminded her of a pug's, but the body was more elephantine. An elephant might have been more reliable. But the boys from St. Anthony of the Desert Destitute Youth Ranch had managed to keep it running, and the bus had become the closest thing to a home that Glory had, and not just for her. For Sam, Peter, Millie, and the whole gang of SADDYR boys. It had even hopped out of 1960s San Francisco with them. But right now, it wasn't hopping anywhere. It was parked with its stubby nose pointed down the hill. Inside, she could see Jude—his dusty-brown curly hair in need of a cut— sitting beside an open window, writing in his journal. Or drawing pictures that he would refuse to share.

Sam Miracle was sitting cross-legged on the roof of the bus. His eyes were shut and his chin was down, touching his chest. He was wearing an old white tank top that left his scaled arms bare. The rattles on his shoulders were still, but both of his arms were twisting slowly, warm and active.

Glory stepped closer to the bus. "Sam?"

Sam didn't move, but his left arm turned toward Glory, tightening into an S, fingers limp and dangling beneath a pair of yellow eyes and scaled horns on the back of his hand. The rattle on Sam's left shoulder twitched.

"Stop it, Cindy," Glory said. "You want me to let him sleep? Too bad. Sam!" Glory whistled and clapped. Sam didn't move. But his speckled, pink right hand crossed his chest and eyed Glory alongside Cindy.

Jude stopped writing and looked out the open bus window at Glory.

"Is he dreaming up there?" Jude asked. "He's supposed to be on lookout."

Glory reached into the case on her hip and pulled out a pencil. Gripping it by the tip, she threw it up at Sam like a knife.

SAM MIRACLE WASN'T DREAMING. HE WAS SEEING. IT MIGHT feel like a dream, it might even feel like reality, but he'd gotten better at telling the difference. First, he almost always found himself acting quickly and confidently in some strange situation, but with no understanding of

3

what his plan might be. And then there were his senses. Pain was almost absent. Fatigue was more like an idea in his brain than burning acid in his muscles. And his sense of smell could be way off.

For example, Sam heard Glory whistling at him, but from very far away. He was standing in an alley at night, walled in by tall brick buildings armored with metal fire escapes and dotted with trash. It was raining. Hard. Getting in his eyes. He spat it off his lip, but the water had no taste. And while his face was wet, his bare arms were warm and dry—hot, even.

"Sam!" Glory's voice was far away, in another time. And he had other things to focus on. Three of them, actually, facing him from the mouth of the alley, lit by a buzzing tangerine streetlight, standing as still as tombstones.

Tombstones that wanted to kill him.

The Vulture stood in the middle, rain streaming off his black pointed beard, a long western coat flapping in the rain behind him like a cape, long-fingered hands poised and ready to draw his twin weapons. The shapes flanking him were harder to make out—both short, both draped in clothing even darker than the shadows.

"Don't be rude now," the Vulture said. "Aren't you going to answer the girl? Invite her to join us."

"Who?" Sam asked.

The Vulture laughed. "Your girl," he said. "The smart one. Glory. I'd be more than happy to take her heart as well as yours."

Sam rocked his head, searching for a memory. "Have we done this before? This doesn't feel like a memory. Not like all the times I tried to cross that canyon in Arizona. It's something different. But it's definitely not real."

The Vulture straightened slowly, his features rising into the light. His skeletal hands still hovered over his weapons. "Boy, this moment is very real. But don't you worry. I'll make it a memory soon." He grinned. "For one of us."

"No," Sam said. "Not real. I can't smell the trash." He looked at the wet filth that had been thrown against the walls. "And I don't remember coming here."

A pencil hit him in the left arm and then tumbled across the ground toward the Vulture. Glory's voice tumbled faintly after it.

Sam smiled. "See?" he said. "We're not really here. Glory is trying to wake me up. You know what? I think this is something that would have happened, but now it never will. It's not a past memory. It's like the ghost of a future that has been undone."

Sam's mind was working hard, straining. All his horrible phantom memories in the Arizona desert had really happened. They had all been real once, until Father

Tiempo had moved his soul back in time and turned him onto a different path to try again. But this wasn't Father Tiempo's doing. Sam hadn't been moved . . . which meant the Vulture had.

Sam laughed out loud. "Wow," he said, pointing at the Vulture. "You were going to die in this alley! I totally had you, didn't I? You're scared! This was going to happen, and now you're running! Well, you can't hide! I have your watch. I will find you, and I will end you. But you already know that, don't you?"

"Running?" The Vulture took one long step forward, spitting his words. "I am eating the whole world around you. You are no more than a worm in the apple core."

"A worm destined to kill you," Sam said. But his humor was cooling. He saw no fear in the hard lines of El Buitre's face; he saw only hate. And impatience.

"*Destined* is an awfully big word for one who has failed as often as you have, Samuel Miracle. And this moment is no ghost future." The Vulture's face twitched into a grin. "I no longer work with simple outlaws and killers as servants. I have greater hunters now. The greatest, in fact. I do hope that you like them. You'll be meeting them soon, because they have found their prey—they have found your pitiful soul for me, here, in this moment of vision. When you wake, your soul will fly back to roost in your physical body, in your physical present . . . and my hunters

6

will be on its heels. Wake, Sam." The Vulture laughed. "Wake. We've prepared you a very real and quite spectacular nightmare."

Sam shook his head. "You can't find me from a dream."

The Vulture raised his bony white hands out to the sides, gesturing to his companions.

"No, but they can," he said. "Now wake, Miracle, it's time you met death . . . permanently."

The shadow shapes that flanked the Vulture began to sway and flap forward, rippling like flags. They had feminine heads and what looked like silver skin. Their arms draped like dark wings, and their bodies weren't present in space; they were absences—holes, gashes in the air that opened on deep space—and they were slithering toward Sam.

"Sam!" Glory's voice was distant. "Wake up! Please!"

"Don't come near me!" Sam stepped back, grabbing for his guns.

But he had no guns. Speck and Cindy slapped his hands against nothing but wet jeans. The two shapes were growing as they approached. Sam wanted to run, to vanish, to wake—

"Sam!" The voice was Peter's, and yelling almost directly in his left ear. "We have to go!"

Cindy rattled and lashed out sideways.

Heat washed over Sam's body. Bright light erased the darkness and the rain and Sam was suddenly blinking in the sunlight of 2013, sitting cross-legged on the hot roof of the white bus from SADDYR, looking down at the side of a massive stadium sheltering tens of thousands of football fans and the sparkling Puget Sound beyond it.

Peter Atsa Eagle Tiempo was standing on the seat and handlebars of an old Triumph motorcycle, leaning onto the top of the bus, his hands slapping the roof in pain.

Sam's left hand had grabbed Peter by the hair, and Cindy was still rattling.

"Sorry!" Sam forced his fingers open and jerked Cindy away from Peter's head. More boys were running up the street toward the bus, a few of them whooping. "I'm sorry," Sam said again. "I really am. I was dreaming and Cindy just—"

"Doesn't matter," Peter said, but his angry eyes were locked on Cindy. "We have a bigger problem."

Sam squinted into the bright sky. "Shadow shapes?" he asked. "They could fly. And he said they could find me."

"What?" Peter shook his head. "No. Cops, Sam. We took too many hot dogs. The police are after us. Now get down and get in the bus! We gotta roll . . ."

Sam looked down at Peter and the motorcycle under

his feet. The bike had a sidecar, and it was overflowing with hot dogs in silver foil sleeves. Peter dropped back down onto the seat and started the motorcycle with one quick kick.

Laughing and whooping boys were jumping into the bus and it rocked beneath Sam as they did. Peter's eyes were focused down the hill toward the stadium. Red and blue lights were flashing. Glory was still standing in the street looking up at Sam.

Sam felt a chill march up his back. Both snakes suddenly tensed in his arms. The gold watch slid out of his pocket and tugged at its short chain, pointing straight forward.

Beneath Sam, the bus spasmed and roared to life.

Peter revved the motorcycle engine. "I'll distract them!" he yelled, clicking the bike into gear.

"No!" Sam screamed. "Wait!"

Peter looked up just as Sam jumped to his feet. A black crack unrolled in the air like a ribbon as Sam turned toward the stadium.

"You have to move us!" Sam yelled. "Right now, Peter! Now! Anywhere but here!"

The dark ribbon became a curtain, and the curtain began to open, pulled apart at the upper corners by two black, winged shapes.

At first there was only darkness. But as the tear in

the sky widened, Sam wasn't looking into nothingness, he was looking into a different *now*. Through the strange widening gateway, he could see the same water and the same ships and the same mountainous islands in the distance—but the ships were sinking and the islands were billowing black smoke and the water was churning. He could see the same stadium with the same vast parking lots full of the same cars. Outside the torn gateway, more cars shone in the sun beneath a blue sky. Inside, lava was crawling through the parking lots and every car it touched exploded.

In one present moment, seventy thousand people were cheering as men played a game with a ball.

In the other *now*, thousands of people were trampling one another, trying to escape a collapsing stadium, only to be met by lakes of liquid fire and armies of erupting cars.

While Sam and Peter and Glory all watched, the window into horror flew toward them, widening their view of the destruction as it approached. It rose up, revealing a sky black with smoke, and raced out and around them to each side.

It was coming for them. It would swallow them.

The binocular case on Glory's hip was rattling, and she pulled out the hourglass, already swirling a long tornado of ghostly sand. She swung it up against the coming change of worlds, but it was smaller than a whip against the tide.

10

"Peter!" Sam yelled. "Move us! Move us now! Somewhere! Anywhere!"

Peter closed his eyes and raised his hands.

The seething, volcanic world closed behind him like a falling curtain.

But Peter was no longer there to see it. He was in darkness, floating between times toward a strange and unknown future.

On the shaking hill where he and Glory and Sam and the bus and the boys and the motorcycle had just been, now there was only a dancing storm of sand.

Now and When

GLORY KILLED THE MOTORCYCLE'S ENGINE. BECAUSE THE old sidecar—and Peter's weight inside it—kept the bike upright, she didn't need to lower her feet. Both boots remained firmly planted on the metal pegs.

Two thousand, nine hundred, and seventy-six hours had passed for Glory Spalding since that moment in 2013 when she and the others had been ambushed by the Vulture and swallowed up by a more brutal time stream. As lava had leapt up out of city streets and volcanic ash had burned her lungs, she had looked at her watch. Moments later, when Peter had somehow managed to leap them years into that bleak future in a harsh swirl of sand, her watch had kept ticking. Since that time, although the watch was now dead, she had logged every twenty-four-hour period in the little notebook she kept with her hourglass. It had been 124 days, and now she and Peter and the idling motorcycle were finally back in time and on the same hill they had been on when the horrors had first come. But this was nothing like those awful moments.

The small white battery-powered kitchen timer that Glory kept in her binocular case was beeping quickly. She popped the bino case open, silenced the timer, restarted it for another twenty-four hours, tucked it back into the case, and pulled out her tiny green spiral notebook and a stubby pencil.

Peter sighed, shifting his weight in the sidecar.

"You missed by centuries," Glory said. "Again. Look around. I'm guessing 1850s."

One more pencil tick and the notebook rejoined the timer. The bino case snapped shut.

Day 125 had begun.

Glory rubbed her hands on her faded jeans and took in the scene around them. The air was warm and the sun bright. Clearly they had dropped in on a summer day. She didn't need the old canvas jacket she was wearing over her flannel shirt, but hopefully she would again just as soon as they moved on.

This Seattle wasn't much of a Seattle at all. The surrounding hills were a patchwork of old timber with heavily logged bald stripes. Most of the bigger buildings—warehouses and shipyards—were down by the water, but a few cockeyed and crooked wooden buildings faced one another across the wide dirt road where Sam and Glory were sitting now. Fifty feet away, a massive team of snorting horses was stamping and straining to pull a barnacle-covered ship's hull that spanned three large wagons. The rear wagon had collapsed and Glory could see the shattered bodies of two dead men pinned beneath it.

Which explained why she and Peter had ended up here. Deaths—the departures of souls—always left a hole, and it was easy for new souls to slip in.

"So . . . ," Glory said. "Try, try again? This is definitely well before the Vulture blew everything up, but I don't think we'll find him setting traps this far back."

Peter didn't answer. He was watching the street ahead of them.

Men were shouting, desperately trying to use poles to lever the ship's keel off the broken bodies. Others were fighting to calm rearing and stamping draft horses, all whinnying anger and fear. Horrified shopkeepers watched

15

from open doors and mothers in dirty petticoats gripped the hands of small children, pulling them well clear of the straining animals and the deadly landlocked vessel.

Watching clouds of soft dust swirl around black stamping hooves, Glory tightened her long dark ponytail, and then she unzipped her jacket, releasing the excess heat. In the sidecar beside her, Peter was perfectly still . . . until his fingers began to drum on the lip of the sidecar.

"Feel free to use your words," Glory said. "Just as soon as you have any. Where to now?"

A red bandana pinned Peter's dark hair back, and he was wearing an old denim jacket. When he stopped finger-drumming and dangled his arms out of the sidecar, sand hissed quietly out of his sleeves onto the ground. He turned his dark face up toward the sun and shut his eyes.

"I would like 2012," he said. "Maybe. Probably. But short distances are so hard."

Glory watched as the first of the spectators of the boat tragedy began to take notice of the motorcycle and the girl straddling it. A woman adjusted her sun hat and squinted. A sweaty barrel-shaped man with a two-gun holster and spurs began to walk toward them. His hands were too twitchy for Glory's taste. She'd seen more than enough old western gunfighters for several lifetimes.

"Girl!" the man yelled. "Did you do this?"

"We should move on," Glory said quietly.

Peter opened his eyes, focusing on the approaching man. "Is this 1884?" he asked. "I'm trying to train my time sense. This tastes a little like 1884 to me."

The man paused thirty feet away, dust settling onto his already dusty trousers. "Indian, you get out of that little locomotive and keep your hands up while you climb."

Peter ignored the man's tone and his command. "What year is it? Please."

Glory turned the key in the ignition and lifted her right foot onto the kick start.

The man squinted. "Seventy," he said. "1870."

Peter turned to Glory. "I was closer. I guessed '84, you were at '50."

Glory smiled. "And you were aiming for 2012? Some time-walker."

The man took another cautious step forward. "I'm not gonna ask you two again. That machine there shouldn't be handled by no girl, and surely no savage."

"You're right." Glory gave the man a serious nod. "So you better steer clear. You're the only savage I see. *No la toca.*"

Glory kicked the starter.

"Excuse me?" The man snorted.

Glory kicked the starter again, and this time the motorcycle roared beneath her, shivering and ready. A dozen already frightened heavy horses stamped and twisted against their harnesses. Not one of them had ever heard any engine like it. Neither had the people. Men shouted as the horses reared. The ship swayed and began to lean. Another wheel cracked loudly.

"Pete," Glory said. "Now would be a good time to move."

Peter had already raised his hands to the sky.

The barrel-chested man was drawing both of his guns.

Glory toe-clicked the bike into gear and twisted the throttle wide open. Dust rose in a rooster tail behind the rear wheel as they surged forward toward the ship and the terrified horses and the even more terrified men trying to control them.

Peter dropped his hands.

Glory shut her eyes as thousands of invisible grains of sand scraped across her cheeks. For a moment, she felt weightless, floating in darkness. And then cold air and rain replaced the warm sand on her skin. She let go of the throttle and opened her eyes on another era of Seattle, this time at night. The bike slid to a stop.

"Wrong again," Glory said.

"Nineteen fifty-two." Peter wiped rain from his face and leaned forward in the sidecar. "But I'm guessing."

"No way." Glory looked around. "I'm going 1930s."

She and Peter were in the same street on the same

hilltop, but now it was wearing shiny wet pavement reflecting old neon signs and dim golden streetlights. The road was a black garden of bouncing raindrops.

A neon motel sign buzzed above them on the left, a bright-yellow furniture-and-appliance store glowed at them on the right. The weak yellow streetlights marched away into the distance. Faintly, Glory could see the same body of water the ship had been heading for.

Steam was hissing out of bullet holes in an old-fashioned black car parked beside them. The windows were shattered and Glory could see blood on the inside of the glass. She didn't look closely. She didn't want to. She had learned over and over again, whenever Peter was practicing, that as they moved through time they would tend to settle into moments with fresh . . . vacancies. Often accidentally. Even old Father Tiempo—Peter as powerful as he would ever become—had found it easier to move into the gaps left in time by recent deaths. And Glory hated it. It made her feel like a crow. Or worse, a vulture.

"How many deaths happened on this hill?" she asked. "Are we going to drop in on all of them?"

Trying to ignore the bloody nightmare in the vehicle beside her, Glory focused on a cop car coming straight up the street toward them.

The windshield wipers were slapping madly, and the car itself was shaped like a rounded snow boot. Glory had seen old gangster movies. She'd seen cars just like it chasing mobsters before World War II.

"Darn it," Pete said. "The cars are very 1930s."

"You're making me nervous," Glory said. "I thought you were supposed to be getting better at this. Not worse. Will you even be able to get us home?"

"It's the dead," Peter said. "I can't sense the hole they leave until after we slip right in."

"I know how it works." Glory blinked away a big raindrop and then wiped her wet mouth on the back of her arm.

"Do you?" Peter asked, his jaw tightening. "You know how it works?"

Glory met his gaze and refused to blink. Even in the dark, she could see the anger in his eyes. "Of course not. You're the only one smart enough. Now put your temper away and just get us back to Sam. We never should have left him."

The cop car lurched to a stop in the street and its lights began to flash. Two cops in blue coats with shiny brass buttons climbed out, one from each side. Both policemen drew guns and aimed them at Glory and Peter over the car's open doors.

"Hands in the air!" the driver yelled.

"I don't understand why it's so hard," Glory said quietly. "Either you can move through time or you can't, right? So why can you drop us into the right five minutes sometimes and then miss whole centuries on the next try?"

She raised her hands and smiled through the rain at the policemen.

"If you can do better," Peter said, "be my guest."

"Don't be stupid," Glory said. "I'm not the one trying to grow up and be Father Time."

Peter sniffed and raised his hands once again. Both policemen stepped out from behind their car doors.

"All right!" the driver said. "Step away from the motorbike."

Peter dropped his hands.

Darkness. Weightlessness. Hissing sand.

And then the rotting stench of sulfur. Searing heat billowed around Glory. Smoke burned her nostrils and chewed its way down her throat.

Peter was coughing. Down the hill, in the ashen darkness beyond where the police car had just been, ribbons of lava leapt into the air. The football stadium was collapsing into a lake of fire.

More than 124 days had passed since Glory and Millie and Sam and Peter and all the Ranch Brothers had escaped from this exact scene of horror and destruction.

"I think we just missed us!" Peter yelled. "We can't have been gone long! The stadium hasn't collapsed yet.

21

And there's that!" He pointed at the short pencil lying in the road, the pencil Glory had thrown at Sam four months ago. Only in this moment, it had only been lying there for minutes.

Glory didn't want to think about it. Not with her eyes burning and her lungs blistering with every breath.

"Stop talking and go!" Glory yelled. "Just go!"

The binocular case on her hip began to shiver. And then two black-winged shapes descended from the ash cloud and landed in the road.

They were women. Short, but long-necked. Small, but clothed in endless shadow. Their features were sharp and silvery, reflecting the light around them. And they were smiling.

The woman on the left slid slowly forward. When she spoke, her voice was a dagger blade. "Where is Miracle?"

"Peter," Glory whispered. "Move us right now. Please."

"Wait," Peter said, and then he raised his voice. "Who are you? Do you serve the Vulture?"

Both women laughed. Behind them, a long tendril of lava snaked into the sky.

"Can death serve a single crow?" The woman on the left spread out her arms wide, draped with black shadow wings. For a moment, she was almost translucent, and then Glory saw something else. The woman was a doorway, a tunnel, and through her, Glory glimpsed the sun still shining on an undestroyed city. She was looking at a different present.

"Speak of the Miracle," the woman said, "and you may reenter the gentler side of time."

"She's lying," Peter said.

"Of course she is." Glory gripped the bike's handlebars tight. "Now get us out of here."

Peter raised his hands, and his sleeves flung sand. Both women flinched, surprised.

"Sister," said the more distant one. "They have been wandering."

Peter dropped his hands and the world around Glory warped and rippled, trying to move beneath her. For half a breath, she was gliding away, but then she crashed right back into the same moment, gasping like she'd been kicked in the stomach. Her vision blurring. Fading.

But she could see that Peter was floating in the air above the sidecar.

And the woman's silver hands stretched toward him on the end of impossibly long dark wings.

"Can he really be the priest?" she heard one ask. "So young and weak?"

"Drink the spirit he has been given," said the other. "Kill him now."

The ground shook beneath the shadow women. The street split and the women shrieked like hawks as white-hot liquid rock leapt out of the ground.

Glory shut her eyes tight, but even through her eyelids, the bright form of the lava remained, standing in the fiery form of a boy.

"Begone," said a voice of cracking stone.

And Glory was gone. In a hissing blink, with that single word the world of smoke and lava fell away like sand and she was back in the cold air of the right time, sitting on the motorcycle beside the pile of toilet paper and cans of chili she and Peter had collected before trying to secretly work on their time hopping.

But she wasn't alone.

Bull and Dog

SOME CIVILIZATIONS TAKE THOUSANDS OF YEARS TO RISE. Some take a few thieves, some stolen brides, and a couple of decades of solid brickwork. Some grow up from tribes and others from lost explorers or colonies, and some from people who simply quit walking or paddling or climbing and decided that they were too tired go farther and that this cliff face or that island or ice floe or desert was far enough, thank you very much.

Some civilizations will never die. Some are doomed as soon as the first tent is pitched. And some grow large and ancient before they rot and collapse into a thousand little tribes if they're lucky, and nothing more than swirl-ing dust if they aren't.

If you live in a nearby century, in one of a dozen dif-ferent time streams, you may have heard of a town called Seattle. You may even live in some version of Seattle now, in your immediate moment. Perhaps you know it as a beautiful city of fish and hills and airplanes and electrical magic built between vast inlets of a cold northern sea and massive snowcapped mountains and lower treed foothills. Maybe you know it as a terrible city of slavers and oppres-sion or a vibrant city of schools and libraries and churches, a rich city or a poor city, a city that loves football or a city that only plays board games. Maybe the city you know is only a great ruin by the sea.

Seattle has been a lovely place, a wild place, and a thriving, bustling metropolis that grew and grew and grew until it discovered that its beautiful mountains weren't so beautiful on the inside.

Sam Miracle knew two Seattles. First a Seattle in one 2013, full of sunshine and sea breeze and the smell of fish, thriving in places, struggling and broken in places. Sam had slept in its parks and on the roof of his bus beneath its bridges and overpasses. And then another Seattle and another 2013 had taken him. The mountains had exploded. Peaks and faces and cliffs had flown up into the sky. And while millions of tons of molten stone had been passing through the suburbs and the city and had been poured hissing into the salty sound, Peter had managed to jump them all forward another twenty-one years—as best they could tell—into 2034. But they hadn't switched time streams. The destruction remained, but it was now decades behind them.

The Seattle where Sam Miracle stood waiting for Glory and Peter to return from their motorcycle supply run had become beautiful again—in a stark and brutal way. Beautiful in the way that graveyards can be beautiful, even abandoned and overgrown. Beautiful in the way that death and resurrection always are. Beautiful in the stillness of the black volcanic rock sprawling around islands of decaying buildings still somehow upright, but edged with ferns and crowned with moss. Lush green life had erupted along the edges of every lava bed, and the mountains still smoked quietly years after their anger, even in the drizzling rain, as if commanding the city never to wake again. Never to rise.

This silent and dead Seattle was the Seattle Sam Miracle knew best. And it made his heart ache like one of the songs of death and yearning his sister sang when she was thinking about the places and people they had both lost. The ruined city plucked sorrows inside him because he knew the destruction was partly of his own making. Sam had failed to kill the Vulture, and the consequences of that failure had been raining down ever since.

Sam knew that if he had chosen to kill El Buitre instead of saving his sister, he would be full of regret, and his heart would have broken completely. Millie would be dead, Sam would hate himself, but hundreds of thousands of other people would still be alive. Cities would have continued on without any sense of how close they had come to destruction.

But that's not the choice Sam had made. He had been so sure that he could have it both ways—Millie could be saved and the Vulture killed. Why? Because that's what he wanted. But wants and wishes cannot erase choices. Sometimes a road forks, and both paths lead to pain.

Since the night old Father Tiempo had said good-bye in the parking lot of a pizza place in California, Sam Miracle had gone to sleep 274 times, always thinking of the faceless thousands who had died because of him. Glory drew a little moon in a notebook every time they all went to bed, and she dragged a slash through it every time they woke. And with every slash, Sam knew that his failure had grown by another day.

Almost half of those days had now passed in this strangely quiet place where an entire city of the west had been destroyed. How many lives were encased just in the black lava Sam could see where he was standing?

He shook the thought away and then shivered. He

didn't feel guilty for saving his sister. How could he? No, he felt guilty for failing to kill the Vulture. For failing to stop the madman before he could unleash his bitterness and violent anger on the world. With every day that passed, Sam was sure that more lives had been lost, that more destruction had been set in motion somewhere and somewhen. And every morning, Sam woke hoping that it all might end before he had to sleep again. Before the next city burned. The Vulture would show himself and Providence would give Sam one more chance to put things right.

But not today. The sun was low, the clouds were high, and while most of the wintry day had been warm enough, the air carried a damp chill on a breeze that was just strong enough to keep Sam's arms tightly crossed under his scratchy wool poncho, despite the red long johns and heavy flannel shirt he had layered beneath. His thick hair, once desert blond, had darkened in the months since he'd traveled north, and it had grown shaggy enough to make him wish for some electricity and a pair of clippers. But right now, the mop of hair was all that kept his head warm. He was wearing dusty jeans and muddy square-toed cowboy boots Millie had given him two months ago—on the day she had insisted was his birthday.

Under his poncho, he always wore a modified two-gun holster, but both of the antique revolvers he had used to face the Vulture were hidden in a sock drawer miles away, along with the last of his bullets. Ammunition, along with food and toilet paper, was quite hard to come by in the volcanic graveyard of Seattle, picked over for decades by territorial gangs and clans. Instead of the old western guns, Sam carried one small, double-stringed black crossbow with worn silver edges—a bow redesigned and repaired by the quick and certain hands of Barto, the most mechanical of the former SADDYR Ranch Brothers.

The bow dangled from Sam's right holster with strings drawn and ready. The holster on his left hip was now a quiver packed full of assorted short and viciously sharp arrows. Some Barto had collected and modified; others he had designed and crafted from scraps. Sam had practiced a great deal with his new weapon. He had even hunted with it. But he had never had to use it in a fight. And that was fine with him. At least until Sam found the Vulture. Or the Vulture found Sam.

Sam was keeping his lookout on a steep hill by the lava-rock shore of the sound, only a few hundred yards from the rusty pier where he had tied his battered metal boat. From where he stood, he could see countless ship carcasses along miles of shore, jutting up from the shallow water or partially trapped in the volcanic beds. Inland, barren rivers and lakes of black lava rock surrounded

30

green hilltop islands crowned with partially burned and rotting structures. And all around, the mountains guilty of such vast destruction were still smoking.

Out in the water, well beyond the wide metal boat he had tied to a steel pylon in the shallows of the sound, dozens of plumes of steam rose from the surface where underwater volcanic cracks lurked like monsters, waiting to ambush prey.

Sam Miracle had seen many things in his many lifetimes, but volcanoes were relatively new. And intimidating. The silent desolation all around him felt like a nightmare. And he knew all about those.

How many people in the city had survived that awful day and the days after? Where were they now, in this version of the future? In the prairie camps of Nebraska? Wyoming? Which was just another way of wondering how many people hadn't escaped. How many souls had been lost in the rock? In the water? Poisoned by the ash? Did the Vulture know? How many of the victims had he counted? And would the guilt Sam was feeling ever fade?

Sam rolled his shoulders, rattling slightly, and put those thoughts out of his mind for now. Glory and Peter were late. He pulled the gold watch with the broken chain out of his pocket and let it dangle against his leg. It didn't float, it didn't tug. The Vulture wasn't near. But it ticked.

He slid it back into his pocket and squinted down at the metal shell of a boat still bobbing in place beside the pier where they had left it. No thieves. No gangsters. Strictly seagulls. A cluster floated slowly above Sam. A few more watched him from the ground, feathers ruffling backward in the breeze.

Beneath his poncho, he slowly uncrossed his arms. Cindy resisted, trying to slip back together with Speck.

Cindy hated Seattle. Even when the sun was strong, there was too much moisture in the air, fresh from the sea. What she wanted, as much as any living creature can want anything, was the feeling of a warm rat in her belly and a hot rock to flatten herself against at the end of a long desert day. All that wanting and never getting kept her angry. She had to settle for the warmth of Sam's blood pumping beneath her own and coiling up against his belly with her pink rival on his other hand. And Cindy had never liked a crowded den, not since that day long ago when she'd wriggled alive from her mother's belly in a tangle of vicious siblings and had immediately fled while her mother fed on the dead. Now, there was no such thing as solitude. She spent all her time listening to the thoughts of the boy she was stuck to, and the muted impulses of the pink idiot who was as stuck as she was. In another life, she would have killed him.

For the last hour, she and Pink had been wound tight

around each other, against the boy's stomach, tolerably warm. But now the boy was trying to stir them both, dragging them out into the air.

Cindy felt the scales on her head plucking against Pink's.

In the darkness below the poncho, she could make out his blue-gray eyes as they passed hers.

Speck. The thought muddled its way into her head from his. *He calls me Speck.*

Cindy would have hissed, but she had no mouth. And she was being dragged out of her warm place.

Pink! she fired back. And then she tried to grab onto the other snake. Together they could fight the boy. They could stay against his belly forever.

Speck blinked, refusing to grab her back. *Idiot.* He had to hate the cold air as much as she did.

Sam dragged both arms out.

COLD. The thought flowed up from both hands, but from Sam's left hand, it blossomed like an angry curse word in his mind.

"Come on," he said out loud. "It's not bad. Just wait till Christmas up here. Then you'll feel cold."

Tugging both arms away from his body, Sam shrugged his poncho up onto his shoulders and pulled a rolled and folded comic book out of his belt with his right hand.

His sister had been thrilled to give him cowboy boots

for his birthday, but Glory Spalding had known him a little better than Millie did. She'd given him a box of ancient comics—mostly Spider-Man and Hulk—and her gift had improved absolutely everything about the last few months.

Speck, the pink rattlesnake in Sam's right arm, contracted and bent his arm into a tight S in the cool air while Sam flipped the comic open.

Cindy, the horned sidewinder in Sam's left arm, was rigid, focusing on the nearest seagull. Her rattle was silent on Sam's shoulder, which meant she was worse than angry. She wanted to hurt the gull.

Kill.

It was Cindy's favorite word, the thought that his left hand sent up into his mind more than any other. There were other impulses from the snakes that he could now understand, but only when they were intense.

"Oh, stop," Sam said. "The bird's not doing anything." He forced Cindy to help with the comic book pages while Speck flexed even harder against the cold.

"I *am* warm-blooded," Sam said, flipping to the first crudely colored page of the comic. "Which means you are, too. So relax. You won't die. You just think you will."

Spider-Man was perched high on a suspension bridge. If Sam had ever been to New York City, he might have recognized it. Mary Jane was bruised and battered and unconscious and draped safely in the superhero's arms. Without reading any of the words on the page, Sam studied the image.

Of course, he liked it. It's what a hero was supposed to do and how a hero was supposed to be.

And given that Sam Miracle was supposed to be a hero, given that he was supposed to have killed the Vulture two centuries prior to the moment he was in now and saved cities like Seattle from total annihilation at the hands of that time-spinning carrion villain, Sam didn't feel anything like Spider-Man. Maybe if the picture was of the hero dropping the girl. Or the hero perched on the bridge looking out over the smoking ruin that had once been Manhattan, now swallowed by lava.

Or maybe if the hero had hands with their own personalities that he could barely control and he was stuck guarding an empty boat in an empty city—destroyed because he had let a villain escape—while a girl who had saved him more than he had saved her was off somewhere on a motorcycle looking for food and toilet paper with another boy. If that was how the hero in the comic had been drawn, then Sam would have felt more like him. Exactly like him, in fact, even without the Spidey tights.

The seagulls still standing on the rough remnants of the street all took a few hops away.

Cindy sensed what the birds sensed. A possible

predator was coming. The boy didn't know. Pink didn't know, either, or he didn't care.

Cindy's rattle shivered slightly on Sam's left shoulder, just enough to get his attention.

Sam lowered the comic book. The animal knew something he didn't.

Where? he asked. Speck didn't seem to care about anything but the air temperature. Impulses flooded up his arm from Cindy. Sam scanned the ruin in front of him. He could feel Cindy's aggression loud and clear. He knew she wanted to frighten, to warn, to strike, but he didn't know what the threat was or where. The only way to know for sure was to let Cindy do as she pleased.

With a gun in his holster, he would have been more cautious relaxing his left arm. He never let Cindy control a weapon unless he was willing for things to die. But Cindy had no weapon to grab, not unless he was going to fight hand to hand using a short crossbow bolt like a dagger.

Sam relaxed the muscles in his left arm. For a split second, he felt Cindy's pleasure. Then his left hand snapped down to his holster and back up, twisting quickly backward and pointing a shiny, short arrow directly behind him.

"Whoa there," a man said. "No need, boy, no need."

Sam turned around, following his arm. Beside a ruined wall a dozen feet away, a scrawny man with a

36

tangled beard and an oversize hooded green raincoat stood fidgeting with a half-raised ax.

Speck was pointing now, too, but the pink snake hadn't bothered to go for the crossbow on Sam's hip. Instead, his right hand held the comic book coiled up in a tight tube.

"Move along," Sam said. "I've got nothing for you to take."

"Your hand shoots arrows?" The man laughed. "Help! Save me!"

"They could have killed you already," Sam said. "You're lucky. So just keep walking."

The man cleared his throat and shuffled nervously, glancing back over Sam's shoulder.

"That's a nice poncho you're wearing." The man's hands twisted on his ax handle as he took a step forward. "I think it might just fit me."

Sam dropped his comic book onto the ground. Instantly, Speck snatched the crossbow off his hip and began to rattle. Cindy joined in. But Speck wasn't pointing at the ax man. Sam's right arm bent his elbow backward, pointing well outside of Sam's peripheral vision.

"Boy," the ax man said, "you're twisted all in a knot."

Exhaling slowly, Sam shut his eyes and tried to quiet his mind enough to sense what his hands were seeing. Cindy was focused on the warm shape of the ax man. But

Speck had three other shapes to worry about. One small and two large.

"You brought friends," Sam said, with his eyes still closed. "The three of you can stop right there."

"Your arms," a girl said. "The way they bend . . ."

She sounded young. And horrified. Horrified was good right now. Sam needed to seem scary. Especially when he had four potential enemies and a bow that could only fire two arrows.

"They don't just bend," Sam said. "They never miss."

He opened his eyes, staring at the ax man but thinking about the shapes behind him.

"You're . . . rattling," the girl said.

Sam didn't answer. If they attacked him, running for the boat wouldn't solve anything. He couldn't leave Glory and Peter, and he had no idea how much longer they would be.

Turning slowly, Sam left Cindy behind to stare down the man with the ax, then focused his attention on Speck's three problems.

The girl had red hair in a loose curly storm around a smooth, pale face. Her eyes were the color of the sun-lit sky behind her, and she was wearing a too-large red down vest and ancient jeans tucked into high rubber boots. Most important, she was flanked by two big bearded men, obviously brothers, both wearing tattered old sweaters and pointing rifles at Sam's chest.

Sam steered Speck and his crossbow toward the man on the right.

"You can't shoot us both," the man growled.

"I don't want to shoot either of you," Sam said. "Or little Raggedy Ann in the middle. But I will."

The girl blinked slowly. "Raggedy Ann?" she asked.

"Red hair. Like the doll." Sam shook his head. "Never mind. My sister had one. In another time. Now why are these guys pointing guns at me?"

"I'm Sam," the girl said. "These two are Bull and Dog and we call that one with the ax Dice. What's going on with your arms and why are you scavenging here? This isn't your turf."

Sam Miracle grinned. "*I'm* Sam," he said. "And if you're friendly, my arms are nothing for you to worry about. I'm just waiting for some friends. I won't be here long."

The big man on the right—Dog—leaned over until his beard was in the girl's red hair. Then he whispered loudly.

"He doesn't have friends. Just wants us nervous. We should take his boat."

"I heard that," Sam said. "And it's the dumbest thing I've heard in a long time. Unless you don't like breathing."

Girl Sam took a few steps forward, crossed her arms,

and studied Sam with curious eyes, slowly taking in everything from the comic book on the ground to the old poncho to the scaled reptilian heads grown into the backs of his hands.

"You're from the comics," she said. "But for real."

Sam shrugged as both his rattles twitched. "I guess," he said.

The redhead nodded at Bull and Dog.

"Well, go ahead," she said. "Shoot him."

3

Super

INSIDE ONE HEARTBEAT, SAM FIRED HIS BOW TWICE, FEELING both triggers depress and both strings jump. Each bolt found its target before Sam could even flinch from the bullets he knew were coming.

One loud gunshot, and one big man's yelp of pain. And then nothing but the distant echo.

Sam looked up from half a crouch, unwounded. Bull was trying to tug a bent and twisted arrow out of his rifle barrel. Dog was sucking on his bloody right hand.

Girl Sam brushed back her curls. And then she smiled. Sam didn't like her smile at all. And yet part of him also liked it a lot. It reminded him of Cindy. Maybe because she had just ordered her men to kill him.

"It's hard to believe you're real. I had to check," she said. "And I didn't think you'd kill them. We aren't safe here. But you have to give us your bow and blind your snake hands or something and you can't be called Sam if you want to stay in our camp."

"I'm not doing anything to my hands," Sam said. "And I'm not going to your camp. So I guess you can keep being a Sam. You won't have to go back to Samantha."

"Samra," the girl said. "Samra Finn. And you're coming. That was pretty awesome, but your bow is empty. You don't really have a choice."

Dog spat blood and examined the gash in his hand. "Leave him. But take his boat. And we should find his storehouse. Anyone with a boat and fuel has a stash somewhere out there."

Kill. The thought flowed up Sam's left arm from Cindy. She gripped her single arrow tighter and her rattle began to quake. Obviously, the ax man was trying to sneak up on him again.

Sam spun, snapping his wrist, letting Cindy do the aiming. The arrow wobbled into a spiral and thunked into the surprised man's sternum, but with nowhere near the velocity needed to do real damage. It barely pierced his green raincoat.

"Whoa!" He plucked the arrow out and threw it on the ground.

Cindy grabbed another arrow with Sam's left hand. "I'm not going anywhere with you and neither is my boat."

Bull finally managed to twist the arrow free of his rifle barrel, and he flicked it away. "He doesn't get it," he said to Samra. "You don't get it," he said to Sam. "This isn't our patch. We're trespassing, too. And if we don't get moving soon—"

Distant gunshots echoed across the lava ruin. The sound of a racing motorcycle engine followed.

Sam and Samra, Bull and Dog and Dice all scanned the surrounding hills. At least a mile and two dark lava flows away, Sam saw the antique motorcycle and sidecar wobble down a broken street between slumping buildings and then shoot out onto lava rock. Only a girl straddled the seat, her ponytail fluttering. The sidecar looked empty.

"Who is that?" Samra asked.

"Glory," Sam said. But no Peter. He should have been in the sidecar. Bracing his crossbow between his feet, Sam reloaded quickly. Two bolts. "You should probably leave. I don't think she's going to like you."

A small rusty pickup riding high above its tires bounced out onto the rock behind the bike.

"Come on, Glory," Sam muttered. "Open that throttle up."

43

A gun fired from much closer and rock sprayed up from the street in front of Sam. Dice collapsed onto the ground beside him, unconscious and bleeding.

"Cover!" Samra yelled, but Sam grabbed her by the vest before she could dive away. The redhead whipped around, swinging at Sam's head, but Cindy grabbed her fist with Sam's left hand.

"Sidearm, bullets, backup gun, anything," Sam said. "I need whatever you have."

Another bullet exploded in the street. Rock shrapnel stung Sam's cheek as the ricochet screamed away. Samra jerked free and ducked against a low ruined wall between Bull and Dog. Sam was left alone with the body of Dice. The motorcycle was growing closer, as was the truck behind it, but Glory was outrunning her pursuer, so she could handle herself for now. Sam dropped into a crouch with his bow raised with both hands and turned in a quick circle, searching for the closer threat. He didn't see a thing, but as the bow passed over what was left of a charred building a few hundred feet down the slope, Cindy jerked it back and held it as still as stone, aiming for a dark second-story window.

Kill.

Sam waited. Cindy wasn't entirely reliable. It could be a cat. Or a dog. Or simply a person with bad enough luck to be watching.

Then Sam saw the barrel and flash and, a split second later, heard the shot as something hissed past his ear.

Cindy aimed the crossbow with his left hand, but Speck pulled the trigger. Once. Twice.

The arrows hissed away, arcing up and then dropping into the square just above where Sam had seen the flash. The shooter's gun tumbled out the window. A limp forearm dangled over the sill.

Sam holster-hooked his bow and refocused his attention on Glory. The truck was gaining on her quickly.

Samra and her bodyguards climbed cautiously back to their feet.

"Bull," Sam said, pointing at one of the big men. "Let me borrow that rifle."

"I'm Dog," the man said. "And make sure you give it back." He tossed the old gun through the air, and it landed heavily in Sam's hands.

The weight of the weapon flooded Cindy and Speck with adrenaline. The scales in Sam's arms rippled inside his long johns as he quickly inspected the old rifle. The wood stock had lost most of its varnish and the metal had lost its black, but it was clean and cared for. The rifle was an old western model with the lever action Sam had seen in every cowboy illustration he had ever studied and in the hands of friends and foes alike in Arizona, two centuries before.

Sam raised the heavy gun to his shoulder.

He held the rifle in his own way, with his left hand pressed tight against the side of the barrel, giving Cindy a clear line of sight to control his aim. Speck was more responsible with the trigger.

"We're not hurting anybody," Sam whispered to himself. "Just shake that truck off of Glory. Shoot at the tires."

The motorcycle was bouncing across the lava too slowly to outrun the truck, but the truck was bouncing too much for the man hanging out of the passenger window to get a good shot at Glory.

Holding his breath, trusting Cindy more than he liked, Sam began to squeeze the trigger.

Cindy whipped the barrel sharply to Sam's left. The butt of the gun bucked against Sam's shoulder like a stung mule, kicking to kill. His ears screamed at each other through his brain. The gunshot was louder than any he had ever heard.

One block away, Cindy's target slumped to his knees. He was big, made even bigger by a huge fur coat. He held a shotgun in his left hand, and his right was raised to throw a grenade at Sam. He fell onto his face.

Speck levered out the empty shell, and Cindy scanned for a new target.

An explosion shook the face off of an already ruined building, burying the man and his coat where they had fallen.

Senses sharpened, heart pumping, Sam spun around and focused on Glory's pursuers.

But Cindy pointed the gun at Glory.

"No!" Sam jerked Speck away from the trigger, then quickly switched hands and shoulders.

Speck grabbed the side of the gun, pressing Sam's fingertips flush against the hot barrel and taking control of the aim. Cindy waited impatiently by the trigger.

"Gotta be quick here," Sam said. "Quick."

The man in the truck fired, and Sam saw Glory wince, jerking her hand off the throttle. The motorcycle swerved dangerously.

His first target was spinning and bouncing at least half a mile away. There was a breeze. Even with Speck aiming, anything could happen taking a shot at this distance. But not taking the shot was sure to be worse.

Sam exhaled and felt his heart slow. The motorcycle veered and the truck turned, showing Sam both tires on the driver's side.

Now, Sam told his hands.

The mule kicked, levered, re-aimed, and kicked again so fast that the two gunshots blurred into one rolling boom.

Sam staggered backward in pain.

Half a mile away, the front and rear tires exploded on the driver's side of the truck at virtually the same time. The two bullet impacts and the torn skin on the backs of Sam's fingers told him that Cindy had levered in and fired a second round as fast as Sam had blinked. And Speck had kept concentration, shifting targets just as quickly. It didn't seem possible, even for them. Part of him was happy when his hands worked together so well, but it made the smarter part of him . . . nervous.

The truck tripped, heaved, and tumbled across unforgiving lava rock. The echo of crunching metal replaced the echo of gunfire. The motorcycle managed to steady and point in Sam's direction.

Dog, now on his feet, took the hot rifle from Sam's hands and studied the barrel.

"How did you sight?" he asked.

Sam held up both hands. "Ask them," he said. "Or don't. They won't tell you."

"This is bad," Bull said. "When the rest of them find out you killed one of their own." He glanced down at the truck. "They're gonna want revenge."

Sam looked at the big man and then at Samra. Her pale face was serious in the center of her red, curly halo. Dog was still staring at the snake heads on the backs of Sam's hands.

"You know," Sam said to Samra, nodding at Bull. "Your muscle here looks tougher than he talks."

Two more rusty trucks bounced out onto the distant lava field, engines roaring. Both truck beds were overflowing with men. All carrying rifles.

Bull and Dog grabbed Dice's limp arms and began to hurry away, dragging his body between them.

Samra stood right beside Sam, watching the new trouble come.

"You know the only reason we came here?" Sam asked. "Toilet paper. That's it. No other reason. At least that's what my friends told me. I'm not sure I believe them." He grimaced, rubbing his right shoulder. "I hope they actually got some." Turning, he smiled at Samra. "It was nice meeting you, Sam. Now I really need to get this boat running. We're going to be leaving in a hurry."

Samra pulled an old pistol out of her vest and pointed it at his chest.

"No." She shook her head. "You're coming with me. We need someone like you. A superhuman or whatever you are. You could change everything for us."

Sam looked at the gun barrel and then stared into Samra's eyes. Both of his rattles began to buzz and hot anger boiled up from his arms and into his skull.

"Listen to me," Sam snarled, and he checked the motorcycle's progress. Five hundred yards and entering a dip out of sight. "If you seriously think—"

Cindy interrupted him.

Kill.

Sam's left hand flashed up, jerking the gun out of

Samra's hands and swinging the butt down on top of her head. She collapsed in a pile on Sam's feet.

"Oh, gosh," Sam said. He glanced at the coming trucks, at Bull and Dog still hustling away, back at the pier where he had tied up the boat, and then down at the curly red hair hiding his boots.

"Glory, if you don't have toilet paper . . ." Sam scrunched up his face, but his anger was already completely cold. "I think I'm going to mind," he said. "A lot."

Kill.

Cindy tried to turn the gun around.

"Oh, shut up," Sam said. He whipped his left hand away, forcing his fingers open despite Cindy's anger. The gun spun over a wall and clattered to a stop out of sight. "You've done enough, you stupid horned snake. Arrows only for you."

In the distance, barely visible through the haze, a jagged ridge spat orange ribbons in a curtain of freshly molten stone.

COUGHING, GLORY WIPED HER EYES QUICKLY WITH HER left hand. The motorcycle twisted beneath her, and she slammed her hand back down to the handlebar. The awful smell of sulfur still burned in her sinuses. Smoke still haunted her lungs. Despite the cool air and the breeze, her skin still felt hot enough to blister.

Peter had been taken. Those winged things had floated him out of the sidecar while the city had puked up lava and gas and ash all around them. She had been sure they were both going to die right there, but then the bright shape had come and had thrown her forward to where that day's time misadventures had begun . . . beside the supplies she and Peter had collected.

Only now, instead of sitting quietly in a heap where she had left them, armed men had been throwing them into the back of a truck. Two more trucks had been rumbling one street away.

The surprised men had given her only seconds to recover. She'd opened up the throttle and peeled away by the time the first bullets had flown, ducking over the handlebars and hoping the sound of shots would warn Sam to get the boat ready.

How Sam had found a rifle, Glory didn't know, but she was thrilled that he had. It had to have been him. Who else could have made that shot? She even knew which hand had been aiming. Cindy would have aimed for the humans, not the truck tires.

The motorcycle settled onto a stretch of smooth rock, running up toward the crumbling buildings where Sam was supposed to be waiting. Glory glanced back at the one already crumpled truck and the two others still in pursuit, loaded with armed men. She knew she was a tough target, but some chump might still get lucky.

Digging into an inside pocket on her jacket with her left hand, Glory pulled out the hourglass Father Tiempo had given her. It was hot in her hand, and the glass had darkened to a deep sapphire blue. Peter had warned her not to use it until she could get some instruction and safe practice; he had made all sorts of horrible predictions about the kind of things that could go wrong. But Peter's older self was the one who had given it to her in the parking lot of a pizza place, with hardly any warnings at all.

Glory was completely over being shot at for the day. And she had done more than a little bit of practicing with the glass at night, when she couldn't sleep, and the moon had been her only witness.

Glory thought about what she wanted and felt the glass immediately begin to torque in her grip. Black sand trickled from one of the open ends. Following the impulse of the glass, she swung it around her head once and snapped it toward the ground. Instantly, the tailing sand became white, spreading into a smoky sheet and then rippling into a webbed shell of hot glass as thin as breath and as gapped as lace. And the strange egg grew in whichever direction the hissing hourglass went.

Inside the growing tunnel of glass, time raced but appeared normal—the motorcycle engine throbbing, shocks bouncing, tires tearing at the rough lava rock. But outside, water vapor hung motionless in the air. Flames emerged from gun barrels like snails stretching slowly from their shells in the morning. The trucks drifted over bumps like space vehicles with too little gravity.

Holding the hourglass high, Glory opened the throttle wide, racing up the slope inside her sparkling, sighing, steaming web of glass, up toward the buildings where she and Peter had left Sam. Just before she reached the top, Glory flipped the hourglass around in her hand and swung it behind her.

Cold wind hit her face as she reentered her original time stream. Behind her, as glass shattered and became sand, her time tunnel was crushed and swallowed by the time outside with a sound like wave foam sucking on the shore.

Ahead of her, with crossbow raised and eyes wide, Sam Miracle jumped back out of her way. But he didn't stay startled long. Wind snapped at his old poncho and forced its way through his thick, messy hair as he scooped an unconscious redheaded girl up off the ground and staggered forward to dump her in the sidecar. Once the girl was in, Sam hopped on the bike behind Glory.

"Her name's Samra!" Sam yelled. "Where's Peter?"

Glory didn't even try to answer. Peter's abduction terrified her. And being terrified made her angry. Being shot at made her angrier. But the fact that Sam had found the time to collect an unconscious redhead somehow trumped everything else completely.

She kicked the bike into gear and peeled out toward the ruined buildings, veering between them down the hill toward smooth dark water, a jagged pier, and the old metal boat.

Glory felt Sam rock back on the seat as she accelerated. She halfway hoped he would fall off, but his left hand slammed into her waist, gripping her tight.

"Peter was taken!" she yelled over her shoulder. "He's gone!"

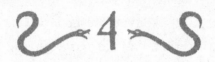

Neverland

Dark evergreen islands rose above the silver water of the Puget Sound, stark against a background of fog, steam, and smoke. Long glassy-backed waves bent and rolled behind the lonely boat.

Glory Spalding sat in the bow on the thick planks where her motorcycle had been tied down. The adrenaline of the chase was fading, but slowly. In her mind, she kept replaying her decision to use the hourglass the way she had. It was one of her closer calls in the last couple of weeks, but she still could have made it without crashing through a faster time stream. Her stomach was still

55

uneasy. Bordering on nauseous. It always was whenever she did something like that. Maybe it was nerves, fear of making some terrible mistake and ending up trapped or ancient and wrinkled. Maybe it was her worry that Peter was gone for good, that whoever—or *whatever*—had saved her hadn't done the same for him. Or maybe it was the simple and inevitable consequence of experiencing something mortals were not equipped to handle.

Or maybe it was the sea.

Glory preferred that option. She was just a touch seasick. If she did throw up, that's the only explanation Sam would be getting. The damp wind snapped Glory's dark ponytail over her shoulder and skirmished with loose strands of hair on her forehead. She traced a bullet dent on her bike's front-wheel fork, and studied the redheaded girl, unconscious on the floor beside Sam's boots.

No matter how she looked at it—at her—bringing the girl back to the island had to be a mistake.

"Did you kill her?" Glory yelled over the rumbling engine.

Sam was squinting into the wind while he steered—Speck on the throttle and Cindy on the wheel—his poncho flapping like a cape behind him. He always stood to drive the boat, even though there was a perfectly good seat. Both snakes obviously hated every minute of the cold wind and showed their hatred with twitches and ripples and shivers that ran up the visible scales on Sam's forearms. Beneath the poncho, he had pushed up his sleeves as high as they would go, and the snakes weren't happy.

"What?" Sam yelled back.

"Nothing!" Glory shook her head. It hadn't been a real question. She'd seen the girl move a few times, and not just her curls being all stupidly gorgeous and picturesque in the wind.

"What?" Sam yelled again.

"You're an idiot!" Glory shouted, smiling.

Sam smiled back. He hadn't heard.

Glory wished that she could sleep just as deeply on the bottom of the boat, but preferably without a goose egg on her skull. She wished for all sorts of things, but most especially that they could come unstuck from this ridiculously broken time and get a move on—or a move back—preferably to a time stream where El Buitre hadn't managed to blow up the majority of the Pacific Northwest.

Sam suddenly cut the engine. The wind died and the boat settled lower in the water, drifting.

"What were you saying?" Sam asked.

"Nothing," Glory said. "Keep going." She looked back toward the ruined city. More than a few pillars of steam rising up from the surface of the sound now veiled the view.

"You looked mad," Sam said. "You did the Glory-is-frustrated face."

Glory groaned and shut her eyes.

"Like that," Sam said. "Exactly."

"This day is the worst," Glory said. "Seriously. We'd have to go all the way back to Arizona and put you back in that train wreck and let the Vulture shoot up your arms to find a worse one." She opened her eyes and raised her eyebrows. "And at least then you were actually fighting him." The boat was rocking gently beneath them. Glory exhaled and put her hands on her head. Her stomach was getting vicious. Too vic—

Glory twisted and lunged for the boat rail. Her stomach emptied into the brackish water and then was suddenly calm. She rolled back around slowly.

"Are you okay?" Sam asked. "Did you eat something?"

"I'm fine," Glory said, and she wiped her mouth on the sleeve of her canvas jacket. She didn't have any better options.

"Glory?" Sam asked.

"Seasick," Glory said. "And it doesn't matter. Do you know why? You shot people today. People shot at me. Why? Were we fighting El Buitre? Did we finally find him? Did he find us? Were we doing anything important at all?"

Sam obviously knew better than to answer. Glory rose onto her knees and plunged her hand into a large green duffel bag inside the sidecar. She pulled out a flattened roll of toilet paper and held it up to Sam.

"That's why!" she said. "For this! One roll! The rest were taken. Peter is gone and we get one roll of toilet paper!"

"I'm glad you got some," Sam said. "Seriously."

Glory threw it at him and Speck snatched it out of the air, saving it from flying overboard while Glory plunged back into the bag and pulled out a yellow plastic package.

"Do you know what these are?" she asked, shaking. "Fig stinking Newtons! The rest was stolen. People tried to kill me for it. Have you ever had one? They're just dried-up fig jam inside Newtons! Why couldn't I get Oreos?"

"I don't know what a Newton is," Sam said quietly. His freckled face was blank—intentionally so, Glory knew. He was judging her but trying not to look like he was.

"Nobody knows," Glory said. "And who eats figs?" She tore the package open, plucked out a soft, cracking Newton, and threw it at Sam. Cindy caught it perfectly between Sam's forefinger and thumb, which annoyed Glory even more. Sam popped the thing into his mouth and chewed slowly. Glory could see the pleasure in his eyes, and then the panic as he tried to hide it. No way he was going to admit to liking it, not while she was being like this.

Like this? Like what? How was she being?

Glory sat down on the planks and flopped backward, looking up through a blue sky crack in the fog.

"I lost Peter in exchange for one roll of toilet paper and a package of grandma cookies while you went all caveman and knocked a girl on the head. You should have left her."

"I couldn't," Sam said. "If I'd left her there, those people chasing you would have killed her."

"Sure," Glory said. "The right thing to do is drag her back to your cave."

"Don't be stupid," Sam said.

Glory closed her eyes again.

"Why not?" she asked. "Everything else is."

"This is all about Peter," Sam said.

Glory laughed, but her tone was sharp. "Of course it is. We can't do anything without him. We're no better than driftwood."

"He's left before," Sam said. "Lots of times." He tried to think of the words Peter Eagle had used to describe his occasional departures from the island. "He goes when he has to go to become what he has to become."

Glory sat up and shook her head. "No," she said. "This was different, Sam. He didn't leave. I told you that already. Peter was *taken*."

Sam stared at her. Glory sniffed and wrapped her

60

arms around her knees. He looked back toward the black hills of Seattle.

"By those people in the trucks? Then why are we out here?" Sam asked. "Why did we leave? We have to go back."

Glory didn't respond.

Sam stepped out from behind the wheel, fists clenched. "Who took him, Glory? What aren't you telling me?"

"He wasn't taken here." Glory looked away, avoiding Sam's eyes. "We went back to the day the destruction all happened. While it was happening. We were on the hill again. These winged creatures came, and . . ." Glory shut her eyes, trying clear the images of sharp silvery faces on shadow bodies out of her mind. But they only grew brighter. "Peter was kidnapped. There was something else there, too. Something strong enough to just send me away."

"You were hunting the Vulture?" Sam asked. "Without me?"

"We didn't mean to be there," Glory said. "We didn't. Not right then."

"Glory, look at me!"

Glory did. And what she saw was exactly what she had expected. Sam's arms rippled into a pair of taut S's, ready to strike. Veins bulged out of his human skin up to the cuffs of his sleeves. His jaw muscles pulsed. His eyes

61

were hard and sharp. Soon, he would be rattling.

"We talked about this. We said no splitting up. We said I would handle things."

"*You* talked about it," Glory said. "We never agreed to anything. And we had our reasons, but they don't matter right now. What matters is that Peter is gone and we're here."

"Where did you go?" Sam asked.

"Around," Glory said. "Peter kept taking us to random years. We were trying to come back when we slipped in right after the eruptions."

"And?" Sam asked. "Was the Vulture there?"

Glory shook her head. "The creatures. They're women. Or strange copies of women. They floated Peter right out of the sidecar like a balloon. I thought we were going to die, Sam. And all of a sudden there was this thing—it was shaped like a boy, but more like a ghost of one. A fire ghost so bright I could see him through my eyelids. Next thing I know, I'm back here and getting chased. Without Peter."

She looked back into Sam's eyes. "The ghost knew what time I'd come from, Sam. He sent me right back here. But he kept Peter. At least . . . I hope he did. Whoever and whatever he is."

Glory waited. Sam's hair shifted with the breeze, but his face was stone.

"I know how you feel," he said. "You're not upset that Peter's gone. You're upset that you were left behind."

"Sam." Glory climbed to her feet. "That's not fair. Do you really want to risk your memory for nothing? Do you want the daydreams to start up again? That's how they found us in the first place, or can't you even remember that? You can't just move around through time like Peter can."

Sam nodded and returned to the wheel. "I'm sure Peter's fine," he said. "Peter always is."

"Are you sure that we're fine without him?" Glory asked. "Because last I checked we don't do much more than survive. We're stuck in the apocalypse and Peter's the only one who could ever have any chance of getting us back."

Samra groaned at Sam's feet and slowly sat up. Once upright, she brushed her hair back, wincing as she did.

"Samra," Sam growled. "Meet Glory. Glory, Samra."

Glory offered the girl a tight smile. "So," she said. "I hear you're pretty awful. If I'd been there, we never would have brought you along."

Samra looked at the quiet water around the boat, and then back at the city.

"You have to take me back." Pale-blue anger sparkled in her eyes. Her cheeks flushed and her voice jumped. "Right now! Take me back!"

"She's a sweet one," Glory said to Sam. Then she

whistled at the redhead and pointed back toward Seattle. "You're welcome to swim."

Samra managed to climb all the way to her feet, blinking in pain and cautiously feeling her head. She stood directly in front of Sam, staring straight into his eyes. He looked away. Quickly. At his feet. When he finally glanced back she was still staring.

"I know who you are," Samra said. "But I didn't think the story was real. I hoped you would help us."

"Let me guess," Sam said. "You read a big old novel about the old west where I almost kill a villain in San Francisco, but he gets away? I've read it. Once, I even liked it. But not anymore."

Glory laughed. Sam ignored her. Samra dropped her eyes to Sam's hands. Cindy twitched, and Sam shrugged his poncho down over her. As for Speck, he was twisting Sam's hand behind him, to get a better look at a seagull.

"I didn't know there was a novel," Samra said. "But I don't read those, anyway. My brother had all the comic books. And we watched the movie. Bull and Dog found it. My father has movie nights when the generator works."

"A movie?" Glory asked. "And who are Bull and Dog?"

"Comics," Sam said. "Like comics. About me?"

"The boy looked a little like you, even though he wore tights. He was better looking. Blonder. And he didn't have freckles. But the snakes in his arms"—she leaned around Sam to look at Speck "—the pink one and the horned one—they were exactly the same as yours, and just as deadly."

Sam looked at Glory. Her face had gone completely serious.

"Comics," Sam said. "Crazy. But I guess it makes sense. Jude's novel hasn't changed since we left San Francisco. I think that story is done."

"You think Jude wrote comics about us?" Glory sniffed at the cold. "Future Jude wrote the novel and Father Tiempo took it back in time to help your memory. How do you explain random comics about us showing up in destroyed Seattle?"

"I'm not trying to explain anything," Sam said. "But Jude has been working on comics. And now comics show up. I doubt it's a coincidence."

"Who's Jude?" Samra asked. She inched closer to Sam. "Is he really old? The comic books are pretty ancient. I think I have one dated 1991. And the movie is on a tape from 1986. Is Jude that old?"

"Movie," Glory replied with a flat monotone. "Right. No wonder she tried to abduct you. You're her superhero crush. We'll have to get you some tights."

"Whatever," Sam said. "We need to see these comics. They could help."

Glory raised her eyebrows. "Help? Did the book ever

help? It changed all the time and got tons of stuff wrong."

"No, we got tons of stuff wrong," Sam said. "How we lived changed what Future Jude eventually wrote. It helped us. It just didn't give instructions."

"I thought you could *help* us," Samra said. "I thought maybe the real you wasn't so . . . *bad*."

Sam flinched. "Bad?"

"Excuse me," Glory said. "What do you mean by that?"

Samra looked at Glory and then back to Sam.

"In the movie, he was an outlaw in the old west. He took whatever he wanted. He stole things. He murdered people. He destroyed whole cities working for a super-villain called the Vulture, enforcing his will, and when he finally tried to rebel against him, he was killed. It's a pretty sad movie."

"Let me guess," Glory said. "He rebelled to try to save his sister?"

"You've seen it?" Samra asked. "Or was that real?"

"Close enough," Glory said. "About the sister, at least. She's still saved."

"Close enough? I'm not dead. How is that close enough?" Sam said. "And I never worked for the Vulture. Never. Not in any life."

"You don't know that," Glory said quietly. "We don't know how far back this time stream goes. Two hundred and fifty years back from right here, Sam Miracle could have easily made a bunch of terrible life choices and gone to work for the Vulture."

Sam shot her a look straight from Cindy's mood. "No. Don't talk like that."

"So the Vulture is real, too?" Samra asked.

Glory nodded. "El Buitre. Yeah, he's real. Real enough to burn and flatten your version of Seattle."

"What do you mean?" Samra asked. "My version?"

"What I mean," Glory said, "is that there is at least one other version of Seattle that has not been blown up and flattened. We were there. This version swallowed us up right when everything was going boom."

Samra's eyebrows lowered and her head tipped, dubious. "But all the eruptions were twenty-one years ago. I wasn't even born yet."

"We hopped forward. If we hadn't, we'd be ash." Glory laughed at Samra's suspicion. "If you've read stories of us in the old west, you should already know we get around."

"The comic books aren't set in the west," Samra said. "They're from the time of tall shining cities, when my dad was young. Before the floods and the shaking and the volcanoes."

"We're taking her back," Sam said. He turned the old rusty key in the ignition and the engine gargled.

"We can't go back," Glory said. "It's already late."

Samra looked concerned. "I changed my mind. I

don't want to go back. Not right now. I want you to show me the other times. Take me with you. But not into the future. Show me the past."

"No," Sam said. "Even if we could, we wouldn't. And we can't. Tomorrow we're taking you back. And you're showing me those comics."

"But I thought you just said . . ." Samra looked from Sam to Glory. "And in the comics . . . So why can't you move through time?"

"Why can't you?" Sam asked.

The engine roared. Glory smiled, shrugged at Samra, and dropped back down onto the planks.

"Wait!" Samra yelled. "If you're here, is the Vulture here, too?"

"If he is," Sam yelled back, "I'm going to end him. Now hold on!"

As the boat surged forward, Samra grabbed onto the side, but her eyes stayed locked on Sam from inside her whirling cloud of red hair. Samra focused less on the snake heads protruding from the backs of Sam's hands and more on the boy who controlled them. In her life, the most amazing things she had ever seen were all left-overs from another time—magical black panels that quietly made electricity from the sun; an escalator in a collapsing building that had suddenly jerked to life and moved ten feet when her father had fired up an old backup generator; movies and pictures that showed her the time before, when all of those things and hundreds more had been as normal to kids as a campfire and scavenging was to her. She had spent her entire life believing in things that she would never see, dreaming of them, yearning to see them. But despite the fact that she believed in things as crazy as elevators and smartphones and credit cards and schools, she had never once believed in Sam Miracle.

Yes, she had imagined her arms with scales and extra joints. She had wondered what it would be like to have a different mind in each hand. At night, she shut her eyes and held out her arms, wandering her father's camp by memory but pretending that her hands could see in the dark and were guiding her. She had read more Sam Miracle comics than the stories of any other hero, and she had decided that she had no desire to be Sam or even someone like him.

No, she would rather be the girl, Glory—guiding the hero, motivating the hero, saving the hero. She was always with him, always at the heart of the adventure, the only one who seemed to understand the complexity of the Vulture's plans and the depravity of his evil agents and henchmen. Glory got to do all that and walk through time wielding a sandy crystal blade sharp enough to sever reality itself.

But if this girl was the real Glory, she didn't seem to

appreciate the incredibleness of her situation. The dark-haired girl was just trying to sleep in the boat. Could she really be that bored with who she was? With who Sam was? How could she sleep after a chase like she'd had? After Sam had saved her like that? If Samra had been in the story instead of Glory, she would have been alert, commanding, standing near Sam with a weapon in her hand so that the artist could fit her in the same picture with him.

She would have kissed him. Maybe. Or at least held his hand. Well . . . maybe not. The real snakes were a bit more unnerving than the drawings. Her gaze bounced down to the yellow eyes above the knuckles on Sam's left hand and below the two snaky horns.

Cindy. In the comics, the snake's thoughts would float out in space by Sam's head, written in italics.

Kill.

Samra wondered if that's what the snake was telling him to do right now. Was Sam thinking about killing her? Were his hands asking permission like she had seen them ask when facing goons on cartoony rooftops and bridges, when facing down monsters in cellars and dungeons and alleys?

For the first time, Samra looked away. Sam's hands might not like her yet, but that didn't matter. She would find a way to keep them. On what should have been a long wearisome day of scavenging, she had met an impossible boy. A miracle. And no matter what, he was not going to slip away. Glory was another story . . . unless she became more interesting. And soon.

Samra carefully reached into her puffy vest and felt for the dense little brick of coiled wires and duct tape and old rechargeable batteries that were more valuable to her father even than his spiked beard or his favorite shotgun. She flipped a crude switch on the side, and she knew that far away, in her father's pocket, a tiny red light would soon be blinking.

Another hour passed, too loud for conversation, as Sam steered the boat through inlets and channels and island chains that he was only just beginning to remember. He would have been happier if Glory hadn't curled up inside her oversize jacket and tried to sleep, because he never knew when he might suddenly forget something, anything. He was fully capable of blacking out and imagining himself—or remembering himself—somewhere and somewhen else completely. It didn't happen often; the incidents usually only happened when he was bored or doing something monotonous—like standing in a boat for an hour listening to the engine's constant whining. But they did happen. And when they did, he tried his best to keep any of the others from noticing. The Vulture had found them through one of those daydreams. They

71

were stuck in a destroyed ruin because of one of those daydreams. He'd be happy to never have another one.

Steering the boat, he was more likely to misremember an island than he was to suddenly believe himself to be standing on a train platform in Arizona two centuries ago, but he didn't want to make any mistakes at all. He didn't want to justify Glory's decision to leave him behind and explore with Peter. And he didn't want to look like a moron in front of the . . . new guest.

Samra followed Glory's example and went to sleep, curled up in the bottom of the boat, and Sam was left alone to watch the water crease in the wind and sea hawks dive after fish. He thought about waking the girls when he saw the distant dorsals of what was likely a pod of killer whales, but he didn't. He focused on finding his way home, and his memory didn't betray him.

The island wasn't entirely evergreen. Oranges and reds and yellows doubled their colors in their reflections on the water as Sam guided the boat toward the mouth of the little island harbor and throttled back. As the engine quieted, he heard laughter and shouting, and he smelled the smoke of a wood fire and the too-familiar scent of grilled fish.

The place was shaped like a crescent moon, if the two tips of a crescent moon ever stretched out almost to touching while still leaving the center empty. Sam and the boat crawled through the shallow mouth and drifted into the small central harbor that held three docks, two boathouses, a waterslide, a waterfall, a fuel tank with pumping station, a torn but still floating trampoline, and perfectly smooth black water.

Above the harbor, imitating the curve of the island, a thirty-thousand-square-foot home of glass and chrome and white leather and gray marble made the place complete. On one end, the mansion had its own power station that no one knew how to run. On the other end, it had a heated indoor swimming pool which was no longer heated or suitable for swimming, having grown itself a thick pool-cover of algae and then dried up. Now it looked like a huge green carpeted hole in the floor.

In between the power station and the dead pool, thirteen boys and two girls had made a home—or at least they had all staked out various claims on various rooms and corners, cooking by firelight, but eating with silver utensils and sleeping on silk sheets.

Sam and Glory docked the boat and led Samra up a wide flight of stone stairs between low walls overgrown with moss and ferns, to the mostly glass entrance to the mostly glass mansion. Sam pulled the wide, heavy door open and stepped to the side, letting the girls enter first. When he followed, the door crawled shut behind him on its own.

The floors were marble. The couches were leather, and thick wooly rugs softened the floors in front of them. A glossy concrete fireplace the size of a small garage held a crackling fire, and six or seven large fish sizzled above it, spread out over a makeshift grill that looked like it had once been part of a metal fence.

The kitchen was vast and steely, a blend of a science fiction laboratory and a Boy Scout campground. The polished white counters looked sterile enough for surgery, but a large plastic trash can was perched beside the sink with a makeshift water spigot screwed into its base. Fish spines and tails were piled on a thick slab cutting board beside a knife gunked with blood and scales. Kindling firewood was stacked up tight between the counter and the cabinet.

Glory crossed the room and stood at the wall of windows that overlooked the silver water and a dozen neighboring islands.

Sam stood beside her at the window, rubbing his left shoulder and grimacing. He was sore from the rifle kick.

"Where's Millie?" Glory asked.

Sam shrugged. How would he know? Millie was probably peeling potatoes outside or searching for spices or washing clothes. His sister was different from the rest of them, always restless without some kind of work. And thank goodness for that, or the Lost Boys wouldn't have eaten most days.

"I'm going to find her," Glory said. "You got the prisoner?"

"She's not a prisoner," Sam said.

"Right," Glory said, backing toward a wide hallway. "She's a big fan of yours. I forgot."

Sam smiled back over his shoulder at Glory. "Just like you were."

Glory vanished into the hall. "That was before I really knew you, Sam Miracle! Not anymore!"

Sam turned back to the window and Samra stepped up beside him on his left.

"Is she the real Glory?" she asked.

Sam glanced at her in surprise.

"I thought so," Samra said. "She's in the movie, too. And the comics."

"Really?" Sam asked. "Well, don't tell her that. She doesn't need to feel famous."

He was expecting a laugh, or at least a smile, but Samra remained perfectly serious.

"You shouldn't trust her," Samra said. "I hope you don't."

Sam tensed. "You better watch what you say. Glory is one of the only people in this world that I do trust. I would be bones in the desert without her."

Samra turned and faced Sam. He refused to give her so much as a glance. After a long moment, she leaned in closer, aiming quiet words up at his ear.

"She is the one who kills you," she said. "In the movie and in the final comic. She loves you and is very sad about it, but she does it to save the world from you. So that she can have more control of the future."

Despite himself, Sam's mouth fell all the way open, but no words came out. He closed it again and focused on the water.

Samra inched even closer and Cindy tightened in Sam's left arm.

"Just be careful," she said, touching his elbow.

Sam's arm jumped, shoving the girl away from him, sending her staggering backward.

"I think you're lying." Sam stared at the girl, noting the fear that flashed in her eyes, and how quickly it vanished and was replaced by disappointment. "I think you're trying to mess with my head. Believe me, I have a lot of experience with that. I know what it feels like. And even if you are telling the truth, movies are made up. And comics? Well, obviously. The story I live is the only story that really matters, do you hear me? Not what other people say about me. Not even people who think they know me. Anybody can call me a villain. I don't care. As long as they're wrong. And anybody who calls Glory a villain is an idiot or a liar."

A cowbell began to clatter and echo through the

house. Shouting voices and thumping feet responded, growing louder and louder until eleven boys slid into the living room. Boys were battling with Ping-Pong paddles and boys were racing piggyback. One was dragged across the marble floor on a soft fuzzy blanket before being flung forward, spinning all the way into the kitchen.

Sam laughed, finally turning away from the window in time to watch his sister, Millicent Miracle, walk into the room beating the cowbell with a wooden spoon. Her long blond hair was in a thick braid down her back, and she was wearing an apron over one of the many dresses she had accumulated on explorations of neighboring island houses. This one was red-and-black flannel with a high belted waist and short sleeves. Millie wore it with cowgirl boots that had come from the same massive closet as the pair she had given Sam.

Millie's eyes widened when she noticed Samra, and she threw Sam a curious look before changing course and approaching them both with a smile.

"This is Samra Finn," Sam said. "Samra, this is my sister, Millicent Miracle."

"Millie, please! Lovely to meet you," Millie said, extending her hand. "Welcome to Neverland. I hope you like fish."

"Fish is fine," Samra said. "Call me Sam."

"Really? I don't think I will." Millie smiled, guiding

the girl toward the kitchen, now overflowing with boys.

Sam didn't see Glory anywhere. There were times when she hated a carefree crowd more than anything. If that meant she ate cold leftovers, so be it. Sam followed his sister toward his rowdy Ranch Brothers, gathered but not yet silent enough to listen to Millie's evening supper instructions.

Through the windows, he didn't see three boats cruising in a distant channel miles away. He didn't see the boats carving slow arrows in the water as they traced an invisible signal.

Moving through dark air and darker water, ignoring the cold spray, standing in the prow of his ship with two shotguns on his back and five thick red spikes in his beard dripping salt water, an enormous man held a duct-taped box with an antenna in his enormous hand. The box clicked against his palm, and a red light blinked.

His name was Leviathan Finn, and some fool had taken his daughter.

5

Dreamers

Neverland was not a democracy. It was a monarchy, and it was run by Millicent Miracle—queen and cook. She had a clear set of rules, which had grown quite a bit and was bound to grow more. Jude had written them down with a fat black marker on the white inside of a roll of old Christmas wrapping paper. He had done it as a joke, but Millie had thanked him seriously, given him a bran muffin—freshly baked, with butter and honey—and had hung them prominently on the kitchen wall with the roll of wrapping paper still on the floor below. When more rules were needed, they would be added. For now, they were as follows:

MILLIE'S LAWS OF NEVERLAND AND HEREAFTER
violators will be gravely punished
No knife Fights
No knife games
No firing Guns (unless on the range and with Peter's
permission.) ← Or Sam's
No gambling
No boting Alone
No Smoking in the house (also, no smoking out of the
house)
No steeling Food
No biting fingernails in the Kitchen
No spitting in the House
No dead Animals in the house (unless they are dinner)
Always Bathe before bathing is needed (with soap)
Always Listen to Millie
Do whatever Millie asks quickly and without
complaining
No breaking windows

Violators *were* gravely punished, even if their spe-
cific crime had not yet been banned and written on the
wrapping paper scroll. First, they were denied Millie's
goodwill. Depending on the gravity of the offense, she no
longer smiled at them, she no longer spoke their names,

she no longer fed them, and she had been known to go so far as to confiscate blankets and force boys to sleep outside in the rain. When the violators managed to do sufficient—and always unspecified—penance, they were welcomed back into Millie's fold with a stern warning, a smile, the sound of their names spoken nicely, and freshly baked goods when available.

The Lost Boys all loved and feared Millicent Miracle. Which Sam appreciated, because his sister kept them busy with assigned chores and jobs that would have sent them into fits of moaning coming from anyone else. The boys were always collecting eggs from the chickens they had brought to the island; milking Neverland's two goats and one cow; tending to the beehives Millie had collected; making candles; churning butter; cleaning fish; clearing brush or felling dead trees and sawing, splitting, and stacking firewood; tilling a new garden or tilling another new garden or winterizing and prepping the old gardens.

Millie Miracle was a girl who didn't even know how to be dependent on grocery stores. For her, the future they had been swept into was simple and overflowing with opportunity. She was a girl who had lived without electricity for years, who had survived winters in West Virginia on pickled watermelon rinds and bone soup with shoe leather. She knew exactly how far away death was when the meals stopped—especially in winter—and she pushed that danger farther and farther away from Neverland with every shelf she loaded with jam jars and jerky and smoked fish. She was tough. She was firm. And she was happy. Which meant she frequently sang while she worked, and every boy within earshot went quiet when she did. Under Millie's government, the boys worked harder than they had ever worked at SADDYR. And they even liked it.

While the boys spent their days working, Sam and Peter and Glory hoped, hunted, explored, searched, guessed, and—so far—failed to find any hint as to where an entrance to a time garden might be, or where El Buitre might be hiding. Although *hiding* didn't seem to describe what he was doing. The time-walking arch-outlaw, with his six remaining gold-and-pearl pocket watches, may not have shown himself, but Sam knew that he was stuck in the time stream the Vulture had chosen for him, along with Glory and Millie and the Lost Boys. Even if he wasn't exactly where the Vulture wanted him, he was generally *when* the Vulture wanted him. Which made him feel powerless. And the fact that Peter had not been able to find his way into any future without a desolate and destroyed Seattle made Sam feel even worse.

No part of Sam regretted saving Millie. But Millie regretted having been saved, and Sam knew it, even though she would never express anything but gratitude to Sam. More than once, he'd seen his sister cry, looking at the ruined city, and he knew that she was wishing that Sam had chosen to save the world instead of her. And he knew why she never wanted to leave the house and bear witness to the destruction.

In the kitchen, Sam watched his sister introduce Samra to each of the Lost Boys in turn. Drew Dill was the strongest of the boys, and he looked it. Built like a guard dog, and with the same personality, he had dark skin and a shaved head, and arms that seemed to get thicker daily. He was missing most of his left pinkie because he'd chopped it off on a dare long ago, but despite his sometimes unreasonable toughness he had a bright smile that lasted for hours whenever Millie asked him to do something because it was too hard for the others. He wore a wide belt full of knives, and his hands were always resting on the handles.

"Which gang is yours?" Drew asked. "Cannibals? Pirates? Raiders?"

"Hush, Drew," Millie said. "Manners."

Drew nodded, but resting his four-and-half-fingered left hand on a bone knife handle, he looked Samra up and down. His loyalties were clear.

Millie dragged Samra on to four boys in a single cluster—all of whom *were* clearly impressed with the redhead. Jimmy and Johnny Z, twins and redheads themselves, were small and silent but always ready for a brawl and the most likely to be banished by Millie for playing knife games. They both blinked and blushed themselves sunburned when faced with the strange new girl of their own complexion.

"Hey," Jimmy said, chin down, rubbing his own matted red hair.

Johnny watched his shuffling feet and didn't bother saying anything at all.

Matt Cat and Sir Thomas had been fighting over a wooden puzzle game, but now they stood grinning, side by side. Matt Cat had a round biscuit face with blond hair perched on top like a pat of butter. Sir Thomas had a face as sharply creased as a paper airplane, and the elbow he popped into Matt Cat's ribs was even sharper.

"Miss," Sir Thomas said, pulling his elbow out of Matt's ribs and bowing with a smile. "Welcome. If you need anything at all—"

"Idiot," Matt grunted. He tugged the puzzle away from Thomas, and then he focused on Samra, lifting his heavy cheeks with an overdone smile. "Did they blindfold you on the way, or are you now capable of revealing our island to the marauder of your choice?"

"Oh, stop." Millie laughed, steering Samra to the next four boys. "Ignore him. They're all just protective of Sam. Now this is Bartholomew," Millie said. "Barto can fix absolutely anything."

84

Barto, tall with brown hair in need of cutting and a pair of rewired glasses, nodded slightly. He pulled a tangle of wire and a pair of pliers out of his pocket, then handed the wire to Samra. Across the kitchen, Sam could see her surprise as she realized that the tangle was actually the intricate outline of a galloping horse. She tried to hand it back, but Barto shook his head, playing it cool.

"What's in your pocket?" he asked, pointing at her vest. "It's heavy. Did they let you keep a gun?"

"No!" Samra said, blushing. "Do I need one?"

Millie stepped quickly between them, redirecting Samra's attention to a broad boy her own height who was all smiles.

"This is Filipe," Millie said. "But we call him Flip."

"Flip the Lip," Flip said. He pointed at his lower lip. "Because I chew it whenever my mouth isn't doing anything. So I talk a lot when I don't have gum. Keeps my jaw busy. And I'm the island wrestling champion."

"Only in his weight class. Which is above mine." A thin boy with long legs and sharp sparkling eyes stepped forward.

"This is Jude," Millie said. "Our historian, storyteller, and comic book artist." Jude had curly brown hair and a notebook and pencil in his hands—both crisscrossed with ugly scars. He saluted with his pencil as Millie tried to move on.

"Wait," Samra said, pulling back to Jude. "You draw comics?"

Jude nodded.

"What about?"

"Things," Jude said. "Things I dream. Things Sam dreams."

"Real things?" Samra asked.

"Sometimes," Jude said. "I think all of them might be real. Somewhere. In different times. Ghost memories from other lives."

"All right," Millie said. "Enough of that." Sam could hear the tension in his sister's voice, and the room grew quiet. She didn't care for the dreams and whispers of her many other endings. And Sam didn't blame her. She had never told him everything she remembered, but he'd seen the graveyard half filled with stones bearing her name. Millie was living the only version of her life that had ever worked out. Of course, so was he.

Millie pointed to the last pair of sharp-eyed, lean boys—Simon, with thick black hair, flattened on one side and fluffed in the back, a style only a mattress can achieve, and Tiago, with a tight, short Mohawk, an old gash on his nose, and two impressive black eyes.

"Simon Zeal and Tiago Lopez are our best hunters, but I won't be happy until they bring me *live* pigs, not dead ones. *And* build me a pen." Both boys wore shirts and pants, heavily pocketed. Neither smiled as Samra nodded at them. They were studying her like they might study a trap.

Tiago squinted his bruised eyes. "How many men in your gang?" he asked.

"More than are in yours," Samra said. "You're all boys."

Simon snorted. "You think we can't kill men?"

Tiago stepped forward, but Millie raised both of her hands and overwhelmed the potential conflict with dining instructions. Then, after offering up old-fashioned thanks for another evening meal, she released the pack. Potato soup was hanging in a pot over a fire in the courtyard. Fish was hot and ready on the fireplace grill. Butter and vinegar and sea-salt beans were in a strainer in the sink. And she had hidden away stewed cinnamon apples for dessert. The boys all whooped, collecting plates and bowls, but Sam hung back, waiting for Glory to show up. He wasn't in a crowd mood, either.

Glory stepped out of the hallway. Her face was pale.

"You hungry?" Sam asked.

Glory shook her head. "Feeling sick. Thinking about Peter."

"He knows where we are," Sam said.

"Not if he's dead," Glory said.

"Not if who is dead?" Millie stepped in close to Sam, handing him a plate of beans. "Peter?" she whispered.

"You said he was exploring on his own. Why would he be dead?"

"He wouldn't be," Sam said. "He isn't."

Glory shut her eyes and exhaled. "I'm going to bed." Slowly, she turned around. "Dream tonight, Sam. Make it a good one. Find out something. Anything."

Millie and Sam watched her make her way down the hall and climb the stairs.

"That's not good," Millie said.

"She'll be fine as soon as Peter comes back," Sam said. "She's just hurt that he left her behind with the chumps."

Sam felt Millie's eyes on him, and he knew her judgment without her needing to say a word. And he was pretty sure she would know that he was lying about . . . no, *downplaying* . . . Glory's version of what had happened. But what good would it do to tell everyone that Peter had been last seen floating helplessly in the air toward two shadow demons about twenty-one years ago?

"You know what I think?" Millie said. "I think my brother Sam is jealous of what Glory and Peter have. I think you're the one who's hurt when they leave you behind to test time."

Sam finally met his sister's look. She was smiling.

"They told you they do that?" Sam asked. "How often do they go?"

Millie backed away. "Eat," she said, pointing to the

plate she'd put in his hands.

Sam looked down and back up at his sister. "It's just old green beans."

"You're welcome." Millie laughed, turning away. "Get in line and get your own food."

SAM'S BED WAS A WEB HAMMOCK STRUNG BETWEEN A DEEP shelf full of dusty, old vinyl records and a window in the corner of what had once been someone's den. He had chosen it because of the western view over the water, and he was most relaxed rocking himself to sleep while watching the moon set. Glory had wanted Peter to make him Navajo charms to protect his dreams from the Vulture's flying watchers. Peter had refused. But he had chosen a heavy rounded rock from the shore and had told Sam to hold it in his hands or let it rest on his belly while he slept. The spirit, he said, can be anchored and kept from wandering too far from the body, although not always.

Tonight, Sam's anchor was on the bookshelf. His foot was on the wall beside the window, and his head was propped up on a pillow, facing the moon. Speck and his right hand wandered the hammock freely, but Cindy and his left hand were bungeed tight to his side.

Sam shared the room with Jude and Drew Dill, and as he rocked slowly, he listened to Jude writing in his journal and Drew dream-breathing like he was in a fight.

89

Sam twisted in his hammock until he could see Jude, writing by low lantern light.

"Read it to me," Sam said.

Jude looked up. After a moment, he shook his head.

"Please," Sam said. "Why not?"

Jude looked at the journal on his lap, and then back at Sam. "Are you sure?" he asked. "I don't want you to get upset. The truth can be hard."

"I'm used to hard," Sam said. "Or don't you know that?"

Jude didn't answer. Instead, he flipped back a page in his journal, sniffed, cleared his throat, and began to read, quietly and quickly.

"'Jude's journal number thirty-seven—fifth entry of November After Destruction 2034 (approx). Still in Neverland. Peter is missing. Sam and Glory returned from a scavenging run without him, but they brought back a girl from one of the scavenger gangs. I don't know why. The boys are all nervous, but pretending like Peter will be fine. Sam and Glory aren't sharing what happened. The girl has read Sam Miracle comic books that I may have written, or that I may one day write . . . in one stream of history or another. She says they are old. I'd like to see them, but I don't think I should. If I am going to draw comics someday, based on what Sam and Glory have yet to do, they should be based on reality, not an echo of some other version that may or may not be real in another time. Millie is trying hard to replace the sun with her mood in this cold weather. But her heart is always heavy and always will be. Millions of people have suffered and died in millions of moments. And all because Sam chose to save her. And for all the times Sam has resolved to do everything he can to set things right, he can't stop a villain he can't find. He had his chance in San Francisco. There are no guarantees that he will ever have another one. Right now, the Vulture is the only one who could choose when to face Sam. All he needs to do is show himself and Sam will come running with his two guns and his last ten bullets and a handcrafted crossbow. Then this could all be over, one way or another, and if Sam fails and another million people die, at least Sam will be dead for good, too, and he probably won't feel nearly as sick about it all as he does now. Of course, I think the Vulture will never live openly again, unsure of when Sam might attack. Maybe he is waiting for Sam to die. Maybe he is trying to trap Sam in a dead time. Maybe he is simply waiting for Sam to stop hiding and show himself.'"

"But I have shown myself," Sam muttered. "I've been all over this place. I haven't been hiding." He stopped rocking his hammock. The Vulture and his floating watches loomed in his mind.

Kill. Cindy tingled the thought up his left arm like an

itch. Her rattle twitched and Sam's fingers splayed.

Yes. Speck's agreement was less itchy in Sam's right arm, but just as firm.

"That's all I've written so far today," Jude said. "I'm sorry."

"Don't be," Sam said. "I will kill the Vulture. I will. You know that."

Jude cleared his throat. "I don't know anything, Sam. Not anymore."

"But you think I could draw him out?" Sam asked.

"Maybe," said Jude. "And maybe he's just waiting for the moment he wants. But trying to draw him out could be dangerous. Are you ready to lose people this time? We could all die. We know that. Millie could die. She knows that. Do you?"

Sam didn't answer. Twisting away from Jude in his hammock, he looked out the window and yawned. Tugging Speck out from beneath his pillow, he plunged his right hand into his pocket, clenching the cold gold watch he'd taken from the Vulture.

Sleeping Drew gasped and then exhaled slowly. Jude's pencil once again began to scratch on paper.

Sam shut his eyes and felt the watch. He focused on picturing the Vulture's face, on his pointed beard and hooded eyes and floating gold chains. He heard train wheels scream and felt the heat of the Arizona desert on his skin.

92

"Come on," Sam whispered. "I know I can find you."

Sam's soul slipped far from the island. His mind shifted.

Sam dreamed, but at first his dreams consisted of nothing more than Glory showing him all the bodies of Father Tiempo turning to ash by the train wreck in Arizona and telling him that every single Peter was dead and that she was going to go explore death with him now and that Sam wasn't allowed to come because he would only slow them down and death would mess with his memories and make him dumber than he already was. Sam argued and argued, but words poured silently from his mouth. Glory and Peter were leaving him. They were gone, nothing more than clouds of ash rolling away in front of the wind. He was alone, in the desert, with Cindy and Speck twisting angrily in his arms. He had no weapons, but Speck was holding something smooth and cold and alive, something strong, pulling him like the needle in a compass pulls north.

Sam turned in place, following the pull, desert rocks dreamily soft beneath his boots. A sky full of darkness was swallowing the horizon, rolling toward Sam like a breaker toward a grain of sand. The watch pulled him toward it. Sam locked his knees and leaned back, but his dream boots wouldn't grip the earth. Saguaro cacti swayed around him in a sucking wind. Dust rolled toward the darkness around his legs.

Speck was taut, extending Sam's right arm like timber. The broken watch chain hummed in the air, pointing out between Sam's knuckles at the heart of the storm. Cindy folded his left arm high and tight up against Sam's shoulder, afraid, ready to strike, shivering her rattle on his shoulder.

"Is he in there?" Sam asked his hands. He looked down the watch chain like a pointing gun. "Will this take me to him?"

Yee naaldlooshii, Cindy hissed. And in his dream, Sam heard the words aloud. He looked at the horned snake with the yellow eyes on the back of his hand.

"I don't know what that means," Sam said.

Yee, Cindy hissed, tightening her coil, *naaldlooshii.*

A wolf loped past Sam, barely touching the ground, vanishing quickly into the storm. It was followed by the twisted and rotten form of a deer with one antler. Then a mountain cat with no lower jaw. Looking up, Sam saw bald-bodied owls and massive ravens and disheveled eagles all gliding into rolling darkness.

A white long-limbed coyote limped to a stop in front of Sam, but only its back had fur. Eyes rolling, it rose to its hind legs, revealing its other half, a girl wrapped in rags—her face peering out of the coyote's jaw and throat, her scabbed shins bare below the knee, but furry and coyote-lean on the calf. The girl looked at Sam's arms and then turned her sour green eyes toward his. When she spoke, her words were nothing but nonsense to Sam's ears.

"English," Sam said.

"Skin-walkers are called," she said, and her words were rough and curdled. "All who would escape the kingdom of dreams and death. Tzitzimime call the *yee naaldlooshii* to live again."

"Am I dead?" Sam asked. "Are you?"

"We are. But we will not be. The darkness will open and the living will flee."

The girl dropped back onto all fours. The animal's eyes focused on the snakes and ignored Sam. Its tongue lolled out the side of its jaw and down bald skin that Sam now knew to be a girl's cheek. Turning away, the coyote limped into a fast-moving, almost floating pack.

Sam stepped forward, but Cindy jerked him back. Speck wavered.

No! Cindy twisted his arm up, meeting Sam's eyes with her sharp yellow gaze.

Speck rose beside her, his eyes granite gray. His voice was quiet, barely hanging in the air. *Killers. Shifters.*

Sam hesitated, looking at both snakes above his knuckles.

"I know I can only hear you because this is a dream," he said.

Cruelest, Cindy hissed. *Kin killers. Curse drinkers.*

"Coming from you, that's saying something. But we're going," Sam said. "I'm sure they're awful, but we have to find the Vulture."

Speck submitted, twisting forward.

Dragging Cindy, Sam began to jog. One step. Two. Three and the ground dissolved. He was no longer in the desert. The air was cold and the ground was liquid. The storm sucked him forward deeper and deeper into the darkness, between a hollow bison and a snorting faceless elk. Then all sight vanished, and even Cindy's rattle went silent.

Sam stood in completely lightless cold air, with cobblestones beneath his feet. He could see nothing, but he could hear steadily splashing water—a fountain, maybe—along with the slow clinking of a heavy chain. He'd heard that sound before, in San Francisco. In the center of a garden, a golden chain attached to a golden clock had been floating above a sundial.

He had found it. Sam was in a time garden, even if only in a dream. And the watch was still tugging in his right hand.

"What do you see?" Sam asked. "Show me."

Two shapes swam into Sam's mind. One large and bent like it was seated, one smaller and standing. Sam recognized them both.

The Vulture and his servant keeper, Mrs. Dervish.

✧ ✧ ✧

THE VULTURE WAS PERCHED BEHIND A STONE TABLE WITH his long black coat over the back of his chair. Both of his guns were drawn and on the table and he had a comic book in his long-fingered hands. Mrs. Dervish, wearing a billowy white blouse tucked in tight to a long black skirt, stood at his side, studying the pages as the Vulture turned them.

"Who is responsible for these?" he asked.

"Clearly someone who would like the boy to be known only as a hero," Mrs. Dervish answered.

"How he is known does not matter to me," the Vulture said. "So long as he is dead, and that death is a more permanent state than it has been in the past." The Vulture stopped over a large full-page illustration of himself in a massive city square surrounded by terraced stone buildings and towers that, upon closer inspection, appeared to be the intricately carved walls and levels of a vast cavern. The square was crowded with men and women with ghoulish animal traits, and the comic book Vulture was retreating through the crowd, firing his guns over his shoulder and barely missing a tumbling Sam Miracle, who was returning fire.

El Buitre did not turn the page. He had no desire to look at any portrayal of his death, even a cartoony and fictitious one. Especially a fictitious one that seemed to be much too familiar with reality.

"Dervish," the Vulture snarled. "I was told no living soul had seen this underworld and escaped." He flattened his broad palm over the page. His lip curled with cold fury. "No one should know of the skin-walkers. Always I am betrayed. Always!" He snapped his fingers shut like a talon, crumpling the comic in his fist and then hurling it away.

"Perhaps there is no betrayal," Mrs. Dervish said. "It may have been written in the future, after this city has been made known and the skin-walkers have reentered the worlds. Father Tiempo could have transported it back simply to make you doubt and fear. And if this presents an opportunity to rethink your strategy, it may be for the best. A monstrous army cannot be controlled once released. If you were willing to once again pursue the approach of patience that we used in San Francisco . . ."

The Vulture lowered his head, breathing hard. Mrs. Dervish continued quickly.

". . . shifting and modifying everything to your design until a rich and powerful future was ripe and awaiting your entrance . . ."

"Dervish," the Vulture said quietly.

". . . there would be no need for such destruction or such a vile army. You are gathering the cursed and damned, William. Werebeasts and shifters and healers who seized their dark powers by murdering those who shared their own blood. They are incapable of loyalty to anything but their own appetites."

The Vulture raised his head. "Have you quite finished?"

Mrs. Dervish sniffed and crossed her arms. "Have I been heard?"

"Heard?" The Vulture laughed. "Woman, how long did I follow your course? I am finished with guile and subtle maneuvering and patience. I will no longer attempt careful surgery on the future with a scalpel. I am an eruption! I am destruction! You may help me with your patience when the time has come to repair the shattered world beneath my feet. But not before! Your patience failed me, Dervish. Do not forget it."

Mrs. Dervish cleared her throat. Her foot began to tap. "Do not act rashly while Father Tiempo lives. Even the boy priest escaped your hammer-fisted assault—"

"Tiempo!" The Vulture spat the name. "Always the priest. Your sky-demon mothers have now promised me his heart before Miracle's. Rest easy. I will not move until the priest is dead and Miracle is trapped in time and cannot escape again. I am done chasing him through centuries. If your mothers cannot do this, then we will find others more powerful who can."

Mrs. Dervish uncrossed her arms, clasping her hands in front of her skirt. "Power is irrelevant. My mothers have no deftness. I was the one who bound time into your heart. I charmed those watches and their chains with artistry. The strength of the Tzitzimime is the strength of a poisonous belch. Your frustration has made you a fool, William."

The Vulture turned, looking into the hard eyes of the only human he allowed to disrespect him, and then, rarely.

"The little lady is jealous," he said, smiling. "You resent my new allies?"

"I think when they have given you the world to rule, it may be no more than a smoking heap of bones. It is their way."

The Vulture sighed. "A globe of graveyards would suit my taste. I told you that I am no longer a surgeon. I am a storm. And when I have taken one time for myself, the Tzitzimime can open me a door to another. When the priest and the boy have both been killed, there will remain cities undestroyed for me to rule."

The broken gold chain whispered as it slid out of the Vulture's vest and pointed across the empty courtyard.

The Vulture looked at it and stared at the emptiness where it was pointing. Mrs. Dervish did the same.

"How?" the Vulture said. He jumped to his feet, snatching his guns off the stone table. "Can he really be here?"

"No," Mrs. Dervish said quietly. "But he is a dreamer. He may be watching us now."

The Vulture sat back down. "Put me to sleep," he said. "Quickly! And summon your mothers!"

"They have tasted the priest and now they are hunting his beginning," Mrs. Dervish said. "You will not be able to trace the boy's spirit back without them."

"Sleep!" the Vulture bellowed, slamming his guns back down. "Now! Before he wakes and is gone!"

The Vulture felt the cold from Mrs. Dervish's hands pour into his temples and he heard the first of her whispered words before his body slumped forward. But his mind didn't so much as blink. While his body fell, his dream-self searched for the foolish invader of his garden.

"Miracle," he said aloud. "My young and ancient friend, are you so eager to finally die that you practice as a ghost?"

6

Ghost Sand

ALL AT ONCE, SAM'S DARKNESS BECAME FIRELIGHT. TORCHES sprang to life all around the cobbled courtyard enclosed by small carved buildings set into cave walls. Torches surrounded the fountain in its center, lighting up a gold chain and clock floating above the splashing water. The Vulture had seen Sam first, and had spoken. Slowly, the tall outlaw—even taller in the dream—rose to his feet. He studied Sam, stroking his pointed black beard as he did, almost smiling.

"Welcome to my dream," he said. "Why have you come? To surrender? To seek peace?"

"This is more than a dream," Sam said. "I found you. And you will never destroy another city or take another life."

The Vulture's eyes sparkled. "Your mind may have found me, but could your body ever follow? Did you come with enough strength to harm me? To even reach me?"

"Face me now, I dare you," Sam said. "I will tell you where I am, to the year, day, and minute. Are you afraid?"

"Afraid?" The Vulture laughed. "You are helpless. Your priest will soon be ash. You will finally be imprisoned in one time without escape. Your heart will be ready for harvest and all those you love will die." The Vulture stepped forward, ghosting through the arm of his chair.

Sam's shoulders began to rattle. Cindy had no weapon, but she hovered in the air, ready to strike.

Kill. The word floated audibly through the air.

The Vulture blinked in surprise. "The serpents speak?"

"Why wouldn't they?" Sam asked.

"Can you always hear them?" the Vulture asked. "Or is this my dream?"

"Always," Sam said.

Yee, Speck hissed.

Naaldlooshii, Cindy answered.

The Vulture froze. "Who told you this? The priest? His brother?"

The torches in the courtyard dimmed and two

shadowy shapes swept into the cave like a cloud.

Sam jumped away, searching for an escape, but Speck and the watch pulled him back. The shadows began to condense into smaller, harder, sharper swirling forms. Sam forced his right hand open, and he threw down the golden watch and broken chain.

The Vulture woke up, seated, facedown on the stone table. Slowly, he sat up. Mrs. Dervish stood beside him, soft hands intertwined with each other. She smiled nervously as she met El Buitre's raging eyes.

"Your mothers," he said, his tone furious. "The Tzitzimime. They swore to me that it was impossible. A dreamer could never enter this place. They swore the *yee naaldlooshii* would be gathered in secret. And yet Miracle was here, and he spoke of the skin-walkers."

"William," Mrs. Dervish said. "It doesn't matter anymore. The boy can't escape you now. He cannot hide. He cannot move through time. He will rot where he stands. My mothers traced the priest to his infancy, to the very day of his anointing as a time-walker."

The Vulture shut his eyes and inhaled through sharply flared nostrils. "And?" he asked.

Mrs. Dervish laughed. "And they are the Aztec Tzitzimime. No Navajo charms and protections could ever stand against them. He's as good as dead. They will halve his infant heart and wield his anointing as their own."

"Sam." Glory's whisper in his ear jerked him conscious. "Wake up!"

Sam blinked the moon into focus, and then squinted at Glory's face. She had thrown his blanket off and was already trying to uncinch the bungee from Cindy and his left hand. Sam's face was drenched with sweat, and Speck was coiled on his chest.

Jude and Drew were both sitting up in their sleeping bags.

"He yelled and threw the watch," Drew said. "Some kind of nightmare."

"Glory?" Jude asked. "What is it?"

Sam licked his salty lips and exhaled, trying to calm himself. His heart was racing and images from his dream were very much alive in his mind.

"The things," Sam said. "The flying shadows. They can find us."

"Tell me later." Glory turned back to Jude and Drew. "We're under attack. There are men on the island. They must have killed their boat motors and paddled in quietly. Rifles, pistols, the works. Go! Wake the others."

Jude and Drew frantically kicked out of their sleeping bags and jumped up, barefoot. Jude was wearing only a pair of old sweatpants and his pale torso was zebra-striped with scars, all shaded by the moonlight. Drew was in tight long johns from ankle to wrist, but he already had a long knife in his four-fingered hand.

"How many?" Drew asked.

"Three boats' worth," Glory said. "Maybe eighteen."

Drew and Jude shot from the room, and Sam listened to their bare feet race away on the marble floors as his left hand slid free. Sam dropped to the cold floor and pain shot up his numb feet. He was wearing a white tank top and he had slept in his jeans but they were unbuttoned. Buttoning quickly, he picked the watch up off the floor and hooked the bent paper clip on the end of the broken chain back onto his belt loop where it belonged. Then he grabbed his bow and quiver holster from beneath the hammock.

"Is the Vulture here?" Sam asked. "Did he find us? I saw him. I told him to fight me."

"Not the Vulture." Glory's brow was damp; her eyes were wide with fear. "He doesn't even matter right now, Sam. We have a bigger problem."

She tugged him toward the door, but Sam pulled back.

"He doesn't matter? Of course he matters!"

Glory shook her head. She was exhaling through pursed lips, trying to stay calm.

"Now, Sam!" she hissed. "Hurry!" And she slipped out into the long gray concrete-and-marble hallway.

Sam didn't walk. He ran. He knew Glory well enough to know that whatever frightened her would frighten him even more. He raced down the hall in his bare feet, ignoring the whispers and warnings from his waking brothers as he passed the doors to bedrooms and bathrooms and an office and a home theater. Grabbing the steel handrail on the stairs, he leapt up them two at a time behind Glory, his heart pounding.

A gunshot echoed through the house and was immediately joined by shattering glass.

Sam wanted to turn around. He wanted to defend his brothers and his sister and his house. But near the top of the stairs, he felt sand slide and grind beneath the balls of his feet. It grew thicker on the landing, and as he slipped through double white doors into the vast moon- and lantern-lit upper floor that was the master suite and gym, the sand grew thicker still.

Glory Spalding shut and locked the doors and scrambled across the room, stopping in an inch of sand beside the wide white bed that she had chosen as her own. Sand was pouring off its sides in dozens of streaming falls.

On the other side of the bed stood a boy Sam had never seen. A boy it was hard to see now, not because he seemed to be made of dying light, but because Sam's eyes—or his mind—just wouldn't process him. The boy was most visible when Sam was looking at Glory or the bed or the sand . . . or the shape that was lying on the bed. The shape . . .

Gunshots and raging voices vibrated the floor beneath his feet, but Sam hurried forward.

Peter Eagle—his best friend, the boy who had been most protective of Sam on the Arizona ranch, the boy who would grow into the time-walking priest who had died and died and died for Sam, the leader of the Ranch Brothers and the Lost Boys, Peter Atsa Eagle Tiempo— was stretched out on the bed in the center of a swirling pool of bloody sand. His face was gray. His skin dry.

"Peter!" Sam brushed past Glory, scanning his friend's body for wounds. "What happened? How did he get here?" He saw no injury, but the blood and sand were only increasing. "Where is he hurt?" Sam looked up at the boy on the other side of the bed, immediately unable to see him. Looking back down at Peter, he grabbed his friend's firm shoulder, and coldness flowed up into his hands.

"He is dying," the vanishing boy said. "Dead in an earlier time but not yet in this moment. His future and his future in the past are spilling out—your futures. You are looking at the top of the tree as it falls, but the ax was taken to the trunk. And when this tree has fallen, so falls the forest."

"What did you do to him?" Sam asked. He jumped

around the bed, trying to force the boy into focus. As he grew closer, the boy vanished completely. "Who are you?"

Glory was leaning over Peter, searching his body for wounds. The blurry figure appeared, standing beside her.

Sam let Speck whip up his crossbow. Cindy grabbed the stock, controlling Sam's aim, tracking the boy's elusive shape.

"Stand still," Sam said. "And tell me what you did to Peter. You better be able to fix him."

"I am not one who fixes," the boy said simply.

"He hasn't been shot," Glory said. "At least not that I can see."

The boy beside Glory suddenly became solid—more solid than a statue of polished black stone. Glory and Peter and the room and the bow and Cindy and Sam's hand and Sam's whole self all seemed to be nothing more than smoke and cobwebs. Speck pulled the crossbow's trigger again and again, trying to shoot at the weighty shape of the boy, but the bowstrings were vapor and the arrows weightless. If the boy had been made of ghostly light before, now he was made of all light, every ray and blast and beam, every spark and every flame, every drop of starlight and moonlight and sunlight that had ever striped dark water at night and burned desert sand in the morning. All of it was gathered into his small shape, and there it stayed. He was not living.

He *was* life.

Glory screamed, but her voice was no louder than drifting steam. The noise of the violence downstairs evaporated. Sam felt his legs beginning to disintegrate, and he sagged toward the floor, his body crumbling in the presence of the boy's enormity. And then, as quickly as the world had gone mad, it was sane again. Sam's weight returned, and he staggered sideways on solid legs like someone in an elevator that had stopped falling too fast.

Peter was still on the bed, but the sand around him had slowed. Thin streams quietly hissed off the bed onto the floor. Glory had fallen onto her knees, but now she rose. She and Sam both focused on the boy.

And that's all he was. A boy. He had black hair, cropped almost to the scalp, and skin two shades darker than a sun-leathered road worker's. He was wearing gray jeans that would have suited a grandfather pulling a trailer into an RV park, bright-yellow flip-flops, and a tan-and-white polo shirt, and he was holding a dirty pale-blue-and-white foam-and-mesh baseball hat in his hands that said "Spokane Yacht Club" on the front.

"Who are you?" Glory asked. The boy moved smoothly to the foot of Peter's bed. Glory and Sam glanced across Peter at each other.

"Did you do this to Peter?" Sam asked.

The boy smiled sadly. "In a way, yes. In a way, no. I did

110

not cause his death. But I am the one who will carry his soul away." He looked into Sam's eyes, and Sam flinched. It was like meeting his own eyes in a mirror. The boy already knew everything about him, already knew him from the inside—and hadn't found it particularly interesting.

"Will he live?" Glory asked. "He has to live. If he doesn't . . ."

"Then many things will unspool. Many pages and many times will burn away. The two of you will be sand spilled on this floor, believed to be no more than characters imagined and created for storybooks. Worse," the boy said, "the Vulture will not be stopped before the world's end. Be grateful that Peter has lived so many moments, that he has so much future to lose. It takes much time for a Father Tiempo to truly die. His soul is and was and will be in many times, and it must leave his body in all of them."

"So it's over?" Sam asked. "For sure? He's hurt and he's going to die and there's nothing we can do?" He reached out and touched Peter's hand, this time letting the cold crawl up his arm until Cindy was shivering and angry.

"The wound is not in this body," the boy said. "The heart and life and anointing spirit have been taken from the infant who became this boy. His thread is cut and now it is falling loose, as will all the other threads he has supported. Yes, he is dying. As are his centuries. Samuel Miracle. Glory Spalding." Sam and Glory both looked up at the boy, but the boy's gaze was focused down at Peter on the bed, and his eyes were wet. When he spoke again, his voice was hard and slow, but full of fury, every word a stone large enough to crush houses.

"Peter Atsa Eagle must not die." He looked at Sam. He looked at Glory. "Not now. Not here. Not until the chosen place and in the chosen moment—there I have already gathered the soul of an old man full of years who laid himself down to save you, Sam, where he died younger and younger in a ring around your fallen body. Now you have been chosen to protect the day of that death. If you fail, Father Tiempo dies unripe. You die unripe. And all the earth will be good for little more than fire."

"But how do we stop this?" Glory asked. "What can we do?"

"And who chose us?" Sam asked. "Peter?"

The boy lifted his foam-front hat and put it on, pulling the faded pale-blue bill down just slightly off center.

"You have been chosen by the one who chose Peter Eagle to become Father Tiempo. The one who chose Sam Miracle to be the boy who would kill El Buitre on a street in Old San Francisco. The one who chose Gloria Spalding as the girl who would be at St. Anthony of the Desert Destitute Youth Ranch to guide his memory through time when all other attempts had failed. The one who sends Brother Segador, Angel de la Muerte, to gather all of your souls in the end."

Sam blinked, his throat tight and suddenly dry. "Who is Brother Segador?"

"I am," the boy said, smiling. "But you can call me Ghost."

"Ghost," Sam said, and his tongue felt numb. Angel de la Muerte, the Angel of Death? Just moments ago, the boy had practically unhinged reality, and Sam hadn't felt as frightened then as he felt right now.

"So, you're a reaper . . . in charge of killing everyone?" he asked, but he knew he was wrong the instant he asked it.

"Not everyone. I have been given certain peoples and lands and times to tend. And I do not kill unless I am directly commanded. I collect. I reap. And I am not in charge." Ghost laughed. "We all answer to somebody," he said. "Some of us answer to fewer somebodies than others."

"How many do you answer to?" Sam asked. "And how many people have you collected?"

"I answer to three," Ghost said. "And when I have collected one hundred and forty-four thousand souls, seventy times, my labor will be complete and I will return home from my master's field. You are one of mine. And Glory. And Peter. And the one who was called William Sharon, but who is now El Buitre, the Vulture. The one who has long used vile powers to elude the death you were meant to bring him. And because he eluded you, Sam, he has too long eluded me. It disgusts me to gather all the untimely dead, cut down by that man who should have been damned to dust and fire an age ago. Still he sends me others in his place, whole cities, and now Peter, and all who will die with no Tiempo."

"So then don't gather them," Glory said. "When the Vulture tries to kill people, just leave them."

"I cannot," the boy said. "I am not the Resurrection Man. Such people would soon rot on their feet. I would be adding a curse to a crime."

The boy gathered a handful of air above his head, and then squeezed it tight in his fist before opening his hand, splaying his fingers wide.

Darkness leapt from his palm, swallowing the bed and Peter and Sam and Glory in a heavy dome. The light inside the dome was just as it had been, but the small space was now truly alone, connected to heavy nothingness in every direction. Sand hissed in trickles onto the floor. Sam's heartbeat was even louder, drumming in his ears.

"Samuel," Ghost said. "Gloria. Listen to me now. Peter

is already with me. But I will not yet carry him from the world. I can delay one day's breaths to focus on a debt, long overdue. The Vulture's debt. Your task is simple, and yet may be impossible. Find Peter in his infancy. Stop the desert demons of the sky, turn back the Tzitzimime before they can take his heart and life and anointed gift. Glory, I will give you the blade you need to find and face such foes. When this is done, you must also find and kill the Vulture. If done quickly, before every Peter has gone to ash, I will see his soul returned, and Tiempo will live to die again. Now step forward."

Glory and Sam inched toward the boy together.

"Glory, you are a time-walker. You must take the lead and move quickly. Sam, you cannot save Peter. But Glory can. And you can save Glory. Without you, she will die on the dark roads between times as surely as you so often died in that Arizona desert without her. Give her your life, lay it down for her, and you may receive it back in the end . . . if Peter rises from this bed. Do you understand?"

"No!" Glory said. "He doesn't understand! And neither do I. I'm not a time-walker."

"That is not entirely true. You have the glass," Ghost said. "You have already used it to make tunnels of slower time or faster time. Give it to me."

Glory pulled the hourglass out of her binoculars case and handed it over.

Ghost stood it up on his flat left palm and studied it.

"Father Tiempo must be an artist," Ghost said. "A time dancer and a pilgrim. But Segador moves as a thief, with silence as well as violence, in and out of time like a blade. There is no door or barrier of time that can forbid my entry." He looked up at Glory. "The blade I will give you can slice through the walls between worlds. It can cut through flesh and bone and even spirit. Will you willingly carry the Reaper's blood? It will be a curse to you, but powerful. Carrying it will mark you."

"If that's what I need to save Peter," Glory said, "then, yes."

"Hold on," Sam said. "Why don't you just kill these Tzitzithings and the Vulture? Isn't it your job?"

"I may not kill," said Ghost. "I gather. And sometimes, like right now, I assist and equip. The Tzitzimime are not mortal, but they gather an army of those who once were. Since Glory is willing, I am giving her a blade sharp enough to carve any being or thing that exists within time, because it parts time itself. Cut the canvas and you cut the painting. Are you ready, Glory?"

"Absolutely not," Glory said. "Let's do this."

Ghost nodded, and held his right hand above her hourglass. His palm opened and black blood poured down out of the wound, as thick and heavy as honey. When it touched the inside of the glass, it immediately began to spin and whirl.

Sam's throat went too dry for speech. He watched the dark, spinning blood fill the hourglass, and then it passed down through it, reentering the boy's other palm on the underside but leaving the glass stained.

Ghost straightened and handed the hourglass back to an astonished Glory. Steam trailed out of both open ends, and Glory winced with pain when it touched her skin, but she gripped it tight. Sam coughed and swallowed hard until he could speak.

"What do we do now?" Sam asked, staring at Peter's gray body. "How do we start?"

The boy called Ghost straightened his cap on his head.

"Glory," he said. "Raise your hourglass."

Glory raised her arm, pointing toward the doorway.

"You will be clumsy at first, but the finesse will come. Think of how far back you would like to see, and cut yourself a window."

Glory moved her wrist in a tight circle, and a small pool of sand spun into a bright glassy hole in the air in front of her. Through the hole, Sam and Glory were staring at the bedroom decades before, with the sun pouring in the windows over the water and a young maid with white earbuds in, singing at the top of her lungs while dancing and pushing a vacuum. The maid bounced, slid to the side, and then looked up at Sam and Glory.

She screamed. Glory dropped her hand, and the window vanished.

"Try not to startle people to death," Ghost said. "Do not slice any mortal into two times unless you intend to, it is necessary, and they deserve such a gruesome death. The power you now hold in that glass would make villains of most men, and I do not intend for you to become a lesser Vulture. With Tiempo's glass and my blood—and much practice—you will be able to exit time and let it move beneath you. But such leapings into the future or tumblings into the past are done by feel and in total darkness. Unless great skill is developed, there will always be imprecision. To see where you are going, choose your direction—forward or backward—encase yourself in slow time, and let the world race past.

"But you will be rooted in one point in space, not safely removed in the darkness between times. Be careful not to shatter yourselves in some collision with a sprouting city or impale yourselves on the rocketing growth of a redwood tree. Become slow in the wrong place and every tree will come up at you faster than an arrow. And, of course, in a fight, or in a rush to travel through space, you can do the opposite. Encase yourself in time so fast that even the light outside your shell slows before your eyes. In the great mortal tragedies, I have gathered hundreds of souls in a single human second. But even more caution is required here. At such speed, even a breath can collapse a skull. A stray touch can disintegrate a limb."

Ghost stopped his speech, and Sam and Glory looked at each other, and then they both looked at the glass in Glory's hand.

"So . . . can you come with us?" Sam asked.

"The two of you are permitted to see me only twice," Ghost said. "The third time we meet eye to eye, I will be carrying your soul away. Then you may see me as often as you like."

"Perfect," Sam muttered. "Let's hang out tons after we're dead."

With her hourglass lowered, Glory leaned over the bed, picking up Peter's hand. "And how much time do we have?"

"One night and one morning," Ghost said. "Now go. Trace Peter to his beginning and prevent his murder. In the darkness between times, trace the Vulture to his present, and deliver him the ending you were meant to. The ending he is owed."

Sam looked down at his friend, pale and cold. Already Peter's body seemed hollow and collapsing, like a melon left in the garden through too many frosts. And before lunch tomorrow, Sam would be joining him if he and Glory failed.

Ghost didn't vanish in a flash; the light he left behind was too slow for that. It spilled onto the floor and washed up the walls and flowed across blood and sand and Peter's still body. The windows in the room warped and wobbled, and Sam's stomach did the same.

Still holding Peter's hand, Glory looked up at Sam.

"Whatever you need," she said. "Grab it now. We have to go."

Sam stared at her. At Peter. And then at the air where Ghost had been.

"I should have told him my dream," Sam said. "The animal people all running into the storm. They have to be the army he was talking about. The Tzitzi-clown whatevers are calling them. That's what the coyote girl said, and then Ghost used the same word. *Tzitzi* . . ." He looked back at Glory. "The Vulture is in a cave, Glory. Another time garden, but this one is underground. And my snakes talked in the dream, too. Out loud."

"Sam!" Glory yelled. Sam blinked his mind silent. Glory tossed back her hair and lowered her voice, but her tone was still fierce. "Just do what I say, Sam. I'm supposed to lead. That's what he said. Get what you need. Let me worry about the rest. Just keep us alive, okay?"

Sam backed away, looking from Glory to Peter, and then around the room as if Ghost might still be present.

"Trust me," Glory said. "Now go! Get more arrows. Get food. Get shoes on. Whatever you can jam in a pack that won't slow you down. Go!"

Sam nodded. And he ran.

Glory focused on Peter's body and his bed of sand. She'd managed to split time's speed before, even without Ghost's infused glass. It had to be easier now. Glory raised her darkened hourglass.

The glass was slick in her hand. Or her hand was slick on the glass. Her palms were cold and as wet as she was nervous. She stood up straight, breathing like a runner before a race, flexing her fingers.

"I know this is dangerous," she said to Peter. "I know I don't have a clue, but Ghost seems to think I can figure it out, and you're not here to stop me, Pete. Sorry." She tried to focus her thoughts on the bed, intent on what she wanted. Her voice sank to a whisper as her concentration grew. "Let's find out what the Reaper did to this thing."

THE SPIRIT OF PETER TIEMPO, GROWN TO HIS FULL STRENGTH and height, stood in the bedroom watching Glory. His invisible arms were crossed. His hair was tied back with a red cloth, and he was wearing the black robes of his priesthood. But he weighed nothing. He breathed nothing. No blood ran through his veins, because he had no veins. Light passed through him as easily as it passed through air.

Ghost stood beside him, his head only reaching Peter's shoulder.

"This is foolishness," Peter said. "She isn't ready."

"Of course she isn't," said Ghost. "Has anyone ever been ready for such a task and such enemies?"

"She will careen through time like a child in a rocket."

"Yes," said Ghost. "As you once did."

"Which I now will never do. And Sam's dream," Peter said. "Skin-walkers are gathering to the Tzitzimime to form the Vulture's army? I do not understand. He cannot expect to control them. Not any of them."

"Sam's words were clear enough," Ghost said quietly.

"The mothers of darkness and skin-walkers from beyond the grave." Peter shook his head. "The Vulture is a Sunday school teacher compared to them. Sam will need a miracle."

"He has one," Ghost said. "In Glory. And she has the weapon I have given her and a boy too foolish to obey his fears or hers. They are only two small sparks, but they may grow into a blaze."

Dead Peter was perfectly still. And then, despite his lack of a body, he shivered.

IF GLORY SPALDING WAS GOING TO RACE A CLOCK, THE FIRST thing she wanted to do was try and slow down the clock she was racing. If she could drag Peter's time to a virtual stop, she would. Of course, she might just end up killing him faster. Or she might end up killing herself. She might end up peeling Peter so deeply into his own time frame that she would never be able to find his moments again. Maybe this would be his tomb. If Peter were conscious, she knew he would be asking her not to do what she was about to.

But he wasn't conscious.

The hot glass grew heavy in Glory's singed hand. She imagined Peter's heartbeats slowing down, each of his breaths wandering for days, and she raised her hourglass, fighting to hold it above her head as it grew even heavier, bracing it with her other hand.

Cold black sand poured down Glory's neck, and then she let the hourglass fall.

The shift in time hit the mattress around Peter like a falling wall. His body bounced. The sand around him spun into a whirlpool, swallowing every sound and ray of light, drawing even more sand up from the floor, mixing it with Peter's blood.

A web of dark glass began to melt and tangle into a small dome around the bed. Glory's senses were fading, but she swung the hourglass again and newly formed glass thickened and grew urgent. Layer after webbed layer whined and stretched and hardened on the dome until Peter and the bed were hidden behind an uneven wall of what looked like crystal midnight stone.

And then, as Glory forced her arms up to swing again, the dome grew faint and vanished, and the hourglass was weightless in her hands. The light returned. Glory's vision sharpened. She was breathing hard, and her nose was bleeding down the back of her throat. Peter and the bed were gone, leaving only a wide hole in the carpet and a shallow crater in the marble floor below. A smell as harsh and hot as burnt hair dominated the room. Only the bed's headboard remained, and it tipped forward slowly and fell, slamming into the crater at Glory's feet.

Glory staggered backward, her heart fluttering against her ribs. Dizzy, she shoved her hourglass back into her pocket and braced both hands on her knees. What had happened? Why wasn't Peter just inside the glass, dying more slowly?

Gagging, Glory coughed gobby blood onto smooth white stone where her bed had just been.

She knew what the problem was. She had slowed Peter's time too much. Peter was slow, all right, so slow that Glory and the house and everything outside the glass had left him behind and moved on into the future without him. And that was the point, right?

Glory pressed her palm to her slick forehead and shut her eyes. Peter would make it to the moment she was in eventually. Wouldn't he? But when? She had peeled the

124

time streams way too far apart.

"Stupid!" Glory grimaced down at the headboard inside the crater. It would still work. Wouldn't it? If she could find the right moment, sure. But now breaking the glass dome and splashing the two times back together again was going to require some serious . . . *math*. Or something just as bad.

"Sorry about the bed, Pete," she said out loud. "I hope you didn't tip off."

She didn't have time to be frustrated. That much she knew. Straightening, she backed toward the doorway. Sam wasn't going to like this. Not at all. But she didn't need to tell him. Not unless they were still alive and the Vulture wasn't in about twenty-four hours.

"So much for *trust me, Sam,*" Glory said, and she turned to run downstairs.

A huge man filled the doorway with his bulk.

Glory jerked in surprise and backed away. She had forgotten about the gunshots and breaking glass from earlier—the invasion of their island.

"Who are you?" she asked. "What are you doing here?"

The man's shoulders touched both sides of the door-jamb as he entered the room, and he had to duck his knobby forehead under the lintel. His red beard had been twisted and waxed into five thick spikes, and his eyes were wide with interest. A crudely sawed-off shotgun with a large black drum for shells dangled from his massive right hand. Three wooden baseball bats had been duct-taped together into an oversize club for his left.

"Girlie." He nodded his head in acknowledgment, grinning as he did. His voice was thick and curdled, and he sniffed at the air with garden hose nostrils as he moved toward Glory. "What have you been burning?"

"Sam!" Glory yelled. "Sam!"

The man chuckled and ran the end of his club across his spiked beard.

"Would that be your Sam?" he asked. "The cursed boy with the viper arms? Or my Sam? My princess? My daughter." His voice rolled into a growl, and his upper lip curled, revealing a thick tusklike canine tooth of gold.

"The lovely girl you fools stole from Leviathan Finn."

DEAD PETER TURNED TO GHOST AS THE BIG BEARDED MAN dragged Glory from the room.

"Brother Reaper," Peter said. "The game is over before it has even begun. Take me from this world now. It is bad enough to die; I do not want to see them killed, as well."

"Have faith," said Ghost, grimly. "Someone has to."

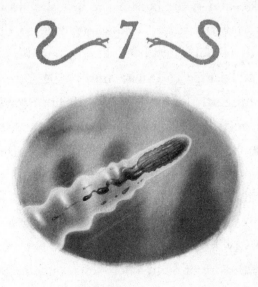

7

Oops

WHEN GLORY OPENED HER EYES, SHE WAS PINNED ON HER side staring at half of a peach from one inch away. She knew that the peach was inside a large jar, along with many others that Millie Miracle had sealed in with it, and when she rolled her eyeball, she could almost see them. Glory's cheek was pressed against the jar, as was the left side of her open mouth. Her tongue moved across the slick flavorless glass.

Coughing, Glory tried to blink some clarity into her throbbing skull, and then she tried to sit up.

It wasn't easy. Her wrists were tied together behind

her back—and tied again to the belt she always wore with her favorite jeans. The knots were so tight that her hands felt like lumps of dough, but she managed to kick and scrape and twist until her legs were under her. Pushing off the hard floor with her elbow, grunting and puffing through the pain, she managed to tip slowly upright, shaking and sweating with the effort, and finally found herself sitting flat on the floor of Millie's biggest pantry.

"Glory." Sam's voice was as dry as one of his rattles, and Glory twisted around to look behind her.

Only the tips of Sam's boots were touching the floor, but not enough to carry his weight. His poncho was gone, and his arms had been strung up to the highest shelves on either side of the wide pantry, leaving him dangling in a painful and helpless Y. Blood stained the chest of his white tank top beneath a messy split in his chin. Cindy and Speck were stretched up and out and thin, and were both completely motionless. Sam's hands were purple and the snakes were lifeless dark stripes of mottled, scaled bruising in his pale arms.

"You were right," Sam gasped. "Shouldn't have brought the girl."

Glory leaned against the loaded shelves, rocking and twisting her way onto her knees. Puffing loose hair out of her eyes, she focused on Sam.

"What happened?" she asked. "Are you okay? Is anything broken?"

Sam blinked. First one eye, then the other. His eyelids were sticky, unpeeling slowly, like his thoughts. What *had* happened?

Gunshots. Broken glass. Needle-sharp ringing through Sam's head, from ear to ear. His brothers hadn't had a chance with bows and bats and knives.

Hundreds of men had entered through shattered windows. Or dozens of men. Sam had recognized Bull and Dog. Or Dog and Bull, and a huge man with a beard like an upside-down spiked crown. His friends were pinned facedown and bound. Millie was yelling. And then Sam was knocked out with a club of three bats.

And then, despite Samra's protests, he'd been strung up half conscious in the pantry. And when Sam had come to again, Glory had been there.

After a few seconds of fluttering, Sam's eyelids slowly opened.

"So," Sam rasped. "I guess that's it."

"What's it?" Glory asked, confused.

"What happened," Sam said. "You asked."

"But you didn't say anything."

"Oh. Well. I thought it. Samra called her dad. Somehow."

Glory knee-walked closer to him. "Is anything broken?"

Sam nodded. "Windows." His eyes were shutting again.

"Hey!" Glory hissed. "Sam! Stay with me. I'm getting you out of here."

Sam's head slumped forward and his weight sagged lower, his legs limp and his arms and shoulders stretching even further. And something bad was going on in his lungs. His breaths were shallow and faint.

"No." Glory banged into a shelf, scrambling up onto her feet. "These idiots will kill him. He'll suffocate hanging like that."

Turning around in the tight space, crowded with Millie's jams and jellies and pickles and peaches and pears, she kicked the door hard.

"Hey!" she yelled. "He's dying in here. Dying!"

Outside, she heard only laughter. She pressed her mouth to the door and yelled again and again, until her throat tore and her forehead throbbed.

"Killers! Idiots! Open this door! You're killing him! Cut him down! Hey!" She kicked the door again and again. She kicked until her toenails split and her bones ached. "I know you can hear me!"

The door opened, revealing a barrel-chested bearded man in a tight sweater. And Samra, with her arms crossed.

"He's suffocating!" Glory shouted. "Get him down!"

130

The redhead's eyes flitted up to Sam and then quickly back down to Glory.

"No!" The big voice echoed across the kitchen from out of sight. "I know who he is. I have read the picture stories. The boy stays."

Samra stiffened and began to turn away. "My father says he stays."

"If he dies," Glory said, "I'm coming for you. I'm coming for all of you." She stepped forward, ready to bite and kick if she had to, but the broad man shoved her back hard, slamming her into the shelves. Jars fell. Glass shattered and peaches and syrup slicked the floor. Glory slipped, staggered, and fell. Unable to catch herself, she landed on her side. After a moment of breathing through the pain, she rolled onto her stomach.

Glass shards were pricking into her forearm, and her cheek was swamped in syrup. Sweetness leaked into the corner of her mouth.

"It's okay, Sam." Glory rolled over, onto her bound wrists, ignoring the glass, ignoring the pain. "I got you."

Sam said nothing. Glory couldn't even hear him breathing. But it would be over soon. She could do this. Hooking both heels onto a shelf, she pulled her hips up off the floor. With hamstrings taut, she wriggled her rear closer to the shelves. Then she stretched her left foot up for the next shelf. And then her right. Slowly, gasping, with her head pounding and her whole body shaking, Glory walked her legs up the wall, pulling herself upside down until her chin was pinned to her chest and only the back of her head and shoulders carried all of her weight on the floor.

Careful not to lose her balance, Glory began to twist and shake and bounce as much as she could, focusing entirely on her right hip. She could feel the hourglass moving in her belted binocular case, but she needed the lid to pop open. It was old. It had popped open on its own many times. And the glass inside had to know she wanted it. It had to. Ghost had said it would become part of her. It would mark her.

Glory shimmied. Bracing her left foot as firmly on the shelves as she could, she kicked her right leg hard over and over in the air above her head.

And there it was. Pop. The flap opened partway. The glass emerged slowly, and sideways.

"C'mon!" Glory grunted. She kicked herself into a backward somersault.

Glory's feet smashed through a shelf as she flipped. Pickles mixed with peaches rained down on her as she managed to land on her knees. Peach syrup spattered out of her ponytail as she sat up, whipping it backward.

The hourglass was swimming with the pickles beside her right knee and the scent of vinegar and brine mingled with the sweetness already in the air.

By the time Glory had the hourglass in her hand behind her back, she was once again lying on her side.

The smells were overpowering and she was trying not to think about the pricking of all the glass. She tried to focus only on what she wanted to accomplish, and where exactly she needed to divide time. Even so, she wasn't sure how much control she would have over what actually happened when time's sands became glass. She could end up cutting Sam's hands off, along with the heads of his snakes. Or it could be Sam's head along with his arms.

But she knew she wanted speed. She and Sam were going to exist at such an incredible rate of speed that none of the thugs outside the door would be able to see them, let alone hurt them.

Maybe.

If it worked.

And if her time blade sliced Sam's ropes, but not Sam.

Black sand began to swirl and stir the mess on the floor around her, whipping the glass shards into itself.

Exhausted, terrified, and hurting, unsure of what she was doing, Glory laughed, and then laughed again out of surprise.

"Let's be peaches, Sam," she said. "The fastest peaches ever. Just need to make a jar around us."

Although Glory could only waggle her wrist, the sand

seemed to understand. She felt it rushing past her. Father Tiempo had told her that he rose out of time and let it move beneath him until he found the moment he chose to reenter. But how much practice had that taken? For now, she knew she could chop. She could fork time's river and slow it down or speed it up before her fork merged back in with the whole. But right now, it didn't feel like a fork. It felt more like she was grabbing part of time's river in a cooler and slamming the lid shut. She and Sam would be like caught fish inside. She sensed the sand rising in a sphere around her, but she didn't take her eyes off of Sam's purple-mottled hands and the knots that bound them.

The temperature jumped as Glory's sand began to glass. It was different being inside a ball, rather than riding a motorcycle through a tunnel, especially when she needed to control its edges perfectly. Syrup and vinegar steamed off the floor. Jars still intact on the shelves melted into the bigger jar Glory was making, spilling their contents as they rose and stretched and melded into the whole.

On both sides of the pantry, the webbed glass rose up through the shelves, cutting through wood and steel as easily as the canned fruit. The crystalizing shell of time bent inward, passing through Sam's bonds within a breath of his knuckles, close enough to blister and scrape the skin.

And then the shell closed its dome just below the

ceiling, absorbing the glass around the pantry's only lantern and extinguishing the flame.

The time inside changed even faster than the darkness fell.

Severed shelves crashed and clattered down onto Glory. Sam Miracle slumped forward and crashed on top of the heap.

It hurt.

But Glory didn't mind. While she fought for breath, Sam was already snoring on top of the pile. He was alive. She was alive. And they were in their own time stream. She was sure of it—hopefully moving much, much faster than the world outside. But she would have to wait for Sam to wake before she could get untied and find out exactly what she had managed to do.

Broken shelves shifted above her. Sam's limp fingers and then one hand and one wrist slithered straight into her face and then froze up against her chin.

"Cindy?" Glory asked. "I know that's you. Don't you dare be nasty right now. I just cut you loose."

In the darkness, Glory felt Sam's hand twist around, sliding Cindy's rough scales and horns across her cheek and neck. The snake pressed against her skin and was still. Cindy wanted warmth and that was all. Glory shivered, but of course, it could have been a lot worse with Cindy. The snake was a killer, and no matter how much control Sam might have, nothing would ever change that.

"Glad I could help," Glory said. "No, no, don't bother untying me. I just wanted to rest here on the bottom of this pile with the pickles and the peaches." And with that, Glory surprised herself by yawning. As battered as she was, holding still was nice. She had successfully used what Ghost had given her. She and Sam might die soon enough. They might fail Peter, and the Vulture might win, but for now, she had wanted to save Sam, she had done something, and it had worked. After months of use-lessness and frustration, it felt good.

Trying to block the sensation of the snake's cold scales against her neck, Glory closed her eyes in the darkness, her mind and body relaxing.

SAMRA FINN STIRRED A COLD BOWL OF SOUP IN THE DIMLY lit kitchen while Bull and Dog and the rest of the men scoured the conquered house and the island for anything of value. Her father reclined on a large, white leather couch. She had stocked the fireplace and put fresh oil in the lanterns, but with the sun down and no electricity, the sleek modern house now felt more like a campground.

Sam's friends and his sister had all been hogtied and laid facedown in the living room. The boys who had tried to fight were all bleeding—some worse than others—but as far as she could tell, they were all still alive. For now.

Samra took a sip of the broth and looked at the pantry door in the flickering lantern light. Sam and Glory. They were the only two her father had separated from the rest. They were the only two he feared. And she didn't blame him. She knew they were real, and it was still a struggle to believe that she had just met two characters that she had known in comic books through her entire childhood. And they were locked in the pantry . . .

"Dad?" she asked.

Her father grunted from the living room. But he didn't sit up and he didn't open his eyes.

"What will you do with them all?"

"I am Leviathan Finn, and I will do with my captives whatever I will." Her father yawned as he spoke, a little too tired to be impressed by his own boasting.

"I know that," Samra said. "But what do you will?"

"He'll do what he's told," said a curly-headed boy who was tied up near the fireplace. The one called Jude with the scarred hands. He arched his back and looked up. "Your father claims he has no master. But he lies. Isn't that right, Levi?"

Samra's father sat up on the couch, looking across a row of bodies to the boy tied up beside the fire.

"Does the Vulture deliver his orders directly?" Jude

asked. "Or does he make you trust messengers? And how do you contact him?"

"Fool." Her father tugged the central spike on his beard. "Do you think I need you alive?"

"Let's say, just as a hypothetical example," Jude continued, "that you happened to capture the legendary Sam Miracle, who has walked through centuries. How do you get word to the Vulture? And what does he pay you to make dealing with him worth it?"

"Dad," Samra said. "What is he talking about? Is the Vulture real, too? Are all the characters in the comics real?"

Drew, the wide boy with the missing finger, rolled up onto his shoulder not far from Samra's feet.

"Hey Barto," he grunted. "How many years can a battery last?"

Barto lifted his forehead up off the floor, with his glasses dangling off the tip of his nose. "Not many. Definitely not, say . . . twenty-one."

"Ha! I get it!" Matt Cat, the doughy-looking blond boy, laughed out loud. "Man, that's embarrassing."

"Get what?" Samra asked.

"Yeah," Flip said. "I'm with you, Samra. I don't get any of this. Why is Drew talking about batteries? Why are we tied up? Why is your dad evil? That must be weird. I never knew my dad but I wouldn't want him to be evil."

The redheaded twins wriggled on the floor, almost completely in sync. "Spit it out, somebody," Jimmy Z said. Johnny Z grunted agreement.

"Levi here is working for batteries," Matt Cat said. Sir T turned his sharp face toward Samra and grinned. He cleared his throat and addressed the room.

"The girl has a battery-powered transponder to signal her pops. That's how he tracked her here, which means he probably has batteries, too. But no batteries could possibly last the couple decades they'd need to since this place blew up."

The boys all laughed, facedown or twisting into backbends and rolling onto shoulders to get a look at Samra.

"Well, well," Jude said. "Leviathan Finn. You work for an arch-outlaw because he pays you in working batteries? Please tell me he gives you more than that. Are you going to tell your battery king you've caught Sam Miracle?"

Leviathan Finn rose to his feet. "Boy, what business is it of yours who I tell? Are you hoping to provoke me?"

Jude rested his face back on the floor and laughed. "I'm hoping to spare you some embarrassment, that's all. If you haven't sent your message yet, I wouldn't bother. And if you have sent it already, well, I'd send a correction quickly, before your daughter finds out just how real the Vulture can be when he's angry."

"Dad . . ." Samra left her bowl and walked around the island in the kitchen, dragging her hand across the cool marble. A crossbow much like the one she had seen Sam carrying in the city, but with four strings, sat on the counter beside a bundle of what looked like freshly made arrows.

"And why would this Vulture be angry with me?" Leviathan asked. "The man who presents El Buitre with the Miracle boy could name his reward. Such a man could leave this century of destruction and live in any time with any measure of wealth he might desire. I could return to the city I love, when it still lived."

"Yes," Jude said. "If you believe the Vulture's lies. But even so, you have one problem."

Samra glanced from her father to the boy on the floor and back to the pantry door.

"I'm pretty sure Sam left," Jude said. "A while ago. After all that crashing in the pantry." He twisted, glaring across the floor at the pantry, and then sniffed. "Sand under the door. I felt the temperature go up. And under all the pickle smell, you can pick up the scent of burning."

Samra's father turned quickly, striding above trussed-up children straight into the kitchen and to the pantry door. Samra followed. When he jerked the door open, she smelled pickles, but she saw nothing. Grabbing a lantern off the counter, she held it up for her father. There wasn't much to see. Shelves had been severed, but the amputated portions were missing. Jars had smashed, everyone had heard them, but there was no mess and no trace beyond the aroma. There was even a shallow crater in the floor where the mess should have been. Up higher, the ropes that had bound Sam's wrists hung slack, with sharply severed ends. And only the top half of the lantern still dangled in the space where Samra had hung it.

"I told you," Samra said, looking at her father. "You should have made friends. And now he's loose."

"How?" he asked, spinning around, anger boiling in his throat. "How did he do it?"

"I doubt he was the one who did," Jude said.

Millie was the first to laugh. Across the living room floor, ten tied-up boys joined in.

"Good luck," said Jude. "I'm pretty sure you're look-ing for someone else you might have seen in the comics. Peter Eagle. He lives here. You don't want to mess with him. And I don't see him tied up on the floor with the rest of us."

SAM MIRACLE WOKE TO THE SOUND OF VOICES. HIS WRISTS were torn on the outside and his shoulders felt torn on the inside. He was lying in the dark, tangled up in a foul-smelling pile of wood and glass and vinegar and sand and . . . Glory.

141

The snakes in his hands were both aware of her heat, and they knew her. If it had been anyone else, Cindy would have been rattling. Or striking.

"Glory?" he whispered. "Are you awake?"

Glory groaned and the pile shifted half underneath him. Sam slid as far away from the movement as he could. The stripe of light beneath the pantry door was enough to watch her struggle to rise. And fail.

"My hands are tied," Glory said. "Behind my back. A little help would be great."

Sam felt his way forward until he had found Glory's arms. Tracking them down to her wrists, he tested the knots with his fingers.

"How long have we been in here?" he asked. "Did I imagine the guy with the spiked beard or is he really out there waiting for us?"

"We've been in here too long," Glory said. "But I couldn't wake you up, and I couldn't untie myself. And yeah, that guy's real. But he can't touch us. We aren't when he left us. I used the hourglass. We've been sleeping for a while, but if I did this right, out there only a couple of minutes have passed. At least . . . if I did it right."

"Can you really do that?" Sam tugged the first knot loose and Glory's left hand swung free and she exhaled relief. Her right—gripping her hourglass—was still tied to her belt. Sam jerked at the rope, hooked a finger through a loop, and then unraveled the whole thing.

Glory rose onto all fours, stretching and rolling her shoulders in the dim light. "As of today, I have done it twice," she said. "Counting this time. But I really shouldn't, because I have basically no control once the glass gets started."

"So when are we?" Sam asked.

Glory climbed slowly to her feet. Sam followed her example, and they stood facing each other, dripping vinegar and peach syrup in the dark. Glory said nothing.

"Okay," Sam said. "You have no idea."

"Right."

"Are we backward or forward in time?" Sam asked.

"Still forward," Glory said. "But like I said, we're faster. And I have no idea what it looks like outside that door. Open it and find out."

Sam looked at the light seeping in under the door. He listened to the muffled sound of voices. Then he found the knob with his left hand, and he pulled it open.

The air in the doorway was more like a wall of water. The surface flexed and rippled gently but it was perfectly clear and incredibly light. Inside the air, floating like fossilized ghosts, like creatures woven from smoke, Sam recognized Leviathan and Samra Finn, both staring his way. While the entire submerged kitchen and dining room was visible, Sam could only see a single light—a lantern on the counter beside his ghostly bow. Long tendrils of fiery string were slithering like caterpillars slowly out from the lantern in every direction. In the entire underwater space, those strings were the only things visibly moving.

"I did it," Glory said. "We're still here, but everything else looks crazy, crazy slow."

"They look like underwater smoke bombs." Sam stepped backward. "What do we look like? Can they see us?"

"If they see us at all, I doubt we're more than a flicker in the corner of the room. Remember what Ghost looked like at first? Basically invisible? I bet we looked like underwater smoke bombs to him."

Glory squeezed past Sam and stood with her face just inches shy of the liquid. She flattened her palm above it. After a moment, she touched the watery wall with the tip of her pinkie nail and flinched back instantly.

"Whoa." Glory looked at her pinkie and then squinted at the water. "It tore the edge of my nail right off. Now it's just floating there, just a little smoky shape." She looked back at Sam. Cindy was creeping forward. Speck was slithering Sam's right arm up toward the ceiling. Sam jerked both of his arms back to his torso and crossed them tight.

"So, how does this help us?" he asked. "Do you have any idea what to do now?"

"Thanks for the confidence." Glory looked back out into the kitchen. "Of course I do. If we can move, this is the best thing ever. I actually kind of know what is going on. I did something like this to Peter, but hopefully opposite."

"Why hopefully?" Sam asked.

"Because if I did it like this instead, then he's already dust," Glory said. "I tried to put him in a bubble where his time would be slower. So we'd have more time out here to save him. We're in our own bubble, but a lot faster." She glanced back at Sam, and then pointed at the lantern on the counter. "Much, much faster. Way faster. So much faster that you can see light waves moving in bundles."

Sam stared at the lantern. "That's light? Moving full speed?"

Glory nodded. "And everything looks smoky because normally the atoms are moving fast enough to make stuff solid. But not from where we're standing."

"What's with the water?" Sam asked.

"Space," Glory said. "Time. Standing still enough that it looks like liquid. That's my guess, anyway. I only got good at this today. I've done little baby versions of this before, playing with the hourglass. But this is the real deal."

"Okay," Sam said. "We're sitting in a superfast time bubble. How do we get out?"

"I'm not sure." Glory rotated the hourglass in her fingers as she tried to think. "But when we do, we have to track down El Buitre and deal with whatever he has done to Peter."

"Look out." Sam's right hand whipped past Glory's ear. Vinegar spattered against her cheek as she flinched away, and the fat pickle Sam had just thrown slammed into the watery surface.

The pickle punched a long cylinder of emptiness into the liquid time before it slowed and became smoke. The smoke passed in a contrail over Leviathan's head, still moving faster than the lantern light, and then it plowed through ghostly kitchen cabinets and vanished, leaving behind a curling crater like puckering lips.

"You shouldn't have done that," Glory said quietly. "That could have killed someone. Were you listening to anything Ghost said? Moving this fast you could literally blow someone's head off with your breath. You just fired a pickle through the house faster than a meteor."

"It had to be a pickle," Sam said. "The peaches were too slippery."

Glory ignored him. Instead, she held up one end of her open hourglass to the wall of liquid time. Slowly, the fluid began to twist and spin, stretching in toward the glass. She flipped the glass around and the whirlpool slowed and reversed direction, retreating away from the pantry

146

door, whirling and widening a tunnel out into the room.

"The Angel of Death gave you his blood," Sam said. "You're getting scary."

"Says the boy with snakes in his arms," Glory said, smiling back at Sam over her shoulder. "Now stay close. We're going to move through here like the Reaper collecting souls."

THE VULTURE STOOD IN A SMALL CHAMBER, FACING A STONE arch filled with absolute darkness so heavy and smooth that the entry looked more like a vertical pool than an opening. Behind him, outside the chamber mouth, torchlight from his cavern courtyard flickered around the fountain and across the empty stone table. Mrs. Dervish waited off to the side, like a servant stationed beside an open door. She wore a long black skirt above riding boots and a lacy white blouse, buttoned up all the way to her plump jaw and pinned with a pearl-and-silver brooch that looked like the moon. Her hair was in a tight ballerina bun, stabbed into place with a thin silver knife.

"The boy found me in a dream, Dervish. He passed through the protective seal on this place," the Vulture said. "Tell me how and I might trust you again." When she didn't respond, the Vulture continued. "He challenged me to face him. And now you want me to do just that, on the ground of his choosing, in the moment of

147

his choosing? And without your mothers. Where is the woman who was preaching patience? Are you so jealous of them that you would push me to risk an ambush?"

Mrs. Dervish sniffed loudly and placed her hands on her wide hips. The Vulture towered over her. "William, you know the charms protecting this realm are of the Tzitzimime, not me. Still I assure you, this is not an ambush. One of my men sent the message! He has Sam Miracle captured, ready to deliver to us. We need only collect him. Kill him on the spot if it will make you feel more secure. Or bring him back here and do it properly. Heave him up on a pole in front of a chanting crowd, I don't care. But get it done, and get it done now! Yourself! Do not run to my mothers for this. Be as strong as you can be, or they will quickly forget you when you have released their army."

The Vulture tugged at his beard between his finger and his thumb.

"The boy is captured? You're sure."

"Yes. And he cannot escape through time. The priest is dead. My mothers are performing their rite with his stolen heart in front of ten thousand drooling *naaldlooshii*, as you dillydally here." Mrs. Dervish stamped her foot. "Do it now, William! Do not let them take the boy's heart as well, and prove you a coward!"

The Vulture growled, a low rumble in his chest that

rose to a lip-curling, spitting snarl when he spoke. "You forget yourself, Dervish. Do not give me orders, laced with insults. I will choose my time and my city and release your mothers and my army out into it like a nightmare. Try pushing me again, woman, and I'll take your heart along with Sam Miracle's."

Mrs. Dervish pursed her lips tight, and then reached back and pulled a black lever on the wall behind her. The sound of clattering metal poured out of the dark entryway, overwhelming the chamber. Chains unspooled in the ceiling as unseen stairs were lowered into liquid blackness.

When the rattling had stopped and the echoes had died, Mrs. Dervish gave El Buitre a smile.

"I have a guide ready," she said. "One of my mothers' many servants. By the time the Tzitzimime have finished with Tiempo, you will be holding the heart of Miracle in your fist."

Hunting Party

SAM STAYED AS CLOSE TO GLORY AS HE COULD WITHOUT actually getting a piggyback ride. The funnel tunnel Glory was using to burrow through the slower time stream was widest where she was standing and the liquid sides sagged in behind her.

With the hourglass extended, Glory moved where time receded. Sam grabbed onto the back of her shirt with his right hand, and wound it tight in his grip.

"Where are we going?" he asked. The smoky shape of Samra was on his right. Leviathan, her massive father, was on the left side of the counter. The slow strings of light from the lanterns hit the tunnel walls and exploded into sparkling reflections as they entered Glory's accelerated time.

"Hold on," Glory said. She was leading him toward the kitchen counter. Her tunnel engulfed the corner and then the top of the counter. The four-string crossbow Barto had made for Sam was swallowed by the tunnel next. Glory grabbed the bow and handed it back. Sam let go of her shirt and took it. The strings were empty. Glory handed back a fistful of arrows and he jammed them point down into his left holster. Then he bent over and began to load his bow. There was a metal loop at the end that he kicked his boot into to hold it down, then he used both hands to pull back and lock the strings in place, one at a time.

He was on string number three when the walls of the tunnel rippled and compressed around him, popping both of his ears.

Glory slipped and sat down. Sam dropped to his knees behind her, grabbing at his arrows and quickly fitting two onto strings as Speck and Cindy rippled and tensed.

"There," Glory said. "Look."

Out in the liquid living room, above the vaporous bodies of the tied-up Lost Boys, a vertical cylinder was spinning in place. It was hollow, it was dividing in two, and as it did, the tunnel around Sam and Glory compressed further. Glory swung her hourglass in every direction, keeping her tunnel open, and slid even closer to Sam.

The two halves of the vertical cylinders separated further, both spinning, spreading darkness in between them like a scroll—like a doorway.

Six golden watches on six gold-and-pearl chains floated out of that black door and the liquid time retreated before them. Sam watched time part as the watches and chains moved with a purpose, like the tentacles of a hunting octopus or the spinners of a spider.

Sam blinked and his memory overwhelmed him. Desert heat and a shattered, smoking train. The room at the top of his tower in San Francisco. How many times had he faced this man and how many times had he lost? How many times had he been a boy moving in slow motion, trying to catch up to the guns of a man who had entered a different speed?

Fear was climbing up Sam's throat. Dizziness was worming into his vision. This was what he wanted. He had shown himself to the Vulture and had begged him to come fight. But his body knew better. His body had healthy responses carved deep into its instincts. His body knew that panic and flight might give Sam the best chance of survival.

Cindy and Speck disagreed. They had their own minds and their own anger, and they hadn't lost to the Vulture hundreds of times. But they knew enough to hate him more than any other man they had ever sensed or seen.

With both snakes taut and rattling, Sam waited to see the man who always followed after the floating watches. His throat cinched up completely and his beating heart thundered in his head.

KILL.

Cindy stopped rattling. She wanted to give this enemy no warning. Speck's rattle shivered to a stop. The snakes agreed.

So did Sam.

KILL.

Glory grabbed Sam's right arm, squeezing Speck and his wrist tight.

El Buitre stepped out of the outer darkness and into the room. His black pointed beard was longer than it had been in Sam's dream, as was the black hair curling on his shoulders. He was wearing a bloodred vest where all six watches and chains attached. A seventh watchless chain dangled past the gun belt at his waist. As the Vulture entered the room, that broken chain rose, pointing straight at Sam.

Sam felt the seventh watch tug forward in reply.

"Shoot him!" Glory hissed, releasing Sam's wrist. "Now! Before he sees us."

William Sharon, the Vulture, onetime king of California's golden age, arch-outlaw king of all ages, looked down at his golden, tugging, watchless chain. And then following the chain's direction, he looked up.

Through twenty feet of liquid time, Sam met the outlaw's hooded eyes. And in that second of seconds, all Sam's fear vanished. How could he be afraid, when fear was what he saw in El Buitre's eyes? That . . . and surprise.

In one accelerated time stream, the Vulture reached for his guns. In another, Sam raised his bow.

The sound was bigger than anything Millie Miracle had ever heard. A single boom, louder than thunder, trailed by a wave of heat and the smell of burnt pickle. And just after, while her bones were still buzzing, she looked up and saw splinters of kitchen cabinet smoking around a large hole in the wall.

But there was no time to even think about what had happened or why it smelled like pickles.

Jude was laughing.

Leviathan was shouting for his men.

The air wobbled like sheet metal in the kitchen and

half of the counter disappeared, along with the lantern. And Sam's bow.

"Sam?" Millie asked.

A foul smell surrounded her, a smell from her nightmares, the smell of the endlessly rotting things lost in the outer darkness that had once been the constant aroma of her captivity.

Millie gagged. Jude had stopped laughing.

Two more explosions split the room, searing the air with bright stripes of fire.

A third boom spun a smoking blue braid between them.

Millie had no time to scream or flinch. She barely had time to blink.

And then the only man she feared in the world was suddenly falling out of the sky, falling from nowhere with a blue arrow in his shoulder.

El Buitre—with a gun in each hand—crashed to the floor across the tied-up bodies of the Lost Boys. Six golden watches bounced on the marble floor around him.

GLORY FELT ONE OF THE VULTURE'S BULLETS HISS PAST HER left ear. His shots sent so many slinky ripples through the liquid time, it was impossible to see Sam's blue arrow fly. Impossible for the Vulture, too, judging from the surprise on his face when the arrow punched into his right shoulder.

The big man staggered backward and slipped, splashing into the much slower time stream, trailing watches from his smoky figure as he fell.

"Go!" Glory screamed. "Finish it!"

Sam was trying to fit another arrow onto a string.

"Now!" Glory grabbed Sam and swung her hourglass down.

The thick, slow time collapsed in around them, slamming them to the floor, filling their lungs and tearing at their skin. Glory gasped, her ears ringing, but not so loud that she couldn't hear the snakes both rattling again on Sam's shoulders. It was like having an ocean fall on her back. Like a car wreck. Like drowning.

Somehow, Sam was already rising to his feet, raising his crossbow. Hanging on to her hourglass, Glory scrambled up beside him.

Leviathan was on the floor with his hands over his ears along with his daughter and her two huge bodyguards. The Vulture should have been sprawled out bleeding on the marble.

But he wasn't. The Vulture was gone.

There was only a rippling mirage in the air above the bodies of her friends, where they had seen the doorway to darkness open.

"Oh no," Glory said.

"Down!" Sam yelled, and he lunged for Glory, but

156

she knew they were already too late. She knew she had made a huge mistake. They never should have left the faster time. Now they were the smoke, the helpless targets, as helpless as Sam had been beside the train when the Vulture had destroyed his arms so many lifetimes ago.

Invisible guns thundered.

The mind is the fastest place in the body. But spirit is faster than all flesh. Faster than thought. Glory's fingers didn't move around the hourglass. Her arm didn't even twitch toward defense.

Her soul moved. As fast as the first light from the lips of the first Word.

Sand pulsed into a glassy swirling window like a shield.

Sam tackled her and they both flew behind the kitchen island, landing back on the marble.

A woman screamed and Glory looked up through the spinning shield that trailed back to her hourglass. A beautiful but terrified black woman stood up against the refrigerator with a platter of vegetables and dip in her hands. She was dressed for a party, in a shimmering dress and high heels, and an amazing pair of gold curtain earrings. The kitchen was full of daylight. The electricity was on. In that strange moment, peering into a happier time, Glory wondered if the woman was the boss of the maid she'd scared upstairs earlier, or if they

157

were from totally different decades.

"Sorry!" Glory said. "Love the earrings, by the way."

"Russ!" the woman screamed and threw the platter of vegetables at Glory's window.

Glory reached up and punched the glass suspended above her. Sand and carrots and spinach dip rained down around her and all over Sam. He sat up quickly, shaking sliced peppers out of his hair and trying to spit sand off his tongue.

The kitchen was dim again. And it smelled like pickles. They were back.

"Glory," Sam whispered. "Hurry! We have to follow him. Do your glass thing!"

Glory grabbed onto the counter and pulled herself up until her eyes were just high enough to see into the living room. She could see the rippling in the air around what she knew was the door into darkness. She thought she could see three shimmering shapes inside it—two shorter ones helping a much taller one. The Vulture had assistants. Of course he did. The idea of trying to follow them through that doorway into the foul darkness was total craziness, and yet Glory knew that's what she was about to do.

Peter's body was upstairs turning to sand. Because of the Vulture. Father Tiempo's life was turning to sand. Sam's life. Glory's. Millie's. Every moment and every year, every city and every nation that Father Tiempo had ever defended or upheld, all of it would be nothing but sand.

Glory twisted the hourglass in her hand. It was her only weapon, but a little more control would be nice. She looked down at Sam. He was seated on the floor, his foot hooked into the end of his crossbow, pulling back strings and slipping arrows into place as Speck and Cindy rattled.

"Go!" Sam whispered. "The train has to make it across the bridge!" He blinked, confusion flooding his eyes.

Great. Could she really do this if Sam was hallucinating?

"Samra?" The voice was Leviathan's.

Sam looked up.

"Are you okay?" the man asked. "Are you hurt?"

"I'll live," Samra's voice responded. "My ears hurt. Who was that?"

"Your father's boss," Jude answered. "The Vulture. El Buitre. The great giver of batteries. That's who."

"Not my boss," Leviathan growled. "A client. An ally. Occasionally."

"Well, he's leaving," Jude said. "Look. You see this rippling business in the air? That's your battery king running away."

Glory focused on Sam's eyes.

"Stay close," she whispered. "And don't let me die."

Sam climbed into a crouch, his bow held with both coiling, scaled arms. Speck was on the triggers, Cindy would be handling the aim.

"What time is this?" Sam was blinking faster now, fighting to understand. "Why do I have a bow?"

Glory bit her lip. She had to make a choice right now. And hiding behind the kitchen island wasn't going to save Peter or kill the Vulture.

"I just had guns a second ago," Sam continued. "In the desert. Pretty sure there was a train wreck . . ." He shook his head, looking up and down and all around.

"Hush," Glory said. She touched Sam's cheek, pulling his eyes back to hers. "I'll explain when I can. Just stay close. Trust me. And don't let anyone stop me."

Sam nodded. "My sister . . ."

"She's fine. We'll come back for her," Glory said. "Later. We'll come back for everyone. Are you ready?"

Sam swallowed, looked down at the bow in his hands, and nodded again.

"Good," Glory said. "Then let's go."

Glory didn't jump out from behind the counter. She stood. She didn't run across the kitchen into the living room. She walked. She didn't lash her glass or swing it like a whip. She held it out in front of her like the hilt of a sword, but instead of a pointing blade, it spun her a shield of living glass. She held it between herself and the

160

Vulture's shimmering door, just in case he could still fire at them from wherever he had gone.

Leviathan had a gun in his hands. The spikes in his beard were bent and misshapen. Five other men stood with him, also armed, along with small Samra—hair a wild, red cloud and face pale with surprise.

SAMRA SAW GLORY RISE WITH THE FLASHING SHIELD SPINning from her hand. She had seen—or felt—everything that had just come before. The Vulture had appeared. The air had blurred, the room had been filled with a vile stink, thunderous gunshots had shaken the windows, and then the perpetually elusive outlaw villain that had long haunted her daydreams and imaginings had suddenly tumbled to the floor with an arrow in his shoulder.

The scream had flown from Samra's lips before she'd even known it was coming. The outlaw had vanished again, almost as quickly, and more gunshots had rocked Samra's eardrums.

And now Glory was on her feet, bright and alive and furious, and Sam was just behind her.

In one of the comic books, it would have taken two or three full pages to capture the battle that had just happened, but in the life Samra was now living, it had all played out in seconds, mostly out of view, and with impossible noise.

And in those seconds, four things became as perfectly clear to Samra Finn as the incredible ringing in her ears. First, this Glory was much cooler and more dangerous than she had first thought, cooler even than her comic book self. Second, there was absolutely no way that Samra Finn was going to get between Glory and Sam, not if she wanted to survive. Third, she shouldn't even want to. Sam and Glory were in a war, and it was a war Samra wanted them to win. If the Vulture was half as evil as the shadowy comic version, every living soul in every time and every world should want Sam and Glory to win. Fourth, Samra was done with her life. It was time to be a hero or die trying.

"Sam!" Millie yelled from the floor. "Glory! Thank God!"

"They're not staying," Jude said.

"We're not?" Sam asked. "Glory, why are they tied up?"

Leviathan Finn raised his shotgun.

"No!" Samra jumped in front of her father, but Sam's right hand was even faster. The arrow hissed past Samra's ribs and ricocheted off her father's knuckles behind her. Levi dropped his shotgun onto the ground, wincing in pain.

"No more!" Sam yelled.

Samra looked at her grimacing father, and then she looked back at Sam. His eyes were wide and startled and even a little worried.

"Sorry," Sam said to her. "You moved quick."

Samra swallowed and nodded. Sam smiled and his pink, snaky right hand twisted up to scratch his horribly matted hair. He was actually embarrassed.

Samra began to rethink her earlier position. Maybe Sam and Glory would be stronger if someone did get at least a little bit between them.

Glory ignored Samra's close call, instead focusing on the big man with the spiked red beard who was squeezing his own bloody knuckles. She pointed at the Lost Boys tied up on the floor.

"Free them all," Glory said. "Now. Or we'll come back in about thirty of your seconds and you'll be dead before you even see us."

"Glory?" Millie asked.

"Sam!" Drew yelled. "What do you want us to do?"

"Kick these chumps out," Sam said. "And be ready."

Glory swung the hourglass up over her head and down again toward the last shimmer in the air. She needed a fast tunnel, one that would give her more than enough time to dive through the Vulture's doorway before it became a mousehole. Webs of glass immediately formed into a tunnel stretching out in front of her, and she began to run. Instantly, inside her own accelerated time, the shimmer vanished and she could see the Vulture's doorway clearly.

The spinning cylinders were almost completely back together, sealing the open darkness between them.

"Keep up, Sam!" She jumped over the tied-up smoky bodies of her friends, preparing to tuck into a somersault and roll in case the Vulture or one of his friends had guns raised or an ambush waiting.

Heavy, sickening blackness swallowed her whole and Glory put out her hands to catch herself. But the ambush was of a different sort. A large, dimly shimmering hole waited where the ground should have been. Glory's hands found nothing. Her feet kicked nothing. She was falling. Twisting, she flailed in every direction, but there was nothing to grab or catch or kick. The air went cold and sharp and clean.

Above her, she saw the tiny pool of light she had fallen into. Sam's shape plunged through it. And then another, with a wild mane of hair.

Glory spun in the frozen air and looked down. Far, far below her, she saw the silvery shape of the Puget Sound, islands and water dotted with the lights of houses and boats. Not far away, she could see the lights and towers and streaming traffic of Seattle, sprawling and alive and magical.

She was back in the living time, but she was falling into it from the height of an airliner, and two more people were falling behind her.

How long did she have before she hit the surface? Thirty seconds? One minute? Not enough. That was all she knew for sure.

Tears were streaming from her eyes. The wind was trying to peel her face off. And she had to do something. Now.

Glory rolled onto her back and splayed her limbs, fighting to balance as she scanned the starlit sky above her, searching for shadows while her ponytail whipped her face.

"Sam!" she yelled again, but the wind swallowed her voice completely.

One hundred yards away, a black shape shot straight down, tumbling and spinning like a thrown knife.

And then a second shape slammed into her legs and grabbed on tight around her ankles. Glory and her passenger began to spin end over end.

"Stop!" Glory screamed. "Let go!"

Desperate to slow down, Glory lashed out with her hourglass. Glass melted into a sphere all around her, and then stretched into a drop as she slowed to a stop inside, suspended in the air like an astronaut.

Samra was still hugging her ankles tight. Her eyes were wide.

"Let go!" Glory yelled. And she kicked her off.

"What's going on?" Samra asked, floating alongside

Glory inside the uneven orb.

"No questions!" Glory spun around. Now without the wind, she should be able to spot Sam and then she'd figure something out. She'd dive and grab him and slow his time down or something.

But it was hard to make out anything through the glass. It was all moving so . . . *fast*.

"Oh, no . . ." Glory realized what she'd done. She and Samra had slowed down, but that just made everything outside faster by comparison. Her glass raindrop was falling just as fast as she had been a moment ago. All she had done was reduce the number of seconds she would have before splatting. She didn't even have time to think.

"Grab on!" Glory shouted, smashing the raindrop with a snap of the hourglass, and she didn't have to tell Samra twice. The redhead hugged her around the back of the knees as Glory went into a dive, searching for any sign of Sam.

And they didn't seem so high anymore. The city lights were out of view. They were above a crescent-shaped island dotted with lights and one massive, glowing house.

"There!" Samra yelled. "To your left!"

Glory saw Sam, limp and fluttering like a shot crow. She shifted her dive toward him, mind racing as fast as the wind, ignoring the screaming panic in her ears.

How could she possibly . . . couldn't make the same

mistake . . . slow? Fast? Back?

She needed a tunnel not a falling ball, a tunnel all the way to the ground, but first, between herself and Sam. And everything inside the tunnel all the way to the ground had to be slow.

Glory focused on what she wanted. With Samra flapping on her heels like a cape, Glory gripped the hourglass with both hands and swung it in a loop pointing toward Sam. She swung it as fast as she could, around and around, until sand and glass hissed and cracked not just beside her but out in front of her.

The tunnel leapt ahead, glowing orange, bending at her direction in pursuit of Sam.

But she was too late. The island was exploding upward now, coming at them like a race car. Glory pushed harder, and the blood drained from her eyes. And then her brain. She felt her body going limp. A cool calm washed through her veins. Her mind latched onto the flickering traces of old memories. Sam at SADDYR. Young Father Tiempo, impatient and bleak. Her right hand was on fire and hissing. For a moment, she wondered if she had been given a snake, too. But then she knew it was just the hissing of sand. And she was unconscious.

GLORIA NAVARRE SAT ON A SMOOTH, YELLOW PLASTIC BENCH in a large bus station. It was her birthday. She was officially eight. She had her heels up on the seat, her arms around her legs, and her face pressed into her knees, watching the bus station strangers flow past her in both directions from behind the frayed holes in her old jeans.

Gloria was wearing her brother's old jean jacket, with patches on both shoulders and the too-long sleeves rolled up, with a purple backpack over the top of it. In the backpack, she had two small action figures—one missing an arm—one small stuffed penguin, one pencil, and one notebook full of pictures and puzzles and the only four photos she cared about from the first eight years of her life. In her belly, she had the remains of her only birthday gift. A donut. From her brother. Given to her four hours ago. Right before he'd given her a quarter and a scrap of paper with a phone number on it and told her to call if there was an emergency.

Before he'd left.

What was an emergency? Being hungry wasn't bad enough to call a stranger. Having no bed, no house, no parents, she'd done without those things before. But being alone in the crowd, being without her brother, well, that felt like the biggest emergency she could imagine.

Gloria had never been without Alex. Never. The first photo in her notebook proved it. It was a picture of Alex, five years old, his hair black and thick, his round face and bushy brows serious and full of worry. His arms were around Gloria—hours old, pink faced and wrapped up tight in a white blanket with blue and pink edges. She took up all of his lap and more. Two days later, they would both be carried out of that hospital by unhappy strangers who were not their parents, but who were more willing to care for them than their real parents were.

Gloria had grown up in bedrooms that were not hers, in beds that were not hers, in backyards that were not hers, in old clothes that weren't even hers. But her brother, Alex, he had always been hers. For real. All the way. Hers. And she had been his. Alex had told her that no one was allowed to adopt them for real, because half of their mother's blood had been older than all the cities in California, and so it was against the law for normal people with normal blood to be their parents. The two of them were their family, the two of them and the long line of ancestors that ran back through desert kings and mountain healers all the way to unknown explorers who had found the New World in the time of unwritten histories. At night, Alex had made up stories for her about those ancestors, so that when they went to sleep, they were surrounded by a family as great and grand as the stars. That was how her life had always been, and that was how it would always be.

Until the bus station.

Telling time was easy, and the big clock was obvious.

But Gloria didn't look at it. Not after the first few hours. Instead, from the safety of her bench, from behind the fortress of her knees, she watched the buses pull up to the curbs and the people file off and the people file on. She smelled the diesel exhaust and she listened to the punch and squeal of brakes. She watched men and women line up at glass kiosks to buy tickets and she watched the tired people inside the kiosks read magazines when there were no tickets to sell.

When men swept the floors, she held perfectly still and made herself small. There was nothing wrong. Alex would come back. He would have food. He would have a plan. He didn't need to explain why he had woken her up in the middle of the night before her birthday to sneak out of the foster house. She had seen his bruises. She had one or two of her own.

Gloria did not leave her plastic chair that day. Not to get a drink. Not to go to the bathroom. The bus station was big and Alex needed to know where she was. If he came back, she had to be where he'd left her. She had to be patient. And so, when the sun was down and the people had mostly gone, and the kiosks were mostly empty, she slept in that chair with her knees up and her backpack on. She slept with a full bladder and a dry mouth and an empty stomach. She slept until a man with a mop and a policeman woke her up and asked

170

her name. And she looked up at them both and she told them what she knew to be the truth.

"It's not an emergency. Alex will come to find me."

Sam Miracle studied Glory. She was curled up in the grass, on her right side with her knees up and her face almost touching them. Her ponytail was in her face, but she was still holding her hourglass tight, and a dark glass blade trailed out of it like a scythe, growing and twisting into a massive, towering glass cylinder that completely enclosed them maybe twelve feet across—grass at the bottom, pure darkness one hundred feet above them, muted daylight outside the thick, cloudy glass walls. Sam didn't know how they'd fallen or how long they'd slept, or even where they were. He didn't know who the Alex was that Glory kept muttering about in her sleep, but he was glad that her sleeping self didn't think that whatever had just happened was an emergency. It sure felt like one to him.

Glory jerked in her sleep like a falling dreamer, but she didn't wake. Whatever was going on in her dreams, Sam was pretty sure it wasn't pleasant.

Leaning forward, Sam reached for Glory's face with his left hand, but Cindy tensed, excited, and her rattle shivered on Sam's shoulder.

Sam pulled her back and made a fist, pressing his

knuckles into the soft ground, leaning his weight on that arm to make sure Cindy couldn't surprise him if she tried. Then he stretched out his right hand, with Speck's curious pink head, and he gently brushed Glory's dark hair out of her face.

"Glory," he said, but he paused. He had meant to wake her. But instead he was focused on her hair. She had a white stripe, an inch wide, that began at her neck behind her left ear. The stripe ran up to and through the rubber band she had used to pull her hair back, and then drifted out loosely through her ponytail.

Sam touched the white patch on her scalp with a single finger, and traced it up. He didn't know what it meant, but it couldn't be good.

"Is she dead?" Samra asked.

Sam looked back over his shoulder. A moment ago, the redhead had been just as unconscious as Glory.

"No," Sam said. "She's breathing."

He looked up the long bent glass shaft at the darkness above.

"Why did you follow us?" he asked.

"Why would I stay behind? You two are superhuman." Samra slid up onto her knees beside him. "I want to help. Have you gone into darkness like that before?"

"Yes," Sam said, looking back down at Glory. She was breathing softly, blades of grass bending away from

172

her lips and then rising again. "We've passed through the darkness before."

"Do you always fall back out?"

Sam shook his head. "We've never fallen."

"What's with the glass tunnel?" Samra asked. "Where did it come from?" She slid away from Sam and placed her hand against the thick pearly wall.

"I'm guessing the tunnel just saved our lives," Sam said. "For now, at least. And it came from Glory. She made it. So she's tired."

Samra returned to Sam's side, looking down at Glory.

"What do we do now?" she asked.

"We let her sleep. I don't think that was easy. And whatever comes next will be harder."

Samra leaned over and reached for Glory's white stripe. "Ha! That's weird. She must dye it in the comics."

"Don't touch her." Sam slapped her hand away. "And don't laugh. Not ever." He shook his head, thinking about what she had just said. "Dye it for the comics? You do realize that comics aren't real, right? Someone colors them however they want."

The redhead sat back in the grass and studied Sam, eyes narrowed, head cocked.

"Sure," she said. "But you've been pretty real so far. And so is she. I guess someone *paints* her hair for the comics, then. Because she has black hair. No white stripe."

"She never has," Sam said. He touched the end of her ponytail. "Until right now."

Samra reached into her vest and pulled a rolled-up and flattened comic book out of an inside pocket. Then she tossed it onto the grass in front of Sam. He flattened it with his hand.

The Song of Ghost and Glory was trumpeted across the cover. But the words didn't matter to him as much as the once bright picture. A boy with snake arms was riding a motorcycle in the upper corner. Sam didn't think it looked like him at all, apart from that fact that the boy was wearing jeans, a tank top, and boots and a gun belt. And he had rattlesnakes in his arms. There was that.

The central image was of a towering boy made of black fire, swinging scythe blades of black fire from both hands. On the right side, a cartoony version of the Vulture was attacking, flying on golden watch-chain wings. On the left, Glory was also flying through the air, deflecting the black fire with a bright whip of glass and sand. She looked amazing.

"You're right," Sam said. "She doesn't have a stripe."

Her hair was completely white.

Glory Hallelujah

EL BUITRE STORMED OUT OF HEAVY DARKNESS INTO AN uneven ring of orange light cast by an iron lantern dangling from a swaying chain. It was the only light visible in any direction. His watches trailed behind and above him in two wings of three, and his right arm hung limp at his side. The sharp point of an arrow was sticking inches out of the back of his right shoulder.

Wincing, the Vulture reached up and pulled the lantern chain. Metal clattered above him and black iron stairs began to lower out of the darkness like a drawbridge

175

while two more shapes entered the ring of light behind the Vulture.

Women. The first was Mrs. Dervish. Her long black skirt was twisted slightly, her blouse rumpled but still buttoned up all the way to her chin. Her cheeks were flushed and the bun on top of her head was fraying.

The second woman was a head taller than Mrs. Dervish, but half her thickness. She was wrapped like a mummy but with strips of shadow instead of cloth, which made her very little more than a shadow herself. But her long bare feet were visible. As were her long-fingered hands, her collarbones and throat, and her sharp jaw and thin parted lips and pointed nose. Yet a blindfold of shadow had been bound tight across her eyes and brow, creating a gulf of nothingness between the lower half of her face and her uneven nest of perfectly white hair.

As the iron stairs settled into place and the rattling of chains and gears drifted away across the unseen world, the Vulture looked back at the women.

"You lied," he said. "Tiempo was there. I thought you said he was good as dead."

"He was not there, William," Mrs. Dervish said, her voice sounding like a teacher addressing a student she fears. "The priest's work has begun to unravel on every side. You have seen it yourself. He is gone."

"Don't start." The Vulture spat and raised a foot

onto the bottom stair. "Shall I leave you out here with your guide? Miracle was waiting in ambush, sheltered in a faster time—a time much faster than any I have ever walked. He knew I was coming, Dervish, or do you not see this arrow in my flesh?" The Vulture began to climb, stomping his anger with each step. "Tiempo was there!" he shouted. "Or another with his powers. Tell me, which is worse?"

Mrs. Dervish moved toward the stairs, pulled up her skirt, and climbed them briskly.

"The girl," she said. "His pupil, he gifted her with an hourglass of his making. That is all. She cannot—"

"A pupil! No consequence of his labors should exist! Tiempo and his line should be no more!" The Vulture vanished into upper darkness.

"William, wait! Maybe there's—"

Mrs. Dervish vanished up the stairs after her master, along with her voice. At the bottom of the stairs, the woman swathed in shadow swayed in place and said nothing. The drawbridge stairs began to rise in front of her. The lamp dimmed and went out above her.

Shadow took her completely.

THE VULTURE STEPPED OUT OF THE SMALL STONE BUILDING that held the iron stairs and crossed his cavernous courtyard paved with cream limestone, pocketing his watches as he went. Damp air nipped his skin as he walked around his large black-bottomed pool with a fountain, heaping up water around the massive sundial in its center and the large levitating golden clock that was chained to it. Thin dagger crystals of ice were visible on the surface of the dark water.

Every square of pavement beneath the Vulture's feet bore an inscription, but he didn't look down. Blood spatters marked his steps as he moved past his stone table toward a stone shrine carved into the opposite wall of the courtyard. It looked like a miniature temple, protected by uneven square columns and a large iron gate.

Mrs. Dervish's quick steps followed close behind him.

"William," she said. "Let me get that arrow out before they see you. William!"

But the Vulture only lengthened his stride.

"William!" Mrs. Dervish yelled. "Do not show yourself weak!"

El Buitre paused at the gate to the shrine. "Madam," he said. "I am as you made me."

Jerking the iron gate open, he stepped inside, letting it swing closed behind him. Mrs. Dervish caught it before it clanged shut, and squeezed herself inside.

El Buitre touched his wounded shoulder and stood in front of a small stone altar beneath a large black carving of a two-headed vulture. Dragging his bloody fingers across the altar, he stepped around it, passed the statue, and faced a heavy black-velvet curtain that served as the shrine's rear wall.

"Respect!" Mrs. Dervish yelled. "William, show respect!"

The Vulture closed his eyes and quieted his breathing, trying to hear his beating heart, trying to feel the six ticking watches in his vest. Then, leaving his right arm limp, he threw the curtain open with his left.

A wall of liquid time rippled and warped in front of him. Otherworldly light spilled through the liquid into the shrine around him—pale, like the sun, but thrown by one thousand unsteady flames. He stood in the back of a small shrine, but if he took three steps forward he would be standing on a stone balcony high above a massive city square in a cavern.

Behind him, Mrs. Dervish was bowing in front of the altar and rushing through whispered chants of respect and supplication.

With the curtain open, the wall of time began bulging inward, probing the shrine. The Vulture stepped forward, standing so close that the fog of his cold breath misted the living wall. Smooth liquid limbs of time as thick as tree trunks slid in above the Vulture's head and on either side. They seemed to taste the air around him, to sense him, to consider his worth.

El Buitre waited. He could have stepped forward himself, but he preferred the embrace he knew was coming.

The liquid limbs wrapped around him, sweeping him up. Warmth filled his nostrils and poured down his throat and stung his wound.

The Vulture blinked slowly, and his eyes adjusted. He was through.

In front of him, the stone balcony rail blocked most of his view of the square, but he could see the massive buildings carved into the walls of the underworld city, and he could see the enormous saffron banners hanging down their columns, and the warm breeze on his face made the black two-headed vultures on the banners take gentle flight.

If things had gone correctly, at this moment, he would have been presenting the heart of the Miracle boy over the rail of this high balcony to the grotesque army assembled below. He would have been announcing the death of Tiempo and the end of his influence.

But things had not gone correctly.

Beside him, two women shaped of shadow spoke.

"Your hurt must be avenged."

"Death is not enough."

The Vulture looked to his left.

Two women barely larger than children watched him. Both women had sharp, symmetrical features with overly long necks. One had large bright eyes of white, and one of black. Their faces were covered with feathers instead of skin, silver and cream feathers that were so tiny and smooth, they were almost imperceptible from where the Vulture was standing. Both had braids of scaled reptilian hair bound back in motionless bundles with wide bloodred ribbons.

The women were also wearing robes of lightless shadow. They were living doorways into the utter darkness. A man could plunge through them and lose himself in the foulest outskirts of time. Blades, bullets, arrows, fists—nothing would strike flesh beneath those robes. Where their shadow robes were open at the throat, they wore thick necklaces of shrunken hearts and faces and hands encased in bloody water.

Tzitzimime, Mothers of Night, star demons cast down from the light of Heaven to the dim light of Earth and from the light of Earth to the deep prisons in Earth's belly, devourers of the newly born, spirit slavers of pregnant mothers, consumers of innocent blood. Razpocoatl and Magyamitl—in darker times and darker ages, when they flew free at dusk and dawn, even to speak their names was to curse the air itself and all to whom the air carried the sounds.

The mothers were guarded by two men dressed all in black except for yellow armbands marked with the two-headed vulture. One of the men was pale and bald. Red scars crisscrossed his scalp, and a short beard covered his wide jaw. The other man had darker skin with thick straight hair that was combed back in a stiff slab. Instead of eyes, both had spheres of clear, shifting water in their sockets.

"The wound did nothing," El Buitre said finally. "Besides, it's a reminder that I am a man."

"No, you are the chosen one," Magyamitl said, and ghostly tails of steam crawled up from the corners of her black eyes. "The one who has gathered us from the deeps and will set us all free."

"Who drew the blood?" Razpocoatl, the woman with white eyes, raised a dark skeletal arm from beneath her robe and held out a smooth rod of watery time in her taloned hand. The Vulture's watches all leapt from his vest and swept up above him, spinning a hazy cloud that held her gaze. "Miracle," she said, and the watches froze in the air.

"That boy again," Magyamitl said, and the feathers on her face ruffled. "But the priest's heart was taken and now hangs in halves around our necks."

White-eyed Razpocoatl extended her rod, touching the feathered end of the arrow in El Buitre's shoulder. He shivered as the arrow liquefied, splashing down his chest onto the stones below his feet.

"Our daughter, Dervish, failed you," she said. "But we will not."

The Vulture filled his lungs and rolled his shoulder. The pain was gone, replaced with the heat he always felt when the mothers touched him—the heat of anger, of rage, the boiling urge to destroy, to shatter, to grind to dust all times and places and people who resisted him.

Tingling with wrath, El Buitre strode to the balcony rail and looked out over the massive city square. The stairs and balconies of every building were overflowing with hollow-faced men and bent women all dressed in ragged black and rotting furs. A crowd as silent and still as it was enormous filled the square like human cobblestones.

The mothers moved beside the Vulture, one on each side. His golden watch wings of chain and pearl spread above him.

"Are they not beautiful?" Magyamitl asked, her black eyes rolling. "Your furious army? The wronged? The vengeful? We have gathered *yee naaldlooshii* from the farthest ages of the dead outer darkness into this, your city of light. We have called them. They will give you the world, and no primitive priest or prophesied boy can stop them. They have no lives to lose, no souls to be burdened with fear."

Razpocoatl and Magyamitl both raised their watery rods. The wind swirled, snapping their robes of shadow and revealing skeletal bodies beneath, and taloned hands where they should have had feet. As one, one hundred crude phalanxes of men and women raised weapons in response—blades and rifles and banners of yellow and black.

"Children!" The mothers spoke in unison, and their sharp voices echoed through the square like the cries of hawks. "What do you desire?"

"Life!" The word erupted from the square, shaking the balcony, rippling the long banners on their columns.

"Who shall give it to you?" the mothers cried.

"The Vulture!" the army shouted, and as one, they stomped the stones and slapped their chests. "The Vulture!" they cried. "The Vulture!" And all over the square, they writhed, taking on animal parts and animal shapes.

The mothers both turned, looking up at the tall outlaw between them, the one who would lead their dead and undying army.

The Vulture watched the beasts chant. He felt the stone rail shake beneath his palms. When Dervish had opened his chest and used the magic of her mothers to chain seven watches to his heart, it had all been for a moment like this. He had thought to release an army into San Francisco long ago, but that moment had been delayed and that city abandoned. It was better this way. He knew that he was being carried by a storm beyond his control. But he was a man who had already awakened volcanoes and quaked the earth. He knew about riding storms. And this one could give him the world.

So long as the bodies of a priest and a Miracle boy were part of the ruin.

"The boy found me here," he said quietly, but he could have whispered and they would have heard him. "In a dream. Tell me how."

The white-eyed mother hopped closer to him, looking up into his face.

"He cannot come here," she said. "The ways are sealed to all but your army."

"But he did," the Vulture said. "Perhaps he is more powerful than you."

The mothers both gargled laughter.

Razpocoatl rolled her black eyes. "And perhaps your fear invented this dream."

"I am not afraid," El Buitre said. "I am ready. When shall I open the doors for this army?"

Black and white eyes sparkled.

"Now," the mothers answered. "The time for doors is always now."

MRS. DERVISH STOOD BESIDE THE ALTAR, HER COLD BREATH curling in front of her mouth. She had respected the altar of her mothers. But she held back. Instead, she looked through the liquid wall and she watched her mothers raise their rods on either side of the great man she had chosen and created. Not for them. For herself. Not to play with for a time and then cast aside, but to elevate, to mold, to wield over history like a scepter. Time's arch-outlaw, William Sharon, the man she had crafted into the Vulture—the one for whom she had created seven gardens and whose heart she had chained to the seven watches powered by the tides of the seven seas—that man stood with his back to her, choosing a path that she had not prepared for him. He was being guided by her mothers, and their toys were used only for destruction. They never lasted long.

Mrs. Dervish had always believed in patience. The Vulture had pursued that patience, but Father Tiempo had been patient as well, and stubborn to the point of foolishness. But in the end, his foolishness and his patience and his Miracle boy had won. But not completely.

Now the Vulture had set another course.

Something cold and fine dragged across the skin inside Mrs. Dervish's left forearm. Flinching, she grabbed her sleeve at the wrist and pulled it up to her elbow. As she watched, crude letters formed beneath her soft pale flesh, inked in blood.

DIDN'T NO HE WAS LOOSE. HAD HIM TRUSSED UP GOOD. U NEVER TOLD ME HE COULD TIMEWALK. IS THE BOSS ANGRY???

"Fool," Mrs. Dervish said. "Stupid, useless oaf." She slapped at her skin and the blood letters vanished, absorbed into her blue veins. A moment later, new letters formed.

DEALS STILL A DEAL. DID MY PART. MORE BATTERIES, ICE CREAM, BULLETS AS WE DISGUST PLEASE?

Mrs. Dervish slapped herself even harder. Reaching up into her loose heap of hair, she plucked out an old bone fountain pen, uncapped it with her mouth, twisted the pen in half, and then opened a flap on the left hip of her skirt, revealing dozens of ink capsules, all dark red. She plucked one from the top row—labeled "Levi"—plopped it into the pen, and screwed the ends back together. With the cap still between her lips and her cheeks, she scrawled down the inside of her forearm in a beautiful looping cursive, but the letters were invisible.

She hesitated, and then twisted her wrist around and wrote across her own forehead.

In front of her, the liquid wall warped and rippled, and the roar of a million soulless voices reached her dimly, as faint as a memory, but as certain as a promise.

Mrs. Dervish capped her pen.

LEVIATHAN FINN STOOD IN THE LIVING ROOM OF NEVER-land, pen in hand. Bull and Dog and two others were with him. Children were trussed up in rows across the floor.

His daughter was gone. Vanished. Swallowed by a ripple in the air. Levi's heart was pounding.

"You should listen to Sam," Jude said. "Set us free or he'll kill you."

"Shut your gob. It's already been thirty seconds," Bull said.

But Levi was staring at his forearm, awaiting his message. When it arrived, it stung with pain like a razor blade, and he knew it was meant to. He gritted his teeth and watched the swooping letters of the woman's hand.

"I can't read these," he grunted. "These aren't English."

Bull looked over his shoulder. "It's cursive, boss. I've seen cursive."

"Then read it," he said. "Now."

"Can't," Bull said. "But I've seen it."

Levi looked at Dog, but he shrugged his sweatered shoulders and backed away.

"I can," Jude said.

"So can I," Millie added. "If you like."

Leviathan strode over the trussed bodies, stepped over Jude, and crouched beside Millie, extending his bare arm with its bloody letters. Millie arched her back and rolled to her side to get a look.

You are hereby sentenced to death, by the Vulture's hand or mine, you donkey fool of a man. I will feed you to the mothers. (You had but one job.)

188

Millie didn't read it aloud.

"It's a threat," Millie said. "She wants to kill you and feed you to the mothers, whatever that means."

Jude laughed.

"Shut it," Levi snarled. And then he twisted in pain and slapped a palm to his forehead.

"Boss?" Bull asked.

Dog hurried forward, grabbing Levi's elbow and helping him upright.

"What's it say?" Levi lowered his hand, glaring at them both. The one word written in capitals was easy for both of them to read. They even knew what it meant.

CARRION

"I think you need some new friends," Jude said, craning his face up from the floor. "Why be hunted by both sides?"

"You have to understand," Levi said. "I never met the Vulture. Never even seen him from a distance. There was just this lady asking me to keep an eye out for a boy with powers. And she gave me things that just weren't possible." Leviathan Finn slumped to the floor and put his head in his hands. "And now my Samra's gone—poof—like that. And all because of that woman."

"And her batteries," Jude said.

"Fair trade." Flip the Lip burst out laughing. "Just saying, I'd take batteries over that girl of yours any day."

"I could like her," Barto mumbled into the floor. "But not more than a pack of nine volts. Man, just imagine actually running something."

Levi Finn tugged on his beard and growled in frustration.

"Forget batteries," Matt Cat said, wriggling forward. "I'm betting that Sam kills this piece of red-bearded beef before the Vulture gets anywhere near him. Who's taking?"

"Nothing wrong with red beards," Jimmy Z mumbled. Johnny Z rolled onto his back and managed to rock himself up into a sitting position. "Agreed," he said. "Red beards are the best beards."

"You boys will never have beards," Sir T said. "What's the bet, Matt?"

"My dessert for a week," Matt said. "Against yours for a month."

"Ha!" Sir T kicked Matt in the thigh. "No way. Week for a week."

"Hush," Drew said, and all the boys went quiet. Sticking his face into the marble floor, he managed to walk his knees forward, get his rear into the air, and then grunt his way upright. Finally kneeling, he looked across the living room at Levi Finn and his men.

"Hey!" Drew said. "Mr. Leviathan, help us out here, and not only will Sam not kill you, I will personally make sure he scores you more batteries than you can carry by yourself."

"You don't get it," Levi said. "You think I would turn a kid I don't know over to people I'm pretty sure are awful just to make a TV remote work when I have enough gas to run a generator to have a movie night?"

"Yeah," Jude said. "I think so."

"Well, I wouldn't," Levi said. "Not me. She offered me a lot more than that. You have to understand, I come from the world before. I've seen it. I've lived it. I remember football and pizza and fresh donuts. Ice cream! Man . . . unless you know what it used to be like, you don't understand what this place does to me."

The boys all twisted, giving one another wide-eyed whatever looks, waiting to see who was going to speak up and make the big man feel stupid.

"I think we can understand that," Millie said. "We—most of us—come from better places."

"Thank you," Levi said. "Years ago, this lady shows up and gives me ice cream. *Ice cream!* Tells me to keep an eye out for a boy with snake arms. I tell her she's crazy, that no boy could have that kind of problem, but I'll still take the ice cream. So she brings me this comic book and shows me pictures and tells me to spread the word to keep a lookout. And every few months she'd check in, drop off more comics and batteries and bullets, pretty much whatever we asked for. And weird enough, even though years and years passed, she always looked the same. Even wore the same clothes, like for her it had only been five minutes when it had been a full year on this end. Well, those comics spread far and wide over the years, and after a while, we hear rumors the snake boy has actually been spotted. The real deal. Sam Miracle from the comics himself."

Levi held up a bone pen, spinning it between his finger and thumb. "She'd given me this pen to send her a message if I ever heard anything like that. And so I did. And she comes running. And that's when she changed everything. She tells me that whoever gets her this boy and whoever he might be running with, well . . . she'll take him and his whole family to a different time when Seattle didn't blow up. A whole new life. The kind I never thought would be possible again." Levi looked around. "And that's what it took for me to say, 'Sign me up.' It was never about the Vulture. I don't know him beyond what I seen in the comics, which is mostly just a man who's mean clean to the bone. But until you can promise me better and make me believe you, that's the team I'm on."

Glory woke slowly, blurring her bus station dream with reality. But it was the dream that seemed more real. One moment, she was hugging her knees and trying to explain that she couldn't leave the station in case her brother came back, and then her knees were suddenly covered with thick grass. Green blades were cool against her cheek and chin. They were in her mouth, tickling her tongue.

Spitting, blinking quickly, she sat up. Sam and Samra were looking at her, both seated in the grass with their backs against thick cloudy glass.

"Where are we?" Glory asked, but she looked around the cylinder and then up to the sky. The darkness high above her was all she needed to remember. "We fell," she said.

"Yes." Sam rocked forward and then crawled toward Glory. She watched the scaled snake bodies in his arms as he did, and the bright eyes on the backs of his hands. "And we're alive," he added. "Thanks to you. But we have no idea where we are or how to get out."

"Why are you here?" Glory nodded at Samra.

The redhead brushed back her mad hair and smiled. "Same reason you are. I jumped through a hole in the world."

"But why?" Glory asked.

"Because you're you," Samra said. "Do you think I want to live my life scavenging in ruins? I've heard my father's stories about the other time, when the cities were alive. You're my best chance at ever seeing the world

193

before." She shrugged. "What would you do if you were me, living on smoked fish and twenty-year-old enchilada sauce, and then two comic book characters show up? Even if you are bad, I'm still glad I jumped through that hole after you."

"We aren't bad," Glory said.

Samra smiled. "I don't disagree, but that's not what my dad says. By the way . . . the way the comic has changed after you is amazing. I can't wait to see your hair all the way white."

Glory looked at Sam. His face was blank, worried. She grabbed her ponytail and pulled it forward, barely visible inches from her face. Black. And then . . . not. She felt the stripe of white hair between her fingers and turned back to Samra.

The smiling girl pointed at a comic book in the grass.

"He's Sam Miracle," Samra said. "Seems nice enough. Creepy snakes. Fast hands. Bad memory. But you . . ."

Glory's right hand was stuck in the grass, bound in place by the glass that wrapped around her fingers and swept across the ground and up into the towering cylinder around them. She picked up the comic book with her left hand, taking in the Vulture, the boy of black fire, the Ken-doll version of Sam, and . . . the woman who had to be her, the woman with the white hair and the whip of glass and sand.

"You can go anywhere and anywhen. That's what the comic says." Samra climbed up onto her knees and brushed back her red hair. "I want you to teach me. I want to learn. I want to see the world before and visit every city. I'll be your understudy."

Glory shook her head. "I can't teach. I have too much to learn and no time to learn it. I have no idea what I'm doing."

Samra smiled. "But you will. You're Glory Hallelujah. That's the name you have in the comics, even though you're really Mother Time."

"And that's not all," Sam said. "Because of the way you move through time and space, and the shape of this blade you create from sand when you fight, you remind some of the poor comic book citizens of a little thing they like to call . . . *Death*." Sam's eyes were weary and worried, but his mouth twitched into a little smile. "I'm not sure we should hang out anymore. You might scare the rattlesnakes."

～10～

Cold Doors to Now

Sitting on green grass in the bottom of a towering cylinder of glass, Glory looked at Sam. Sam looked at Glory.

"Should I call you Hallelujah?" Sam asked. "Or Death?"

"Stop," Glory said. "But I'll take either over Mother Time. That's the weirdest." She looked back down at the comic book. "And the dumbest."

Sam climbed to his feet and then tapped the thick glass wall with the toe of his boot, sending a tight echo darting up into the darkness.

"I don't know how you did this, or what you even did, but thank you." He smiled. "I'm pretty sure we're not dead, because Ghost isn't here, and I don't see any pieces of myself splatted on the ground."

Glory sighed. "We might be alive, but this isn't great. I tried to slow us way down. I have no idea how fast time has been moving outside of this thing. For all I know, every one of your heartbeats could be taking an hour out there. Which is bad news for Peter. And us. We could turn to ash as soon as we step outside."

"Right," he said. "Good thing you're Mother Time. Take us backward as far as you can before you crash it open. We have to go back in time, anyway. Then we can start hunting for baby Peter."

"Yeah, easy as that," Glory said. "Sure." She tried to stand, tugging at the hourglass, but it pulled her right back down to her knees. It wouldn't break away from the blade that grew into the cylinder wall. She scrunched her mouth up tight and jerked at the hourglass with both hands.

"Do you need help?" Samra asked, scooting closer.

"No!" Glory tossed her hair back and pointed at the redhead. "Don't touch me."

"Glory?" Sam moved to the glass blade between Glory's hands and the tunnel wall, and he raised his boot to stomp on it. Glory shook her head and fired him a look of sweaty irritation. The last thing she needed was for Sam to break her hourglass. If anyone was going to do that, it would be her.

"Put your foot down." She pointed at a spot in the grass. "Hard. Grind it in deep." When Sam obeyed, Glory sat down on the ground and spun her legs around, bracing her feet against the outside of Sam's foot. Then, shutting her eyes, she focused on what she needed the glass to do.

She was pretty sure that they had landed on the island—she remembered seeing it flying up at her before she blacked out—but she was also pretty sure that she and Sam and Samra and the glass cylinder were just as invisible to anyone in the normal time stream as Peter's body and the bed had become to her. If the cylinder were visible, the Lost Boys would have smashed the glass by now.

"Kill the Vulture, save Peter," Sam said. "That's all you have to do."

Glory opened her eyes and looked up at Sam. "What? Why are you telling me this?"

Sam grinned. "I'm being Glory Spalding. Helping you keep things straight. Maintaining your focus. Just like you did for me."

Despite the situation, Glory laughed. "You think that's my punch list, Sam?" she asked. "Because it isn't. I need this cylinder to move us back in time before I break it or we're dead. Hopefully more than a century, because then

I need to find a way through time and a whole bunch of space to get to Peter in the moments before his heart is taken. And then I need to find a way to the Vulture. You and Cindy and Speck are going to be doing the killing and saving."

"What will I be doing?" Samra asked. "How can I help?"

Glory shrugged. "Follow your heart. Believe in yourself. Whatever floats your boat. Stay out of the way and try not to cause problems."

Samra cocked her head. "What? Seriously?"

"I can find the Vulture," Sam said. "I mean, maybe. I can in a dream. We should try it in the darkness between times."

"No, Sam. You will find the Vulture," Glory said. "But first things first." Closing her eyes and gritting her teeth, Glory tried to pour her loudest desires into the glass in her hands.

Backward. Don't break. Don't collapse. Grow stronger. Backward.

As the hourglass grew warm in her hands, Glory pushed with her feet against Sam's boot and pulled with everything else, like she was rowing an oar. She was half expecting to lurch backward beneath a wave of cold sand. Or to lurch backward with the crack of broken glass and bleeding hands. Instead, the hourglass bent slowly toward

199

her. Her arms trembled with the exertion, but she was strong enough. She opened her eyes and saw that the glass blade connecting her to the wall was still intact. It pulled her forward again, but she fought it, pushing off of Sam and flexing her body backward, dragging her hands and the hourglass and the blade up to her chest.

The tunnel tower groaned. Warmth became heat and it flowed through her, buzzing her ears and roaring behind her eyes.

Glory fell onto her back, looking straight up, blinking. The hourglass was still in her hands. The massive uneven cylinder was turning in place around them. The ground quaked, bouncing her on the surface.

"Glory!" Sam shouted. "Glory!"

He leaned in above her, grabbing her shoulders and jerking her to her feet.

"Ow," Glory said. "Sam!" She knocked his hands away, and saw that the glass blade still trailed her hourglass, but it was molten, barely more than thick water.

All around her, the glass of the cylinder had gone clear. And it was moving.

"Oh," she said, and she turned in a slow circle. As she did, the cylinder accelerated. Sam hopped in the air next to her. And then Samra. And then Sam again. The slow groan of the glass was deafening, loud enough and deep enough to disrupt her stomach. She felt dizzy.

"Glory!" Sam yelled again.

"Make it stop!" Samra screamed. "Please!"

Glory looked down. The glass blade was spinning around her at ground level, attached to the turning tunnel wall. It had already cut the grass down to mud. Sam jumped it again. And again. It would take his feet off. And it was winding a tight glass shell around Glory's feet.

The glass was still accelerating. Sam wasn't jumping anymore; he was running in place, like a kid trapped inside whirling jump ropes that were only getting faster. Samra was crying.

"Jump high!" Glory yelled. "Now!"

Sam and Samra both did. Glory spun, whipping the blade even faster. The groaning of the tunnel hummed suddenly to a higher frequency. The blade became a slippery, solid, spinning floor. Sam and Samra both landed on it, whirling around twice before stopping in a pile as it throbbed beneath them.

Glory stood on a glass floor, slick and alive, like the icy floor of an elevator, but manageable.

Sam and Samra pulled themselves free of each other and tested the floor. Cindy was rattling on Sam's shoulder, and as he stood, his left arm bent into a tense S, eyeing Glory, clearly hoping to strike.

"Are you seeing this?" Glory asked. She moved as close to the turning but perfectly clear glass wall as she could.

"It's like we're in a tornado," Sam said. "But we don't touch anything."

Outside, Glory watched the modern world flicker like fire.

"Watch," Glory said. "Just watch."

"Are we fast?" Sam asked. "Or slow and they're fast?"

Samra rose to her feet, but Glory barely noticed her.

"No," Glory said. "We're slow. We've slowed to still while everything else moves." She was looking at the world. At first, it was like something from a movie, played at high speed. Clouds snapped and lashed at mountains like frantic whips. The sun rose and fell and rose and fell until it suddenly became an unflickering, solid fiery band in the sky that wobbled south and then north and south again as years passed as fast as breaths.

"And we're getting slower," Sam said. "The sun is a solid ring."

Glory watched the water, and the faster everything else went, the more solid it became. The forests on the mountains were the new liquid. Green forestation ebbed and flowed up and down hills like a splashing tide while the sea looked as still as stone. She'd seen the same thing standing in the Vulture's tower in San Francisco.

202

And then every single thing moved at once. The planet began turning beneath them, spinning from east to west. Glory and Sam watched Seattle coming toward them, shrinking as it came—buildings vanished, roads erased themselves, flattened hills rose back up. By the time the city passed around them, it was barely more than a village, and it was moving at high speed.

"Is this good?" Sam asked. From the fear in his voice, Glory knew he didn't think so. Neither did she. "Are we breaking away from space *and* time?"

"I think we're getting slow enough to hang on to our spot in space. The planet is moving back through its motions," she said.

"Should we stop?" Sam asked. "This is far enough, right?"

Seattle was gone. They roared through ghostly mountains, over a desert, and into Montana.

"Whoa!" Samra grabbed onto Sam's right arm and pulled herself close to him. "Are we flying?"

Cindy lashed out across Sam's body and smacked Sam's palm into the side of Samra's head, knocking her down onto the glassy floor. Samra looked up, shocked and angry, while Cindy rattled at her for good measure.

"Sorry," Sam said, but he didn't even look down.

"Usually best not to touch him," Glory said. "Ever." She gave the redhead a glance before looking back out at the world. "See, I'm teaching you already."

Samra climbed back to her feet, but this time she put Glory between herself and Sam.

"So are we?" she asked. "Flying?"

"Yes," Sam said.

"No," said Glory. "The world is."

"Stop, Glory," Sam said. "Make it stop."

"Next time around," Glory said. "We're already in Minnesota. Or . . . somewhere."

Glory didn't just see the movement, she felt it. It was like having her hand inside a waterfall, if waterfalls could be perfectly smooth and more powerful than planets. She was seeing the world how angels must see it. She was watching a dance and hearing a song that was too big for human eyes and too grand for human ears. And there was more, ever so much more.

Europe rolled beneath them as close and as quickly as yellow paint on a highway.

"We're slowing down," Glory said. "In space."

"It feels faster." Sam looked at her. "A lot faster."

"Exactly. Because we are becoming more and more still. I wonder if we'll completely stop." Glory reached out and put her hand on the glass. Russia. The Pacific again. North America.

"I didn't even see Seattle that time," Sam said. "Glory, stop us anywhere. Please."

But Glory wasn't sure how to stop it. She didn't really even know how she had started it. The Earth turning beneath her wasn't just a day. Not even a year. Each turn was the blur of centuries unwinding. Just as the sun's path had become a solid ring, the years were uniting.

And in a blink, the Earth was gone from beneath them.

"Oh gosh." Sam wobbled on his feet next to Glory. She yanked his left arm tight, and Cindy pressed the back of Sam's hand into Glory's waist, hiding her eyes. In Sam's right hand, Speck went limp and cold.

They were among stars. Massive stars. Tangles of stars. The blackness was vanishing.

"No," Samra said. "No, no, no." She dropped to the floor and curled up, eyes squeezed shut, hands over her ears.

Sam caught his breath and Cindy grabbed Glory's hand around the hourglass as the planet—with the moon a stationary, tangled pearly knot around it—screamed toward them and then passed by inches from their feet before vanishing behind them.

"Can you stop it?" Sam asked quietly.

"In space?" Glory asked.

"Anywhere." Sam let go of her hand.

The planet swung around, orbiting faster and faster. The stars became a blinding blur. Samra was crying.

205

Glory shut her eyes against the light. The hourglass was hot in her hand. Burning. But she couldn't even uncurl her fingers to let it go. She had to move the cylinder forward again, all the way forward, back to where they started. But how could she?

"We're dead," Glory whispered. "Dead."

"No!" Sam said. "Glory, you have to try something. Anything."

"Ghost," Glory said, opening her eyes. "Come on."

"Twist it again," Sam said. "Turn the tunnel the other way."

But Glory wasn't listening. She lifted the hourglass up to her face, watching the thin liquid blade spin out of its open end.

"Ghost," she said again, leaning her mouth as close to the glass as she dared. Earth and its moon rings were coming back around. "Ghost. Angel de la Muerte. Brother Segador. If we die here, who will collect us? God. Please. Send him. Send anyone."

The tunnel shook. Glass was cracking. Melting. Glory looked up, watching the tunnel burning away into sand from the top down. The darkness was descending. She dropped to the floor, pulling Sam down with her by his shirttail.

There was no impact when the tunnel hit Earth. One moment, the glass was shaking and cracking and smoking away around Glory and Sam. And the next, every single bit of glass shattered into sand, revealing the shape of a boy made of black fire in a trucker hat, standing beneath the moon.

Glory was curled up on her back in tall cool grass. A breeze danced across her skin, giving her goose bumps. She could hear water lapping at rocks. And the timer she used to count days was beeping in her binocular case. Her arm was around Sam, holding him tight, but he was snoring. Cindy and Speck both slid his hands up into the air, assessing Glory and then focusing on the boy made of fire. Samra was curled up tight on her side, completely motionless, except for the slow movement of her hair in the wind.

"Was I unclear?" Ghost asked, his voice tinged with anger. "What were you attempting? Have you given up on Peter? On the future?"

Glory swallowed, trying to open her throat and loosen her voice.

Glory shook her head. She felt tears filling her eyes, but she blinked them away quickly. "What was I supposed to do? I chased the Vulture. I did! But I fell, and then . . ." She trailed off. "Are we dead? Are you here to take us?"

The boy's fire dimmed and he became flesh. He took off his hat, brushed back his hair, and pulled it back on.

Ghost stared at Glory. After a long moment, she shifted in place, glancing down at Sam and Samra.

"What's wrong with them?" she asked.

"What is wrong," Ghost said, "is that you moved back through more time than any human is meant to and more than most could ever survive. I put them to sleep. Otherwise, I would be collecting their souls. But I don't want to collect their souls. I want to collect the Vulture's soul. I want Peter alive!" His voice rose and rose to a gale-force wind. "I do *not* want to harvest millions more men and women and children because you have failed them. But I will. As he kills, that is exactly what I will be forced to do, but I will carry your soul along with me so you can see every one of them."

Glory curled up, throwing her hands over her head. Speck and Cindy were both rattling, coiling Sam's limp arms above him.

"Do you understand me, Glory Spalding? Glory Navarre? Glory Hallelujah?"

Glory looked up at him. "Do you think you have a right to be angry with me? How much have you given up in this fight? How much have you lost? Now tell me how much Sam has lost? How much has Peter?" She rose to her feet. "How about Millie? How many times have you had to die, Ghost? Matt and T? Jimmy and Johnny? Drew and Flip and Barto? Tiago and Simon? Jude?

Heck, even Speck and Cindy have given up more than you have. Do you know what happens at the end of this fight? I know you do. We die." Glory pointed at Sam and Samra. "We all do. Maybe we die winning. Maybe we die years after winning. Or maybe we lose, and we all die right away."

Glory turned, stepping toward Ghost. "All of us will die, and you'll be the undertaker. Yeah that's scary, but so what? Being mortal is scary. The Vulture is terrified of it. But do you know what scares me even more? Not being one of the good guys. That would be so much worse." She sniffed, jaw clenching, ears hot and head ringing. "You talk like we're all apples falling off a tree, and yeah, maybe we are. But if you think it's hard being the guy who has to pick us all up, try being one of the apples."

Ghost didn't move.

Glory stopped, trying to gauge the boy's reaction. He was more stone than fire. "Do you understand me, Reaper? Help me save Peter and kill the Vulture or just take my soul now."

"I have helped you," Ghost said. "As much as I am allowed. I am not permitted to write the stories of your mortal lives or take the stage in your mortal plays. But I have armed the glass of Father Tiempo. I am lengthening the process of collecting his soul. I have paused your careening time walk rather than collect you dead. I cannot kill the Vulture for you."

"Why not?" Glory asked.

"If I break the commandments to which I am bound, then I am no better than he is, writing what is not mine to write, touching what is not mine to touch, wielding power that was given to me with the strictest of limits. I will be cast down. I will never fulfill my duties and take my seat in the coolness of the stars. I will be shadow, not light. I will become as others have become before me, less powerful but as vile as the Tzitzimime, who once were mothers of the sunrise and sunset, keepers of all that bloomed. The Vulture would be dead, but I would replace him. Is that what you want?"

Glory sniffed. Now that her anger was easing and no one was shouting, she assessed her surroundings. She was standing on solid ground on the moonlit island with cool earthly air in her lungs and the scent of salt and water clearing her mind.

"Promise me," she said.

"Promise you what?" Ghost asked.

"That you will do everything you can," Glory said. "Even if it isn't enough. And I will do the same."

Ghost smiled suddenly, walking toward her. He stopped in front of her and held out his hand. "I will. Now you have seen my face twice, so I may as well make the most of it. The next time our eyes meet, your earthly time will be no more. So take my hand."

Glory looked at the boy's thin wrist and brown skin, at his long fingers. Then she looked down at Sam, snoring in the grass with Samra behind him. Cindy and Speck met her look one after the other.

"Don't worry," Ghost said. "Sam will be fine. I'm showing you something, not taking you anywhere. Taking you would be impossible."

"Why?" Glory asked.

"Because you are already there," Ghost said. "I going to show you one of my memories."

Glory reached for his hand but paused.

"If I die," she said, "do what you said. Take me with you to collect all the people who are killed because I failed."

Ghost's eyes widened in surprise. "Why?"

"Because they aren't just apples. It will be awful and they'll need someone nice," Glory said. "You'll just yell at them."

Ghost laughed and his fingers closed around hers. Cold stopped her blood. Black fire raced up her arm. The world around her vanished.

THE VULTURE SAT IN A HIGH-BACKED RED CHAIR, HIS LONG legs stretched out under the middle of a wide stone table in front of him. His watches were all pocketed, his elbows were resting on the arms of his chair, and his fingers were tented in front of his face, sharp thumbs nesting in his dark pointed beard.

Behind him, the fountain in the center of the courtyard splashed and the gold clock swung from the sundial, catching the red light thrown by the torches and flinging it back. Dozens of tall torches had been set into the courtyard pavers, as much for heat as for light. Strange woven symbols and grids of sticks and bone hung from the torch poles—all freshly hung wards and dream catchers. Another fire had been set in a bronze bowl in the center of the table, and it was at this fire that the Vulture was staring.

The black curtain behind the Vulture's altar had been drawn on the cavernous City of Wrath. But much to Mrs. Dervish's consternation, El Buitre had invited the mothers to leave the city and join him in his garden. The shadow-clothed sisters and their two generals had passed through the shrine's protections Mrs. Dervish had so carefully maintained against them. Now they and their generals were seated at a stone table with the Vulture, filling the cave with their stench and staring at the untouched wine, cheese, grapes, and sliced apples that Mrs. Dervish had provided. Four furious eyes drifted to the enormous horsehide maps the mothers had unrolled across the table ends. The man with the white beard and the scarred scalp was on the Vulture's left. The younger one, with his hair slicked straight back on the top of his head, sat on the Vulture's right. He had both hands on the table, his fingers quietly tracing lines on the hides.

Mrs. Dervish stood behind the Vulture's chair, clasping both hands tight at her waist.

Razpocoatl leaned forward across the table, the bowl of fire throwing fingernail shadows behind every feather on her face, her white eyes glowing orange. "We promised you an army," she said. "And we have gathered you an army."

"You offer me soulless locusts," the Vulture said. "Well and good. I will loose them. But your dead and damned werebeasts and skin-walkers must remain under my control even after the conquest is complete. I will achieve the rule of new mankind with the souls still in. This is a necessary term of your service."

Mrs. Dervish nodded. "Even if he should banish them back into darkness, they must be sworn to obey."

Magyamitl did not lean forward, and her shadow robes and black eyes made her face look like a mask. Her two taloned hands were playing with a necklace of flesh at her throat. "It is our power that chains time to your heart and soul. It is our labor that has gathered you an army of devourers and our two sons who will command it. It is our wrath that will give you the world. We have felled the priest and fed on his anointing. We have terms, as well."

The Vulture plucked an entire cluster of grapes off a platter and leaned back into his chair. "I am aware. Play your parts and I will hear them." He looked at the two men. "Alexander, Young Son of Night, and Scipio the Scarred, you are a pair of frightening outlaws indeed. Are you ready to begin this war in earnest?"

The two men nodded. The Vulture popped a grape into his cheek and smiled.

"Then let us begin," he said. "Prepare me doorways through the darkness into my chosen Seattle. Our rotting army will enter her streets in a frenzy with the rising sun. Mothers, find me storms. Cold storms. Despair. Then tear open the skies between times and let their brutality join our invasion. Snow and ice will suit me better than lava for now. And fetch me monsters from ancient seas. Biggest is best. Fill the sound with boat killers. There must be no escape from the city onto the water." He stretched a hand out over the horsehide to his right, finally tapping the spot he wanted. "Begin with the Miracle boy's island. Storm his moment. Find him. Cut him down."

The two mothers smiled.

"When his heart has been taken," the Vulture continued, "and a living city belongs to me, we will move to the next, and the next, and the next. Until even you have fed enough and I banish the gorged walkers back to their hells."

Both mothers smiled and the shadows hardened on their feathered faces.

"But you have yet to name your price," the Vulture said. "What must El Buitre pay the mothers in exchange for the world?"

The smiles widened.

"These things only," Razpocoatl said.

"Give us our choice of servants from among the living and the dead," said Magyamitl. "And give us a city to rule them as we please."

Razpocoatl stretched out a shadowy hand flat above the fire. The flames disappeared into her palm, like they had vanished up through a hole. She looked into the Vulture's eyes, her own white orbs sparkling.

"But most of all," she said, "give us the girl called Glory. She will be our daughter, and we will make her a queen of night and darkness."

11

Mother T

GLORY HAD NO FEET, NO HANDS. BUT HER SENSES WERE still alive enough to see and smell and feel. She was in a cave city she had seen before, lit with hundreds of torches; and she was floating up a narrow street, weaving around men and women and children and dogs as she passed between dozens of small stone houses. The warm desert air was dry on her skin and the smoke from the torches burned in her lungs . . . but she had no lungs. She wasn't even breathing.

She was following an old woman. How she knew

this, she wasn't sure, because the woman was wearing a hooded black robe and only her hand—gripping a tall cane—was visible.

I know this place, Glory said. But her voice was a thought that never touched the air.

Yes. The voice belonged to Ghost.

This is the cave where Sam got his arms, she said. *Manuelito and Baptisto lived here.*

Yes, said Ghost. *Cities die as well as men.*

What happened?

Do not be distracted. Watch.

The woman in the robe stopped at the curtained doorway of a small cubicle house. Raising her cane, she tapped lightly on the wall, and then the old woman pushed back her hood and scanned the city around her, as if she may have been followed.

Her thick, perfectly white hair was pulled back in a ponytail, and she looked directly at Glory, her eyes focused.

Glory was looking into the face of a much older version of herself.

And then the curtain was peeled open, revealing a tall young boy, with black hair, no shirt, and a thick tangle of necklaces. The boy smiled, bowed, and stepped aside. The old woman entered.

Be calm, Ghost said. *You are seeing what I have seen.*

Glory couldn't respond. She was sweating from nervousness, wanting the dream to be over, but instead, her vision closed in on the house. She floated toward the door, and then through the curtain and inside.

The house was warm. A cooking fire devoured twigs beneath a small clay pot. The tall boy was there. And a woman seated on a beautiful rug on the floor—woven all of black and white and red. She held a baby boy, clothed in white and red, and the bottom of a wooden barrel sat empty on the rug beside her. Glory noticed all of this, but barely. Her focus was on herself, her very *old* self.

The woman spoke a language like wind and rocks and falling water. Glory watched herself kneel on the rug before the mother and hold out her thin bony hands to take the baby. Glory winced at the splotches on her skin, at the coarseness of her white hair and the hard creases on her brow.

I'm so . . . Glory's thoughts trailed off.

Beautiful, Ghost replied.

Horrible, Glory said.

Lovely as a ripened field, said Ghost. *Rich as an ancient tree still bearing fruit in her final season.*

Glory felt embarrassment at the strange compliment, but the scene in front of her overwhelmed her self-reflection. Her older self was singing to the baby, holding him tight to her shoulder, swaying gently on her knees, singing into his neck. Tears striped her old cheeks with a much younger shine.

Wait, Glory thought. She looked at the tall boy by his mother. This was Manuelito's cave city. The boy had Manuelito's face, his eyes, even his height. And Manuelito's brother . . . she looked back at the baby as her older self leaned over, placing him in the bottom of the empty barrel. He kicked and punched with displeasure, arching his back.

"Peter Atsa," Old Glory said, and her aged voice carried a scratch like a breeze carries leaves. "It is strange to meet you now when I have known you so many other times. You will meet me again when I am younger and you are older. I have seen you lay your life down in victory. To do that as you must, you need courage beyond measure, and a heart always pouring but never emptied. Little Eagle, be stubborn enough to outcircle the Vulture." Sand trickled out of Glory's hands and down the sides of the barrel, and the boy became still. "Be selfless enough to save us all. Be my friend and my teacher. Be faithful to the Maker of stars and men, be strong and fearless and full of song. Be Tiempo, Father of Time. May you receive a double portion of the spirit of seers and walkers that I have been given and carried for you until now."

With that, Old Glory cupped her shaking hands in the air above the barrel. A liquid clearer than water welled up from her palms, mounding up into an orb before spilling down into the barrel in two streams.

The barrel began to fill and the baby was still as it did, mouth open and eyes wide. It rose above his eyes and then lapped over his face, but he did not fear and he did not fight. The falling streams became trickles and then drips. The old woman's hands were empty, and once more, she began to sing.

The baby, Glory said. *How can he breathe?*

And then half of the house was swallowed in darkness. A cold stench filled Glory's nostrils and she tried to pull away.

Two winged, shadowy shapes swept shrieking out of the darkness, down toward the baby. The old white-haired Glory threw herself forward, shielding the baby with her body. She raised her hands and sand swirled, but not before black blades flashed. She fell limp to the ground, and so did the rest.

Enough, Ghost said. And the room and the house began to recede. The vision was shrinking, the sound of a mother's screams fading in the expanding distance.

The room was small and far away, but it was full of death. Two female forms dressed in shadow bent over the baby. Feathers rippled across their laughing faces as they reached into the barrel with bloody taloned hands.

Ghost let go of Glory and the black fire leapt off her

arm and vanished in the cold night air. She was exactly where she had been. Sam and Samra were still asleep in the grass beneath a silver moon. Glory doubled over, gasping, trying to forget what she had just seen. It was too much. All of it. Seeing herself die. Hearing a mother wail in agony as her sons were attacked. But worst of all, seeing those monsters over the baby, over Peter. Tears fell into the grass between her feet, and she could have dropped to the ground on top of them, paralyzed by sobs. But there was heat inside her, too. Anger.

"Are those the same shadows who tore open the sky in Seattle?" Glory asked. "The ones who trapped us here?"

"Yes," Ghost said. "The Vulture's darkest allies, or so he thinks. Tzitzimitl Razpocoatl and Tzitzimitl Magyamitl. Blood goddesses of the Aztec. Long ago cast out of the light. Now returning."

"How many are there?" Glory asked. She didn't look up.

"Only two that matter now," Ghost said. "There were once many."

"And they work for the Vulture?"

"He might think so. But his abilities are no match for theirs."

Glory exhaled, wiped her face on the back of her arm, and stood up slowly.

"I died," she said.

"Yes," said Ghost. "And your death is not what must be changed. If we are victorious, that will remain your end just as Peter's end was beside a smoking train, defending Sam's broken body."

"Then what?" Glory asked. "Stop them from killing Peter?"

Ghost pulled off his hat and scratched his moonlit hair. He could have been just another boy. Just another boy with power over light and time, standing on an island in the wrong millennium, talking to just another girl.

"Stop them. Destroy them. Banish them. Do anything that prevents them from taking Peter's heart and the time-walking anointing you gave him."

"But how did *I* get it?" Glory asked. "I thought Peter would be the one to teach me."

"You gifted it to him," Ghost said. "Always. He returned some of it in that glass you hold, and I filled it."

Glory inflated her cheeks and shook her head. Sam's right hand was drifting in the air, with Speck's eyes focused on her. But Cindy and his left hand were lightly striking Sam in the face. He sputtered and yawned and stretched. Samra remained motionless.

"Tell me," Glory said. "Who gave the spirit to me? Who teaches me?"

"Your mother left it to you and to your brother," Ghost said. "Laila Navarre, daughter of seers and conquistadors on her mother's side. Daughter of the Nightway, descendant of Baptisto, son of Manuelito on her father's. You have no teacher but me."

Glory's mouth went dry. "*My mother?*" she asked. "And Alex? From Manuelito? But Alex *left* me. He promised we would always be together, and then he left me in a bus station."

Ghost's head slumped. "Alex abandoned you because I told him who he was. I told him he had been chosen for this fight." He looked back up. "Your mother had desirable blood and much loss. A Tzitzimitl found Laila's dreams and drew her in, promising her strength enough to avenge her losses and remake her life. Foolishly, she abandoned the life that remained to her and fled into the ancient Night instead of the Light, and the darkness betrayed her. Laila was bound in shadow and enslaved."

"But Alex?" Glory asked. "Even if this is all true—no. Whatever." Glory raised both hands. "I don't believe you."

Ghost sighed and dropped cross-legged onto the grass. "He had abilities. He was needed. But he also had pride."

"Needed for what?" Glory asked.

"For Sam Miracle. For Peter Eagle. For the Future and the Past. You and he would have eventually been at SADDYR together. Alex would have been Sam's guide, standing shoulder to shoulder with Peter. But when he learned that your mother was enthralled in shadow, his

223

focus changed." Ghost tore up a handful of grass and threw it away. The sky behind him was beginning to glow red. Glory could see the black shadows of islands and mountains on the horizon against the first warmth of dawn.

"He went to look for her," Glory said quietly.

For years, she had tried not to think of her brother. He had left her. Alone. She had left that pain as undisturbed as possible. She had let it settle in her soul and after the first year, she had not allowed herself a single tear—for her mother or her brother. They had not wanted her. They had thrown her away.

But now, it was all threatening to explode out of her. To her young self, Alex had been huge and fearless. When they had run from their first foster home and had lived in the streets, she had never been afraid when he was in reach. How many times had she seen Alex frighten grown men? No one on the streets had ever tried to touch her without suffering. How many times had he broken the two of them out of homes and even police stations? How many miles through how many streets and along how many railroads had she ridden on his back?

Alex would have fought for their mother.

"What happened?" she asked. "Was he killed?"

"Yes," Ghost said. "And worse. Like your mother, the

darkness made him promises that took root in his anger and turned him. He was taken. You still went to the Spaldings and the ranch in Arizona and Sam Miracle. Father Tiempo was surprised to meet a girl with such a mind for time. He never knew that you were descended from his brother."

"You're awful," she said. "You think you can just use people up like that? Try my brother until he breaks and then try me. Hey! Now let's see what happens? Who's next in line when I turn evil?"

"No one," Ghost said seriously. "You must not turn."

Glory closed her eyes. Her right hand began to tremble, and she realized that she was still holding her hourglass tight. The glass was twisting and shaking inside her grip. Someone was moving time nearby....

"Glory?" The voice was Sam's. Two rattles began to buzz. "Glory!"

Glory opened her eyes. The sun was not yet up, but the world was brighter and the moon above her had gone ghostly faint in the bluer sky.

The air was getting hotter. Much hotter. And thickening quickly.

"Is this our island?" Glory asked. "Where did you put us?"

"Where you will live," Ghost's voice whispered. "Or

where you will cease. Here you will glimpse Peter's killers, searching for Sam. And for monsters. Move quickly."

He was gone. And the next time she looked in his eyes . . .

SITTING UP, SAM SQUINTED AGAINST THE BRIGHTNESS. THE sun hadn't even risen yet, and the day was already brighter than any he'd ever survived in the Arizona desert. The grass around him was strange, too—the blades were long and plump, but curled up into tight rolls like snail shells. As the temperature climbed and sunlight began to spill over the horizon, every blade began to unroll up into the air, stretching for the warmth.

Glory was just standing there with her back to him and her face toward the sunrise, with a thousand grass snakes unrolling up around her legs.

Sam's arms whipped around him, charged with energy. Speck was excited, but Cindy was afraid. "Glory!" Sam yelled, trying to get her attention.

"Is this our island?" Glory murmured. "Where did you put us?"

Eyes watering, Sam rose to his feet and the grass he had been holding down jumped up past his knees. Samra was on her side a few feet away, and her skin was flushed from the swelling heat. Her comic book flopped open awkwardly, lifted up by the rising grass.

"Glory?"

Sam grabbed her shoulders. Both of his arms were writhing, his rattles shivering. The heat was too intense; even Speck was getting nervous. Sand dribbled out of Glory's right hand.

Sam had memories of stars and darkness and spinning glass, but that could have all been one of his dreams. Glory's unblinking eyes were streaming tears. Her face was turning red. The white stripe in her hair was too bright to look at.

"When did you take us?" Sam asked. "Glory! Wherever it is, we have to leave. Now!"

Glory turned in a circle, raising her left arm to block the dawn. She seemed half-asleep. "Where's Ghost? Did he leave? Did you see him?"

"No idea," Sam said. "But we're going to crisp into jerky soon if we don't get out of here."

Glory looked at the hourglass shaking in her hand, spilling sand.

"Someone's up to something," she said simply.

"Glory!" Sam stepped back, and then spun, looking for shelter, for shade. Anything to protect them from the sweltering sun.

The island was almost identical to theirs—a crescent moon around an inner harbor—but the land was much lower. Or the water was much higher. They were standing

227

on the western crescent tip with the dawn coming at them from across the little harbor. There were no trees, just the armies of snail grass, and a massive tubular lava formation the color of scabbed blood sprawling across the top of the island where the house would eventually be, but taller, and much longer.

"There!" Glory pointed with her hourglass. Sam turned, looking out across miles of water to the west.

"What?" he asked. "Is it a boat? What am I looking at?"

Glory didn't answer. But whatever it was seemed to be waking her up. She cocked her head, finally blinking her glistening eyes.

Sam saw a black shape that could have easily been a ship, if ships could grow longer on one side while the other side remained exactly where it was. The dark shape was expanding unevenly but quickly across and above the surface of the water—rising and falling and bending in a great curve that stretched for miles. It was moving quickly.

"It's a doorway," Glory said. "Between times." And then, from one end to the other, the black hole opened like a zipper, lowering its jaw below the surface of the sound. Water crashed together in a chain of angry geysers, all of it beginning to slowly swirl into a great whirlpool.

"That can't be good," Sam said.

Behind Sam and Glory, the sun rose, and the force of the heat almost knocked Sam to his knees. Needles of light pressed into his bare arms and the back of his neck. Cindy and Speck both tucked in tight to his belly, trying to stay in the shade.

All around, the plump vertical grass began to hiss and steam, and the smell it gave off was like rot dragged up from the bottom of a pond. Glory gasped and doubled over.

Stretched across the highest point of the island, the massive, tubular, scab-colored lava rock shifted and stretched.

It wasn't a rock.

The island shook as an enormous spiny tail rose up and up and up out of the water, flinging a small lake of spray over the dark red blotchy body that was draped all the way up and over the top of the island and down the other side.

The head was out of sight.

The tail slammed back down into the water.

Sam stood in the animal's rain and forgot his blistering skin and his hiding arms. He was watching the serpentine tail longer than three semitrucks—finned between brutal spikes along the top and bottom—sweep up another load of the salty water and launch it in a sprinkler explosion over the basking monster. Much of the water began to evaporate immediately in a fog, but the rest came down in fat drops of hot rain.

Sam bent over beside Glory. He was dripping sweat, but she was dry, and her skin was rough with salt.

"Take us somewhere!" he hissed. "Before we boil or this thing sees us!" Forcing Speck and Cindy to obey him, he lifted Glory's right arm with both of his.

"This is our island," he said. "Just move us forward! Forward, Glory! A long way *forward*!"

She looked at him, blankly, like she was frozen with fear. Sam swung her hand around for her. Sand seeped out of the hourglass, but nothing else happened. He swung her hand harder.

Finally Glory jerked her hand free from Sam's grasp, slipping and dropping to one knee as she did. As she snapped her wrist like she was cracking a whip, a veil of sand spun and melted into a small glassy dome in front of her, but they were stuck on the outside of it.

Within the dome, there was no snail grass. There was normal grass. And ferns. And one orange, very surprised chicken, cocking her head and looking out. Sam knew the chicken. Millie had named her Carrot because of her color, and then Carrot Cake because of how fat she had gotten.

"Sam, it's the right time," Glory said, and she laughed. "I thought about when I wanted and it worked! That's Carrot Cake! I did it!"

"Great," Sam whispered. "But we're still out here with a monster bigger than this island! We need to be in there with that chicken!"

Another shower of hot drops rained down from the beast, but this time, the tail didn't slam back into the water. It remained in the air, like a scaled train standing on its head, twisting slowly, taller than a water tower.

The bloody red body bent in the middle, and the other end of the creature rose into view from the other side of the island.

The head.

The Head.

Was Smoking.

The monster yawned, flapping a spiked membrane mane like a deadly collar just behind a horsey head. Scab red outside, the inside of the creature's gaping mouth was black. The upper and lower jaws were lined with jagged, broken, yellowing tusks, and translucent skin-flap cheeks were as taut as drums on both sides. The throat was scaled and baggy, lined with dozens of vertical black vents. The nostrils were wide uneven triangles, both flaring. The beast's eyes were pupilless and knobby, the size of large pumpkins, but jaundice yellow. And they were both leaking steam from the inside corners.

Sam tried to focus on those eyes, but he could barely stand the stifling heat, writhing and twisting his back almost as much as the snakes were twisting in his arms.

Glory was still staring at the chicken inside her little glass dome.

"Do it again!" Sam whispered. "But around *us* this time!"

Glory raised her hourglass and swung a slow loop of hissing sand around her head.

Samra began to whimper, stirring in the scorching snail grass.

The beast shut its mouth and flared up its spiny collar. Its baggy throat inflated, widening dozens of vertical black vents like pleats in a skirt.

"We're burning!" Samra's eyes were still closed, but she sobbed, thrashing in the steaming snail grass. And then she began to yell. "Put it out! Put it out! Put the fire out!"

And at the sound of her yelling, the jaundiced eyes rolled open. What Sam had thought was eyeball was actually lid. The lids opened sideways, from the inside out, and sharp yellow eyes focused vertical pupils on Sam and Glory and the kicking Samra.

Glory looked down at Samra, then up at the monstrous animal, and then straight into Sam's eyes. Her face was the color of Valentine's Day and he knew that his must be, too. But he could see her mind clearing in her eyes, the fear and realization and memory all crystalizing at once. And he knew exactly how that felt.

"I know," Sam said quietly, and he pulled his crossbow off his hip. "Do your best as fast as you can. I'll hold it off as long as I can. But if that's not long enough, jump in the harbor. Get back to the others. I'll stay with Samra." Hooking his foot in the nose of the crossbow, he made sure all four strings were drawn and had arrows in place.

Samra sat up in the grass, wiping at her tears. "It's so hot. Hot."

The beast leaned its towering head and ballooning throat forward, eyes narrowing beneath their own steam. Its throat pulsed with a sound deeper than any drum.

Samra screamed and Glory swung her hourglass, cracking a long whip of sand around herself. The creature lunged forward, firing two spinning clouds of white sparks out of its nostrils with a blast that would have broken windows. The sparks sizzled and hissed over Sam's head into the snail grass, turning it into ashen char. The beast roared and leaned closer.

Sam raised his bow, letting Cindy aim. The first bolt disappeared into the corner of the animal's left eye. The monster bellowed surprise as white-hot sparks erupted in a whistling stream from the wound. The second bolt vanished into the right eye, but black blood boiled from the wound instead of fire.

"Get over here!" Glory yelled. The sand was melting into a web around her as she worked. Samra, comic book in hand, was crawling toward Glory's feet.

Sam darted toward Glory, letting Speck take aim and firing two more arrows. After they launched, he pushed through the stinging sand and hot glass, into the center of Glory's little dome.

"Look!" Glory pointed down at her feet. The snail grass was gone. They were standing on thick, cool, Puget Sound grass. There was even a fern. Samra was kneeling on it, her face as red as her hair.

"You look." Sam pointed up. Mostly blind, the huge animal was keeping its head down, but its spiny tail was climbing high. "Can we thicken the glass? Or move away?"

Glory backed up, holding her hourglass tight with both hands.

The dome half grew and half dragged with her, leaving a stripe of beautiful grass behind them to shrivel up yellow in the heat.

Carrot Cake watched them leave, in her own little dome of glassy time.

The monster's tail came down like a hammer as thick as a building.

The ground shook. Sam and Glory bounced. Samra yelped and hid her face with her hands.

Fluttering orange feathers appeared in the air inside Glory's dome, along with the smell of chicken.

Glory looked at Sam as the massive tail rose back into the air, trailing sand and smoke and feathers.

"Well," Glory said. "I tried."

12

Mama Leviathan

MILLIE AND JUDE STOOD OUTSIDE THE GLASS HOUSE, STUDY-ing the silver water of the moonlit sound. Leviathan stood beside them, sharpening the thick spikes in his beard one at a time. Bull and Dog and the rest of Levi's men were loading the boats with the food and blankets and towels that Millie had given them.

"Again, Mr. Finn," Millie said in her most formal voice. "You have our thanks for releasing us."

"Don't thank him," Jude said. "He never should have attacked and tied us up in the first place."

Levi sniffed at the air. "You had my daughter," he said. "What's a man supposed to do?"

"Clearly," Jude said, crossing his arms, "he should take a group of innocent people hostage and then summon a bloodthirsty, time-walking arch-outlaw from the outer darkness."

"Seemed reasonable," Levi said. "I don't trust that boy with the snakes and I don't trust you."

Jude laughed and began to answer, but Millie grabbed his arm.

"You should trust him," she said. "Mr. Finn, he saved your daughter's life. And that's according to her. Do you trust her?"

"You mean *before* he kidnapped her?" Levi cracked a smile. "I know he's your brother and I respect the love you have for your blood, but he has snakes in his arms. *Snakes*. In his *arms*. He's a comic book freak, and my daughter is still missing. So is he. Maybe you haven't noticed."

"I am sorry about that," Millie said. "I don't know what she was thinking, running off with Sam."

"Don't apologize," Jude said. "He's a pirate and I'm sure his daughter is getting whatever she deserves, wherever she is."

Levi bent his center spike into a hair hook and then turned to face Jude, looking down his beard into the boy's face.

"Talk like that, boy," he said, "is likely to get you trussed back up. Is that what you want?"

Barto coughed politely behind them all, leaning against the outside of the living room window. His mostly homemade glasses were strapped onto his head with elastic and he was wearing a blue-and-green knit beanie with a pom-pom on top. Most important, he was cradling an oversize crossbow in his arms.

"If you try anything, starfish face, I'll try out this new bow I've made," Barto said. "And I *really* want to try out this new bow I've made." He grunted, hefting it up. "Twelve strings, two arrows per string, four triggers, three releases per trigger. I could shoot you with twenty-four arrows right now."

"Put the bow down, Barto," Millie said. "We have a deal with Mr. Finn. If he honors his side, we will honor ours."

"I don't know how he could help us and I don't know how you could make any promises for Peter like that," he replied. "Maybe Peter won't want to move the pirate into a better time. I mean, it wouldn't be nice to the people already there. And maybe Peter'll be too dead to try, anyhow."

Millie gave the boy her iciest look. Barto immediately lowered the crossbow, letting it dangle at his right leg. "The rest of the boys are arming up," he said to Millie. "Just like you said."

"In case of pirates," said Jude.

"In case Sam and Glory need us," Millie said.

"And Peter," said Barto.

Jude laughed and looked back out at the sound. "Peter can take care of himself. Sam and Glory have been in some messes. But that other girl—what's-her-face, the redhead—she'll be the one needing help."

But Levi was ignoring him, sniffing at the air and then squinting at the silver water.

"When I'm older," Jude said to him. "And El Buitre is dead and we're done jumping times, I'm going to find a nice time to settle down in and I'm going to write a story for you."

"I don't read," Levi answered, but he was distracted.

"Comics," Jude said. "With pictures. I'll make up characters and one of those characters will be you. I'll name him Levi, but he'll have tiny bony shoulders and a little belly and only five red hairs on his chin. He'll love cats, and he'll share their food and he'll work for the Vulture, doing something not at all cool. Something boring. Or gross."

"Cleaning his ears," Levi said. "And filing down his toenails."

"Perfect," Jude said. "You're good at this."

"No," Levi said. "I have seen that character in my daughter's comics before. He's nothing like me, so it's not insulting and you did not even make it up." He looked

239

around at the three kids and pointed out at the water. "Are you seeing this?"

Millie tried to follow the big man's thick finger, but the moon glare on the water was too bright. Raising one hand, she blocked the stripe of reflection and immediately saw what Levi was worried about.

In the darkness, the water was churning and swirling beneath a long bandage of rising fog on an otherwise clear night.

"This air," Levi said.

Millie already knew what he was going to say and she shivered. The breeze had an icy bite to it.

"Snow," Levi said. "And a lot of it, unless I'm wrong, which I am not. A winter storm is building high above us. But the water out there is hot and tossing up steam."

"What's your point?" Jude asked.

Leviathan leaned down until he was eye to eye with Jude and his hooked beard spike bent back against the boy's chest.

"My point," the big man said, "is that someone is playing games. Someone very large, because these are very large games."

A boom shook the ground beneath their feet. Every window in the house beside them rippled and clattered. Jude slipped but caught himself. Barto jumped away from the wall of windows.

Millie dropped into a crouch, bracing herself against the ground. Her heart was fluttering with adrenaline, trying to fly against her rib cage. "Was that an earthquake?" she asked. All over the island, her chickens began to squall.

"No," Barto said. "That was just here."

"Large games," Levi said, straightening back up to full height. Boat engines roared to life on the other side of the island.

"Time for you to go," Jude said.

A second boom rolled across the island. This time, windows cracked.

"It came from the other side." Barto turned around.

"Did you bring bombs?" Jude asked.

"Always," said Levi. "But they don't sound like that."

Levi, Jude, and Barto were all still, listening to the cluck-screamed fear of chickens. Millie was the only one who moved, inching back toward the house, passing Barto. With Sam, Glory, and Peter all gone, she had to be in charge of more than just the kitchen. And the gardens. And the house.

"Don't you think we should find out what that is?" Millie paused, clearing her throat to raise her voice. "Jude? Bartholomew?"

The boys didn't hear her. Two large shadowy shapes flew above the island, above the water, above the islands across the water, and out of sight. The sky tore open along their path with a sound like a traveling waterfall. A vast darkness spread along the tear, rippling like a curtain, swallowing even the moonlight.

Cold frosty air roared out of the black opening, combing the steaming water with wind.

Billowing in behind the frost, flashing worlds of snow attacked the air in armies thicker than clouds.

In seconds, the moon was gone.

Cindy and Speck were dragging Samra backward by the shoulders while Sam ran and Glory shuffle-walked the glass dome back with them. The blind monster's throat bulged and pulsed and bulged and pulsed as it sneezed the air above the island completely full of twisting white sparks the size of birds. Snail grass was burning on every side, and Glory's glass had molten streaks where sparks had made contact.

The beast had its tail raised for a third strike.

"In the water!" Sam yelled and he veered with Samra down the bank toward the little harbor, banging his shoulder against the glass to force Glory along.

The third blow from the beast's tail glanced off the outside of the island and splashed into the water of the sound, sending a sheet of foam and spray up as high as the sparks.

"I don't know about this," Glory said.

"I do," said Sam. "Come on! Come!"

The glass warped and elongated with Sam's pressure and Glory's movement, all the way down to the water's edge and then into it.

Water lapped up the side of the dome, but the ground beneath Sam's feet was still the lush grass and fern from another time. The grass path they were leaving behind almost instantly lost its moisture and yellowed in the heat. And wherever the white sparks landed on it, low red fire sprang up and spread beneath curtains of black smoke.

The glass between times held back three feet of water. Four feet. Sam slipped, slamming against the side, jolting Glory and Samra further down. Cold water finally splashed around Sam's toes. He had found the water level. Even better, he had found an iron hook set in concrete—the corner of the dock. He might not be able to see, but now he knew where he was.

Samra slipped down beside him. Glory came more cautiously, stopping at the water line. Sweat was pouring from her flushed face and she gripped the hourglass with both hands, concentrating more than Sam had ever seen.

Six feet of water lapped around the glass that encased the three of them. Above their heads, the raging beast swayed against the sky and a storm of sparks crackled with heat. Below them, cold, cold water sucked the warmth right out of the air.

Glory may have stopped moving—one foot on a mossy rock and another wedged below a thick driftwood limb—but her focus hadn't broken. Puffing two quick breaths, she managed to blow droplets of sweat off the tip of her nose.

Sam did nothing but breathe hard and enjoy the brief bit of coolness.

After a moment, Glory spoke, without taking her eyes off the hourglass in her hands. Sand was trickling out of one end and tumbling across the ground to be swept up into the glass wall, and sand was peeling off of the glass wall and being sucked into the other end.

"Samra," Glory said. "Could you push this hair out of my face?"

"Are you kidding? We need a plan," Sam said. "There's a for-real dragon monster out there, and you want to fix your hair?"

"I'm not kidding," Glory said. "It's driving me nuts, and I can't believe I haven't screwed this up yet. We're talking life or death, Sam. Do you want to get all the way back into the right time or not? I have to figure out how to close that time all the way out and open this one all the way up and I have no clue how to do it and all I'm think-ing about is my stupid hair!"

Samra climbed up beside Glory and carefully pushed

the loose clusters of black hair back behind her ears. Glory flashed her a quick smile, but without shifting her eyes.

"It's not a dragon," Samra said. "It's a leviathan, and they're in the comic books, too. Where do you think my dad got his nickname?" She pulled the rumpled comic book out of her hip pocket and flipped to the back, holding the book open for Glory. "See? It's pretty close. Of course, I never thought they were real. But then, I never thought you two were real, either."

Samra tossed Sam the comic book, pulled a rubber band off of her wrist, and then sat down on a rock by Glory's feet, pulling her own wild hair back into a curly, pom-pom ponytail while sand streamed across her feet, coming and going from the hourglass. When she had finished, she looked up.

"Now what?" Samra asked.

"Good question," Glory said quietly. "Sam?"

Sam had his feet in the cold water up to his shins and his shoulders pressed against the glass holding back six feet of warm water. He was flipping pages, glancing over the Ken-doll version of himself and his trusty band of outlaws doing battle in the streets of Seattle with thousands of gun- and sword-wielding men and women in matching black uniforms. Flipping toward the front, he paused on a full-page illustration. He was leaning forward, driving a motorcycle and sidecar—Father

Tiempo's old Triumph—across the smooth surface of the Puget Sound. Glory—with all-white hair—was leaning out of the sidecar, hourglass in hand, spinning sand onto the water beneath the bike.

A redheaded beauty was on the bike behind Sam, with her arms around his waist. But she was twisting in her seat, looking back at what was pursuing them.

Leviathan—massive and spiny and spewing sparks, its scab-colored body the size of a train tunnel—was mounding and dolphining after them with its tusk-lined mouth agape.

"Sam?" Glory said again. "Talk to me. What now? I don't think I can just hold this until that monster gets bored."

Something hard knocked against the glass behind Sam. Samra bit a scream in half and covered her mouth.

Sam scrambled forward, twisting around and sitting on the slope beside Glory. Cindy buzzed on his shoulder.

"What is it?" Glory ask. "Sam?"

"Another one," Sam said. "A smaller one."

A lesser leviathan ground its face against the glass, and then swam on, bending and rubbing its serpentine body against Glory's dome.

Glory looked up from her hourglass as the tail disappeared in the dark water.

"How big was that?" she asked.

246

"Telephone pole," Sam said. Cindy began to buzz and flex and twist Sam's arm into a striking position, and then another shadowy snake swam into view, levering its mouth open to slide and scrabble its young tusks on the glass.

Kill. Poison. Pain.

Cindy was communicating with it. She was announcing her intentions. But the serpents didn't care. To them, she was tiny.

Suddenly two more similar-sized shapes were approaching. And then two more. Even Speck was buzzing his rattle now. All the beasts tested the glass with open mouths, rubbing their scaled skin against it as they circled back around.

Slower, longer, thicker shadows were gliding past in the background.

The sand had stopped moving in and out of Glory's hourglass. The glass dome was hardening, becoming brittle, cracking a little every time a beast touched it.

Glory wiped her sweaty forehead on the back of her forearm.

"Okay, so I think our harbor is a hatchery." She looked at Sam. "Man. If these guys are babies, I'd hate to see the mother." Her mouth twitched. "Oh, wait . . ."

Sam snorted in surprise and then slumped back onto his elbows and laughed in exhaustion.

Glory grinned, tried to make her face serious, and then grinned again. "We are in serious trouble, Sam."

Sam nodded and bit his lip, trying not to laugh. His cheeks were streaked with hot tears, his belly shaking. Samra was gaping at him, and then at Glory.

"How is this funny?" Samra asked, eyes wide. "Are we going to die?"

The ground shook with another Mama Leviathan tail quake. The thirty-foot-long babies twitched into a split second of rapid speed before slowing back down into a steady prowl.

Glory dropped onto the ground beside Sam, leaning back on her elbows.

"You know," she said. "This little glass ball we're in is going to break."

"I know," said Sam.

"So we are going to die," Samra said.

"Well, we're alive now," Sam said. "Focus on that."

"You want to know something else?" Glory asked him.

"Maybe." Sam shrugged. He smiled. "But the way things are going, maybe not."

Glory held up her right hand, gripped tight around the hourglass.

"I haven't been able to let go of this glass. Not since we fell in the darkness and . . . all *that* happened. It's like the glass burned through my skin and is growing into my bones. And I can feel sand in my veins, Sam. *Sand.* I can't even handle sand in my shoes, and now it's in my blood. I am living itchiness."

Glory laughed but Sam's face was serious. He sat up, taking Glory's hand in his two, testing her fingers with his own. Glory was watching Sam's hands and he knew it—Cindy's horns and angry eyes, Speck's bright eyes beneath rosy pink scales.

"Funny," Glory said. "Me complaining to you about having something stuck in my hand."

Sam grinned, tugging at her fingers. She wasn't lying. Her fingers were frozen in a death grip around the open-ended hourglass.

"This is sweet and all," Samra said. "But is there some kind of plan?"

"Good question," Glory said. "Maybe she should have asked it before she jumped into the outer darkness after us."

"There's a plan," Sam said, his eyes brightening. "And she already knows it." Leaning forward, he picked the comic book up off the ground where he'd dropped it. He flopped it across Glory's lap, open to the picture of the motorcycle on the water.

"That's the plan," he said. "According to the comics."

The glass groaned, and then squeaked with the gnawing of tusks. Glory studied the picture.

"Think you can do that?" Sam asked.

"Two questions," Glory said. "First, where's the motorcycle?"

Sam pointed straight at the leviathan aquarium wall. "Out there. Still strapped into our boat that's tied up to our dock at a water level that's about six feet under this water level, and I don't even know how many thousands of years in the future."

"Just as many years in the future as we are in here," Glory said. "I got us to the right time, Sam. You saw Carrot Cake." Glory sniffed and then nodded. "Okay. Second question." She tapped the version of Samra in the picture, with her arms around Sam's waist. "Who the heck decided to let this Finn girl into *our* comic book?"

"What?" Samra hopped and crawled forward, looking over Glory's shoulder. Sam watched the girl's eyes widen. "I was never there before," she said. "Never!"

Samra laughed out loud and grabbed the book out of Glory's hands.

"I'll have to read the whole thing over again." She beamed beneath her burnt skin. "I wonder if I could find other copies. Do you think that looks like me?"

Sam and Glory didn't answer and Samra didn't notice.

A white spark landed on the dome's clear roof and the glass popped loudly as the fire slid down and died, hissing, in the water.

"As soon as you're ready," Sam said. "We should try this."

"Right," said Glory. She looked down at the hourglass locked into her palm and inflated her cheeks. "Just give me a minute."

"Sure." Sam understood. He could give her a minute. Hopefully, the water pressure and the beasts outside would give them all a minute. Or ten.

Something freezing cold slapped into his forehead and then melted down into his eyes. As strange as it was, he didn't even have time to wonder what it had been.

Thousands of snowflakes simply appeared inside the little dome, flying at high horizontal speeds, peppering Sam's singed bare arms and face with icy cold.

"It's snowing in here," he said. "Hard."

Glory blinked flakes out of her eyes and shook snow out of her ponytail.

"All right," she said. "I can't hang out in a snow globe. Time to get out of here."

MILLIE MIRACLE STOOD AT HER KITCHEN WINDOW AND stared down through the blizzard at the island's little harbor, and the two prongs of land that almost encircled it.

The boys had all armed up to go looking for Peter on the mainland. With Sam and Glory gone, what else would they want to do? Peter hadn't come back in the boat. Therefore, Peter needed some finding. Or the Lost Boys needed some looking. When the snow had come, they had all disarmed themselves, bundled up, and then rearmed.

The dumb boys wanted to load up the boat and take off in a freak blizzard, even after Jude had described the massive whirlpool that he and Millie had seen before the snow had hidden it.

Even Levi had announced that he and his men would not be leaving. They'd taken possession of the living room, building up the fire in the fireplace to a roar. They had promised to help find and fight the Vulture, but deadly blizzards had not been included.

"A woman's job is not to be liked," Millie said to herself. It was a phrase her mother had used often when she'd had to take command of drifting farmworkers who were less than eager to get the crop in before the first freeze.

And so Millie had staunchly forbidden the venture, to much loud dismay and complaining. She had entered the kitchen intending to begin work on a vat of chicken soup that would erase all disappointment from her Lost Boys, but instead she had ended up at her window, watching mysteries unfold on the island.

Despite the thick snow, there were red fires burning down in the grass, but only inside a strange yellow path of curly, ashen grass that veered first one way and then another before finally veering down into the water. And there was one charred circle down there where the snow was burying a flattened mat of chicken feathers that had once obviously belonged to Carrot Cake.

"Millie . . . ," a voice behind her began. She knew it belonged to Matt Cat, with his lumpy floury face and the butter-colored hair.

"No, Matt," Millie said. "No one is taking that boat anywhere in this."

Another minute passed.

"Millie . . ." The voice belonged to a different boy, but the tone was the same.

"No," Millie said. "Go sharpen your knives or something. I'm making soup and I'll need help peeling."

"Millie . . ."

"No."

"Millie . . ."

"No, Barto."

"Millie . . ."

"No, Tiago and Sir T and Drew and Flip. No, Jimmy Z and Johnny Z. No, Jude. No, Barto. Why not? Because I said so, and someone has to be sane. Don't worry, I'll make soup. Peel me potatoes. Fetch me a chicken."

Millie was the sane one. But she wanted to scream in anger and then cry in fear.

Her brother had gone into the darkness after the

Vulture and she had been left with an impatient tribe and some less-than-friendly guests ever since. She wanted to know where her brother was and why it was snowing and what the whirlpool in the sound meant and how the sky had been opened to let in the storm.

But she didn't know, so she made soup. A huge vat of soup, for too many men and too many boys to eat. While she cooked, she thought about the Vulture and Mrs. Dervish, and she wondered how all of this was helping them, because she knew that it had to be. The Vulture loved chess. Millie had spent too much time bound in a chair while he played chess across from her. This blizzard was a chess move. And so was that whirlpool, somehow.

Millie wasn't good at chess—it was hard to even remember how the knights moved—but she was good at people. She hoped that Sam and Glory were still alive and playing chess right back. But even if they were, even if they were excelling beyond belief, they would still benefit if their opponents began to doubt themselves. Doubt was a destroyer of men and armies.

"Levi!" Millie yelled suddenly. "Leviathan Finn!" She picked up a large wooden spoon and began to stir her vat of chicken soup.

A moment later, the big man with the spiked beard stepped around the counter and entered the kitchen.

"What?" he growled.

Millie smiled. "If you're going to eat, you're going to help. Now stir!" She handed him the spoon. Grumbling, Levi began to stir and Millie leaned across his body to grab some salt.

While she did, her hand slipped quickly in and out of his pocket, emerging with his bloody fountain pen in hand and tucking it immediately up her left sleeve.

It was time Millie Miracle sent the enemy a message.

Levi stirred long enough to complain and beg to leave.

Millie let him. Then she slid up her sleeve and uncapped the pen filled with Mrs. Dervish's blood. Hesitating only briefly, she went with her first thoughts and memories, mashed up as they came, all in the tight regal cursive her mother had insisted she practice daily, and she filled the inside of her forearm with red.

We will walk safely, and our feet will not stumble.
We will not be afraid; we will lie down and our
sleep will be sweet. We do not fear sudden terror,
nor trouble from the wicked when they come
against us. The curse of the Lord is on the house
of the wicked, but he blesses the home of the just.
Surely, He will break your teeth and feed you only
dust and sorrow. Fear the one who can destroy soul
and body. Shame will be the legacy of fools. You
shall surely die.

For a moment, she struggled with her conscience,

because she didn't want to lie and she knew that she hadn't quoted any of the old Scripture verses even close to correctly. But this was war. So she signed her work quite simply:

Father Tiempo.

After all, Father Tiempo was the only person she knew who might be intimidating. And she was sure Peter wouldn't mind. Wherever he was. If he was alive, she'd tell him later.

Capping the pen, she read over her writing once, and then pulled her sleeve down over it and tucked away the pen.

Millie Miracle was feeling better already.

"Millie . . ."

"No, Matt," she said cheerfully. "No one is leaving. Soup will be ready soon."

"It's not that," Matt said behind her. "I was just outside, putting out fires."

Millie turned around and looked Matt Cat square in his biscuit face.

"And?" she asked. "What set them?"

"No idea," Matt said. "But the motorcycle is gone."

See the Song

W HEN THE ELEVATOR DOORS OPENED, SIX GOLD WATCHES floated out of the Vulture's vest and trailed behind their master like wings as he crossed the restaurant lobby. Time slowed around him. Laughing men and women became statues and their voices deepened and prolonged, finally becoming silent to El Buitre's ears. As for the waiters and waitresses and the diners awaiting tables, when the Vulture passed by them, they felt only a shadow, bleakness. But when he touched them, even slightly, their bones cracked with the force of it. Joints were unknit, and he was gone before his victims even felt their pain.

El Buitre entered the dining area with long strides, a western buffalo-skin overcoat flapping behind him. Mrs. Dervish followed closely, quickstepping on her toes, clutching two rolled-up horsehide maps in her arms.

The restaurant at the top of Seattle's Space Needle was crowded with tourists, but the Vulture wasn't there for the company or for the food. He was there for the view. From the top of the Needle he could see out over the water of the busy port and he would witness the release of the first ancient monsters. From the right window seat, he could see the bustling downtown traffic of the thriving city, and he would witness the chaos caused by the release of his werebeast army. It was a new and pristine time, a version of 2017 that he had never touched, ripe for his picking.

"Here." El Buitre stopped in between two tables for two beside a wide window. An awkward teenage couple in prom outfits occupied one. A white-haired couple wearing fanny packs and matching orca T-shirts were seated at the other. The Vulture dealt with them first.

Grabbing the backs of their chairs, he dragged the old folks away from the table and heaved them out of their seats into the air. They drifted away like half-heliumed balloons—eyes barely beginning to widen in surprise.

The prom couple was launched in the other direction.

The Vulture pulled the two unoccupied tables together, pushed them against the window, and then stood, stroking his beard and studying the city while Mrs. Dervish unrolled the horsehide maps and drew up a chair.

The hide map on the Vulture's left was a great deal simpler than the map on his right. Hairless lines marked borders and rivers, and the hide imitated topography perfectly, with its own small foothills and mountains. The hide was a complete map of the world, and was also completely changeable. When the Vulture wanted to see a particular city more closely, he simply looked at it on the map and desired it. The entire hide would ripple and change, becoming a map of any part of the world he might desire to see.

Right now, a tiny horsehair skyline of Seattle bristled in its center. The Space Needle was as easy to spot as the real one.

The map on the right was a map of time, the hairs on it constantly moving and flowing like fluid.

But the time map didn't matter. The Vulture had already chosen his moment to seize the world. He had begun preparing it before he had agreed to join forces with the mothers. It was the geographical map he would be using most now, a map he could use to view his invasion more closely from on high.

"Excellent, Dervish," El Buitre said. "Thank you."

Mrs. Dervish smiled primly and nodded. The Vulture's watches slid back into his vest. Time leapt back into full speed around them.

Four bodies bowled through the tables on both sides, and the restaurant was filled with screams. Windows exploded.

In the streets below, horrified people watched two plumes of tables and chairs and people fly out of the Needle and begin to fall.

Inside, the Vulture inhaled deeply. A cool wind flowed through the restaurant now, fluttering the tails on his horsehide maps and billowing his heavy buffalo coat.

Through all the screaming and the sobbing and the cries for help, the Vulture heard footsteps approaching from behind. He turned around to find Alexander the Young walking briskly toward him, scanning the chaos on both sides with liquid eyes.

"Well?" the Vulture asked simply.

"The great storms are being released," Alexander answered. But his voice was edged, faintly uneasy. "The oceans have been opened. The great beasts you desired will come. Scipio is preparing to move your army out of the City of Wrath and into the streets below."

The Vulture shrugged the buffalo coat higher up onto his shoulders and narrowed his eyes at the young man with the dark hair.

"You are withholding something," El Buitre said. "What is it?"

Alexander raised his jaw and met the Vulture's look. "The boy you fear. He is coming for you."

The Vulture growled. "I do not fear him."

"You should. He continues to surprise." Alexander leaned forward, smoothed the hide map of the world with his palms, and then stepped back. The hide contorted itself, revealing large islands and rippling water between them. A shape was moving quickly across the surface of the hide sea.

The Vulture leaned forward, studying the tiny hairs on the map. It looked like a motorcycle. Behind it, a pack of monstrous serpents was in pursuit.

"He rides across the water?" El Buitre asked.

"He does," Alexander said.

"And he moves through time?"

"He does. Despite the priest's absence."

"Tell Scipio to release half the army now. Hold back the others until he comes." The Vulture prodded the tiny hair motorcycle with a long finger. "They can all partake in his devouring."

"They may," Alexander said. "And they may not. The mothers have summoned *yee naaldlooshii* and many others like them—skin-walkers and shifters and werebeasts all allied. But the boy is part beast, is he not?"

The Vulture froze in surprise, but then his face thawed, and he laughed. "You think they will see the boy as one of their own? He was broken, not bitten or cursed. And the *yee naaldlooshii* slew family members to gain their powers. Miracle . . . he's not capable of that."

Alexander shrugged. "Perhaps."

The Vulture looked around the chaos in the restaurant. Dozens of eyes were on him now. He saw many hands with phones raised as cameras and others using their phones to no doubt call the police. A manager flanked by waiters was approaching.

"Kill all of these people and return to Scipio," the Vulture said, turning away. "But leave me one waiter and one cook. I may grow hungry."

Alexander stamped once, dropped his chin to his chest, and then drew two long knives and turned to face the manager.

The Vulture shut his eyes and focused on the coolness of the breeze, ignoring the sounds of shattering glass and toppling tables and screams of pain. People were fleeing or dying. The space would soon be as quiet as he needed a roost to be.

"William." Mrs. Dervish was leaning over his shoulder, breathing hard in his ear. Leaning away, he gave her a glance. Her face was hard and furious. And . . . *afraid*. She was wearing a cream blouse pinned high with a vulture brooch amid the lacy fringe that encircled her thick neck, and she had her left sleeve pulled up high.

"Leviathan Finn is dead," she said. "Or he'd better be."

The Vulture raised his thick brows. "He was a petty criminal. Why should I care?"

Mrs. Dervish extended her bare forearm, covered in crisp blood-blistered lettering.

"Because this was written with the pen and blood I gave him."

The Vulture squinted, scanning the words without interest.

"The signature, William," Mrs. Dervish said. "The priest is alive, and he is near."

The Vulture growled in frustration. "Of course he is." He looked back down at the tiny shape, turning in circles on the hairy hide sea. "Then the long hunt ends. The boy and his priest must both fall here."

Inside their tiny private blizzard, Sam had reloaded his bow while Glory had tried to reawaken her glass and Samra had reread her now-soggy comic book twice.

Glory's task was the hardest, but the brittle glass had finally broken away around her newly spun dome.

While leviathan young—from tangled dozens of ten-foot hatchlings to thirty-foot elder siblings—bumped and pecked at the fresh warm glass, Sam and Glory and Samra had blinked away falling snow and shuffle-waded around the steep bank and up onto the snow-slick dock that was only visible inside the glass and beneath their feet. The leviathans had become more aggressive when the humans had moved out into the water and down the length of the dock.

Tusks scraped and tails whipped, denting and bending Glory's glass.

Glory was sweating despite the snow. Sam stood beside her, Cindy clutching his bow, ready to grab onto Glory and swim if the glass broke. Samra followed behind, constantly touching Sam's bare shoulder, and receiving a quick buzz from Cindy's rattle every time she did.

"I wouldn't do that," Sam said, shrugging her touch off once again. "I'm holding this bow and my hand really wants to shoot you every time you touch me."

"What? Why would you want to shoot me?" Samra took a step back, and then yelped as a tail slapped the glass behind her.

"Not me. My hand. Cindy. She wants to shoot you. I can hear her loud and clear." Sam glanced back over his shoulder. "Grab my belt if you have to. Just don't touch my left arm anywhere."

"Or his right," Glory said. "Speck might not kill you, but he'll make it hurt."

"Can't you just tell them not to?" Samra asked. "They're your hands. In the comic—"

"Shut up about the comic," Glory said. "Or I'll vote with Cindy."

With Samra hanging on to Sam's belt and Sam hanging on to his bow and Glory hanging on to the sand-spinning glass that was hanging on to all of their lives, the three of them inched down the dock through sand-salted snow until they found the ropes tied to the dock cleats that secured the still hidden metal boat.

"Now what?" Samra asked.

"Now . . . ," Glory said. "We hope this glass is really bendy."

Sam looked at her. "Can you just step up and in?"

Glory shook her head. "I don't know."

"Do we jump?" Sam asked. "Count to three and go?"

"Pick me up," Glory said. "From behind. Around my legs."

Sam hooked his bow back on his right holster and then Samra moved forward and he moved back.

Crouching, he put his head on Glory's waist and wrapped his arms around her legs, twisting Cindy and Speck into a tight braid before grabbing onto his forearms.

"Slowly," Glory said. "Samra, watch your feet."

Sam straightened his legs, lifting Glory six inches, then twelve. As Glory rose, the glass dome rose, too. The curved sides left a smaller and smaller circle of dock to stand on.

"Higher," Glory said.

Sam stood all the way up. Samra hopped back, slipped on the glass as it sloped in beneath her, and sat down hard. She slid into Sam's feet.

Samra yelped. "Ow! I hate this. There's a better way. There has to be."

Only a two-foot circle of dock remained, snowy and slick under Sam's boots. The rest of the glass held back warm water and hot rippling air.

Spitting snow and blinking away melting flakes, Sam lifted Glory up to his right shoulder. The dock under his feet was replaced with glass, and he crow-hopped dangerously as the sphere snapped shut beneath him.

The leviathans were still angry. And the snow was still falling, but now it was accumulating in the bottom of the ball.

"Set me in the boat," Glory said from his shoulders. "Then dive in after."

Sam moved forward, boots squeaking on glass, and the ball bent in, folding over what had to be the side of the boat, at least two feet below the leviathan water.

266

Glory's weight shifted forward.

"Glory, no!" Sam's feet slipped and scrambled. He couldn't stay up. Samra screamed, Sam threw Glory forward, and the glass ball buckled and cracked.

Sam fell.

Warm water washed around his legs.

Glory was shouting.

Sam felt two hands grab onto him and pull. His kicking feet collided with something as solid as a slithering log. He pushed off of it and wriggled up slick glass, before tumbling down into a pool of water and two pairs of feet. He was on his back with his boots in the air.

"Sam!" Glory was yelling. "Sam!"

He spat out a mouthful of salt water and looked up. A pair of hatchlings was writhing between his feet, fighting each other to get into what was left of the glass sphere.

Speck had already drawn Sam's crossbow. Cindy was already aiming. Two bolts punched into two heads, and the serpents flopped away in a shower of white sparks.

Samra dragged Sam's feet all the way inside as Glory desperately spun sand.

"Don't!" Sam said, and he scrambled to his feet. On one side of his body, the air was scorching, and on the other, snow was still pelting him. "We're in the back of the boat, find the motorcycle first!"

Knee deep in hot water, Sam forced his way toward

the bow, pushing on Glory's glass, bending it down and rolling it forward.

Samra screamed and Speck shot something Sam couldn't see, but he didn't need to see it to know what it had been.

"Bigger!" Sam yelled. "Glory, make it as big as you can!"

The motorcycle was strapped on to a platform in the bow, so the water wouldn't be as deep. Inches. Maybe a foot. The leviathans might not even be able to reach them.

Sam kicked the glass hard, and more water flooded in around his boot. Reaching back, he dragged Glory forward, and they both took a big step up and banged into a motorcycle tire as glass re-formed around them.

Speck fired Sam's last arrow and white sparks shrieked past Sam's head, dying in the water.

Samra half crawled and half swam up onto Sam's boots.

The blizzard was back. They were standing in shin-high hot water on a plywood deck. Snowflakes were steaming into it. The motorcycle and sidecar were intact inside Glory's dome, with water up to the exhaust pipe. The glass had cut the straps that tied it down.

Gasping and drenched, Sam looked around. Samra had her eyes closed tight. A severed leviathan tail was floating against her back.

"Are we alive?" Samra asked.

"Yeah," Glory said. "Barely. Sam tried to kill us all, but we beat him."

Sam spat into the water. "I'll try, try again." He looked at Glory. She was breathing hard and dripping sweat, her work nowhere near done. Her stripe of white hair had at least tripled its width.

"You okay?" Sam asked.

"I'd like to eat a bushel of pasta and sleep for a year," Glory said. "But first I need a shower."

"A shower," Sam said. "How about a towel?"

"Do you have one?" Glory asked.

Sam didn't answer. The snow and the warm water were fogging up the inside of the glass. But at least they were more elevated now. Water lapped barely more than a foot up the glass. Fewer tails and tusks could reach them at one time, but the animals were still trying.

Samra sat up in the water. "I lost the comic book. Oh no." Splashing up onto her feet, she rubbed condensation off the glass and peered outside. "I was in it. I was in that book."

"You still are," Sam said. "But for real." Reloading his bow, he counted the bolts remaining in his left holster.

"Sam," Glory said. "Start the bike. Now."

The huge blind beast on the island was swaying above them—fanning her collar and pulsing her throat.

"Right," Sam said quietly. "You stay put, Mama. We'll be gone soon."

"Not there," Glory said. "Behind you."

Sam turned, looking out the mouth of the harbor. Through the steam, a massive rolling wave was approaching. He wiped the glass quickly. A scab-colored head the size of a bulldozer was plowing through the water, followed by a moving mountain range of body.

"And that must be the Papa Smurf," said Glory. The animal bellowed across the water, knocking the steam off the inside of the glass with the sound.

All across the harbor, hundreds of spiny heads rose from the water, bellowing in reply.

Angry and blind, Mama joined in directly above the glass dome. Samra tucked her chin and covered her ears.

"Start the bike," Glory said again. "I'm ready."

Sam hopped on, turned the key, and kicked the starter like Glory had taught him. The bike coughed. Again. The bike grumbled. Again. The bike woke briefly.

"Kick it hard," Glory ordered.

Sam did, and the bike roared, spewing black exhaust above the water. Every spiny head in the harbor turned their way.

Samra tried to climb on behind Sam, but Glory grabbed her with her left hand.

"Sidecar," Glory said. "Quick."

"But in the comic—"

"Don't care," Glory said. She threw her leg up and over the back of the bike and hugged Sam's ribs tight with her left arm. "Sidecar or stay behind and feed the beasties."

Sam's eyes and lungs were already burning from the fumes when Mama Leviathan slammed headfirst into the harbor next to them, like a train diving into an Arizona canyon. His heart jumped and memories slammed into him even faster than the wave—hot fog clouding his mind.

The motorcycle was rising. It was tipping. On the other side of the canyon there would be a train wreck and smoke and ruin and pain and a man with guns faster than impossible and seven watches floating around him like wings.

No. He had six watches now. And Sam's hands were faster.

The motorcycle was in gear. And Speck had already opened up the throttle wide. Behind him, Glory was leaning away hard. The bike was turning across the wave. Water was rising in two glistening sheets around the front wheel.

AT FIRST, GLORY THOUGHT THAT SHE HAD DIED. THE STILL-ness that surrounded her was cool and perfect. And then she opened her eyes.

Immediately in front of her right eyeball, there was a snowflake, shining in the sun, hanging in the air as firmly as a star in the heavens. Like a star, it was beautiful, and like a star, she knew it was one of uncountable billions.

Sam was still in front of her, and her arm remained around him. Inside his chest, beneath her palm, a song was playing in his heart, a song that told a story, that rose and soared, that battled and rejoiced and then sank into peace. Every beat was more intricate than any opera, as simple as something played perfectly by a galaxy of orchestras, and she knew that it was only one part of a single heartbeat. Even as still as the world had been made around her, it would take her countless lifetimes to learn the first movements of just one beat.

Two sheets of water hung in the air, like museums of light. Beside her, a red monster was fixed in both the sea and the air, surrounded by foothills and planets of water. Looking at that beast, she saw its glory like she had seen glory in the desert, in the great painted rocks heaped between the ground of Arizona and the blue-bellied sky of lesser Heaven. And lesser red serpents, intricate statues of anger and ignorance and fear and hunger, had been placed all around her, across the polished skin of the harbor.

The beauty of it all ached inside her, although it

throbbed like death and sorrow, but with it came a deeper joy than she had ever dreamed of. Hot tears spilled down her cheeks like laughter and new sun-filled rooms opened in her soul. Until this moment, she had never known how dead she had been. Now she was alive. She felt . . . *real* . . . *new*. Like a dragonfly feeling her wings unfold in the sun for the first and only time—wings that could never be forgotten and would forevermore be felt.

She was a dead girl, rising from an unknown grave in a garden world.

"Well done," Ghost said. "You can now be still and see with a sight that cannot be taught. And seeing, you can now move with a movement that is given only to a very few. Like a bird in flight, like a fish in the sea, like the winds in the sky, so Glory Hallelujah can now soar and swim and storm the limitless roads of time. Do you feel alive in this world? Are you a life in this world?"

Glory was scared to look for his face, because she had been warned about seeing him again. But when she turned, she saw only black fire, dancing across the water near the mouth of the harbor.

"I think so," Glory said. "Where are you?"

"I am burned into your bones and into your blood. And you do not 'think so.' This is knowing. This is being known. That is what *this* is. Knowledge of the words written inside the words and the Word outside all words, the notes inside the notes and the song outside all songs. This knowledge is given and in turn, it opens. Taste and See. Hear. Touch. Move in this song. Make your own songs inside of it."

The black fire moved between the heads of young leviathans before stopping a dozen feet away.

"Glory Hallelujah," Ghost said. "Dance with darkness, because you are the dawn. May every tongue of your fire burn white-hot against the chains imprisoning others. When your time is done and your life is spent, this will be the song Ghost sings of Glory when he gathers you in."

"Amen," Glory said. The word rose out of her, and it felt right.

"This is the purpose for which you were made," Ghost said. "You will soar in this song of ours where only a few can hear, but those few are everything, and when you soar, you will make the rest more beautiful. To many, you will be a wind unseen. You will be the aroma of hope. To others, you must be fierce protection. And you cannot be that without also being destruction and fearless fire. Like Peter after you, you will learn your gifts and your own ways, but his strength will only be a portion of yours, so carve a mighty way. There will be much pain. And in that pain, you will find your deepest joys, like the grapes find their wine. Open your right hand."

Glory looked down at her locked fist, and her fingers

finally obeyed her, spreading wide and flattening her palm. The hourglass was gone, but its shape remained, burned into her, still burning, with flames of black fire. Her flames poured out and leapt across the water to join the others. Heat and sorrow and laughter surged through her when fires met.

"Your war awaits you," Ghost said. "But do not forget your joy. Make the song more glorious with your every touch, and the name of Glory Hallelujah will always be the truth."

Ghost's fire dwindled, gathering in on itself.

"Wait," Glory said. "When does it all go back to normal?"

"This is normal," Ghost said. "But not everyone sees."

"I mean the speed." Glory looked around behind her. Samra was head down in the sidecar with her feet in the air. "How do I make it faster again? I'm pretty frozen."

Ghost's fire began to spin into a whirlwind. "You may slow as you like and speed as you like. Exist in any moment for as long as you need to. Neither you nor I nor any but the Three above us can adjust the true tempo of this song. It is only our tempo that changes inside it. Act with the agility of light as you do now. Or fall behind the slow percussion of the planets, as you already have. Now go, be as you were meant to be."

With that, Ghost's flames shot into the sky. And the

275

harbor exploded with movement.

The snowflake hit Glory's eyeball. The leviathan thundered into the water like a collapsing volcano. And the wave flung the motorcycle, trying to catch it in its foaming mouth.

But Glory moved faster.

14

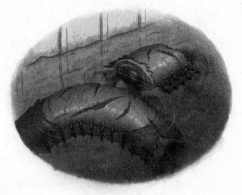

Song

GLORY'S GLASS DOME WAS FLYING APART IN SHARDS, LEAVING them in the hot ancient time, but she no longer needed the protective shell. Leaning off the motorcycle, she plunged her hand into the hot water, slowing its time.

The water firmed, spitting the wheels up to the surface as the engine roared. Fishtailing and sliding and flinging a massive, chewy fountain from the rear wheel, the bike rocketed forward on a darting path of sandy glass that dissolved to foam behind it.

Sam swerved around the first snapping spiny head and accelerated toward the harbor mouth, racing the monster approaching on the outside.

Samra was trying to right herself in the sidecar.

"What's going on?" Samra yelled. "Where are we?"

"Can you get us out of here?" Sam yelled over his shoulder.

Glory didn't answer. She wasn't exactly sure how to do it, but she was sure that she could do it. And Ghost had said that she could take as much time as she needed inside a single moment.

Mother Leviathan erupted from the water on her right, white fire blasting, jagged yellow tusks bared. Father Leviathan dolphined out of the water in front of them, spitting a cloud of sparks the size of turkeys across the surface toward them. Sam hit the harbor mouth and banked left, sending a sheet of water up into the air like a shield. The sparks ripped right through it.

"Glory!" Sam yelled. "Hurry!"

Glory knew what time she wanted. She knew its feel and its taste. Raising her right hand from the surface of the water, she swept fiery black sand in a wide arch above the motorcycle.

A door opened between times.

The motorcycle shot through it and dropped six feet, landing hard and splashing harder. Glory smacked her face against Sam's spine and Samra almost flew out of the sidecar, but landed upright. Around them, day became night, cold knifed their skin, and snow pelted their faces.

"Ha!" Sam laughed. "Glory, you're amazing."

She smiled, licking blood from her lip.

Immediately, Sam veered the bike back around in a big loop, sliding and bouncing across the water toward the island. Even through the blizzard, the glass house was visible on the top of the island, a few of its windows gently glowing.

"We're back!" Sam yelled. "Back!"

Glory looked at the storm all around them. Really looked. Every flake was coming from the wrong time, blowing through a massive tear in the sky. And the water was wrong, too.

"You left it open!" Samra yelled. She was pointing back at the wide arch Glory had made for them. Sunlight was pouring through it.

And so were the leviathan.

But Glory didn't care right now. She was focused on the two birdlike shadows flying along above the motorcycle almost faster than sight. Glory slowed her moment, and she saw everything.

With the shadow wings spread wide, the skeletal bodies were laid bare in the center. The creatures had arms for legs and arms for arms, with taloned hands on all four. Each rib was feathered and the rib cages were stuffed full of gory trophies—the young feet and faces of those who had been killed in sacrifice. Their heavy heart necklaces flapped against those rib prisons as the two ghouls dove and crisscrossed in front of the bike, tearing open the air in an X just barely above the water.

The mothers were too fast for Sam's eyes, but Samra pointed and shouted a warning.

"Glory!"

The bike was going to career right into the freshly gaping darkness.

Glory swept her hand forward, and the motorcycle and its passengers dropped into the sea.

It wasn't wet. And it wasn't thick. All around them, the water wafted and curled away like transparent vapor. Behind them, the leviathans' huge bodies twisted slowly above them like monstrous sculptures. Young curling leviathans floated in the vapor like balloons.

Sam yelled in surprise, and the sound of his voice was as gargly as any underwater shout.

Glory focused. Flinging glass balls was clumsy. She needed precision. She was already touching the bike with her legs, and Sam with her knees, and her free arm and the water with almost all of her. Clamping her knees tighter, she let go of Sam and reached into the sidecar to grab Samra. They had passed well under the Tzitzi trap, but they were dropping fast.

The bike and its passengers were enveloped in a sleeve

of rapidly accelerating time. The water around them thickened, and the bike chewed its way forward and up.

One moment, Glory was watching a pair of massive monsters behind them, the next moment, the bike erupted from the sea like a leaping shark, slamming back down onto the surface and wobbling, sliding, and then rocketing away.

The air was cold and sharp, but breathing was easier. Snowflakes dangled in the air, barely moving, like ten billion hung ornaments waiting for the celebration.

Glory let go of Samra and hooked her arm back around Sam's rib cage.

Sam laughed. Snowflakes and droplets trailed his hair, and Glory's ponytail snapped like a damp flag.

"Where to?" Sam yelled.

"To Peter in the past!" Glory yelled. "In Arizona. And then back to the island to pick up our crew!"

Samra slumped as deep into the sidecar as she could, head down, arms around her legs.

Sam bent the bike south and accelerated across the water. Glory accelerated more.

THE LOST BOYS AND LEVI AND HIS MEN HAD GATHERED AT the dock, studying the pieces of sea monster that were somehow floating in strangely steaming water inside the hull of the metal boat. When they heard the motorcycle, every one of them had run through the falling snow, up from the harbor onto the arm of the island, and every one of them had seen the same thing.

Which didn't mean they all believed it.

Sam was racing the motorcycle across the water, trailing a watery rooster tail of epic proportions. Glory was riding behind him. Samra was in the sidecar.

Two massive sea monsters with gaping mouths and sparking nostrils plunged and leapt behind them and a wide sunlit arch sat open in the night air, half a dozen feet above the water. Steaming water from another sea was flooding in.

And so were dozens of long red-bodied serpents.

"Lord have mercy," Levi said. "Leviathan."

Only Jude saw the shadowy trap and the motorcycle vanish under the surface just in time. A split second later, he heard the engine again and turned to see it launching from the sea much too far away. And then it was gone, lost in the blizzard, hidden by its speed.

All other eyes were on the beasts that followed, with bodies as wide as the archway itself and nostrils spraying fire whiter than the falling snow.

"Fetch every weapon!" Levi bellowed. "Load the boats and say your prayers! We cannot allow those beasts in our waters!"

Excited boys and stunned men leapt into action.

Only Jude and Levi remained.

"They vanished again," Jude said. "Your daughter is alive."

"I saw her," Levi said. "Have no fear for your friends. My Samra's smart as a shark. She'll look after them."

"Maybe." Jude looked up at him. "Sharks aren't very smart."

Levi laughed and slapped Jude's back. "But they're winners! Ask anyone. Nothing beats sharks."

Jude watched the pair of train-size monsters twist and turn in circles. Clearly, they had lost the trail. "Those do," Jude said.

"And I'll beat those," Levi said, tugging his beard spikes. "I've seen them in books. Now don't you try and tell me that you wrote those books but not yet. If you did, you'll know to aim for the eyes and stand by for fireworks. Come on, then, before they realize they aren't meant for cold seas, and they try to lay claim to this island."

In the harbor, boat engines were already firing and the Lost Boys were whooping.

15

Hunt's End

THE MOTORCYCLE WAS STOPPED HIGH ON A LAVA HILL OVER-looking the Puget Sound. Sam and Glory stood beside it. Samra was standing up in the sidecar.

"I'm coming," Samra said. "I'm staying with you, Sam. You can't stop me."

"Yeah," Sam said. "I can."

"You think I can't keep up?" she sneered, lifting her chin. "You think I'm scared of the dark?"

Glory shook her head. "But you're a princess who thinks she's tough because she has always had Daddy's big old thugs standing behind her. You might have grown up in a hard world, but it was soft on you, Samra."

Samra flushed red. "You think my life was easy? You think you're better than me?"

Glory laughed. "What I think—"

"Glory," Sam interrupted. "Leave it." He turned to Samra. "I need you to stay."

Samra sniffed.

"Listen," Glory said, calming. "We're going into the darkness. All the way in. Not just diving through. If you come with us, you could die. Worse, you could get sick and terrified and be lost in there forever. I totally collapsed my first time in. I might again, and Sam can't carry both of us." She paused. "And I'm sorry I called you a princess. I'm sure your life is hard."

"A nightmare," Samra said. She brushed back her curls. "I hate it."

"Samra," Sam said. "Stay and guard the bike. We won't be gone long."

"Or we'll be dead and gone forever," Glory said. "Give us a few hours and if we're not back, take the bike. Keep it. Try to be a hero, not a punk like your dad. Make your world better."

Samra slumped down into the sidecar.

Glory shut her eyes and inhaled, smelling the air. Then she crouched down and flattened her palm on the rough stone. Scraping up some dust, she licked it.

"What are you doing?" Sam asked. "You look like you're about to start chanting."

Glory laughed. "I'm marking my place. This spot in this moment is unlike any other. To come back from the darkness, I need to remember it to reach for it again."

Sam looked around the volcanic destruction. "It looks like a lot of spots."

"I know," said Glory. "Which is why I'm doing this. I don't want to miss by years. Or miles."

"Why not just leave the door open behind us?" Sam asked.

Glory dropped her voice to a whisper. "Because your soul mate over there will definitely follow us through. And other things might wander out."

Samra sat up, listening closely.

"Soul mate?" Sam whispered. "Don't even joke like that. She'll take it seriously."

"Sorry." Glory smiled. "And if I throw up on you in there, I'm sorry again. In advance."

Black sand poured out of Glory's glassy palm and spun into a short rod and the long hooked blade of a scythe. Sam stepped backward and watched as Glory raised the blade and swung. The tip vanished into the air with a sound like a knife in watermelon. Glory pulled on the blade, the air peeling open like cut skin. The dark entrance gaped at Sam and Glory and a smell many miles beyond rot oozed out around them.

"Gosh. You're going in there?" Samra threw her arm over her face. Cindy and Speck both rattled.

Glory bit her lip and stretched out her left hand to Sam. He took it with his right. For a moment, Glory simply gripped and regripped his fingers. He could feel her nerves, her fear. And he could feel her determination.

"We can do this," Sam said. "Peter needs us to. We need us to."

Glory nodded, but she didn't speak. And then she ducked through into the darkness. Sam followed, and a moment later, while only Samra watched, the wound in the world's skin healed.

Sam kept his eyes shut, holding Glory's hand with Speck and relying on Cindy to see in the darkness . . . if there was ever anything to see. When Glory threw up, it didn't even make the smell of the place worse.

"You okay?" Sam asked. "What can I do?"

"Nothing," Glory said. "I just . . . keep your head clear. Listen to your hands." Gagging, she dropped to her knees. "Ghost gave me his memory, marking the moment. And we've been to the place." She threw up again, and Sam listened to her spit and then try to talk. She rolled onto her side, pulling her knees up as she spoke. Her voice was fading. "I just need . . . to focus."

Sam crouched, scooped Glory up, and tried to help

her walk. But he only succeeded in staggering sideways and tripping over her feet. Finally, sliding Cindy under Glory's legs and Speck under her arms, he picked her up. Still with his eyes shut, hoping Cindy and Speck would steer him clear of any pits or snares, he began to move forward.

"We don't need to move," Glory said slowly. "Anywhere . . ."

"Yeah, we need to move. Some places are worse than others," Sam said. "Just focus, and tell me when you're ready."

Glory's breathing slowed as Sam walked. He followed a low incline until he seemed to be rising out of the worst of the smell. Or maybe he was just growing used to it.

He understood Glory's reaction. He had felt it before himself, and without the snakes, he knew that he'd be dizzy and lost in the darkness forever.

"Okay, Glory," Sam said. "It won't get better than this."

Cindy rattled. Speck tried to coil away, almost dropping Glory.

The heat image of a heavy bear rose up Sam's arms from the snakes. The big animal rocked slowly toward Sam, growling and snorting. As Sam backed away, the bear rose onto his hind legs and bent and warped into the hunching shape of a man.

288

"*Yee naaldlooshii*," the bear-man slavered. "Leave your prey. The Vulture calls us to join his army and feast."

"Um." Sam took a step backward. "I will. Soon. I'm on my way."

"The doors to the living are open to us," the man said. "Tzitzimime desire our strength."

"Yes," Sam said. "I'm going to see them now."

After a long moment, apparently satisfied, the man dropped back into his beastly form and heaved himself slowly away.

Cindy's rattle stopped, but her tension didn't.

"What was that?" Glory whispered.

"A dead werebear," Sam said. "Off to join the Vulture's herd. I don't even want to know how many of those things he has by now, but I'm sure we're going to find out. Can you stand?" He dropped Glory's feet to the ground and held her arm while she tried to balance.

"Yeah," she said. "I'm sorry, Sam."

"Don't be stupid," Sam said. "Don't worry about it. I'll carry you wherever you need to go."

"Here," Glory said. "I'll try to open a way to the memory Ghost showed me right here. I just need to . . . focus."

Sam heard Glory drop to her knees, and warm images floated up to him from both snakes. The glass in Glory's right palm burned white-hot when she held it up. Her whole arm grew white. And then a long, curved, sandy scythe blade grew from her hand. Sam stopped paying any attention to the snakes and used his own eyes. The outer darkness now had a light even his eyes could see. From her knees, Glory swung her blade straight down, glowing orange and trailing sparks.

The darkness parted, and the blade slammed into the ground, parting it, as well.

Heat, the smell of fires and food, and the sound of laughter all entered the darkness.

"Is this right?" Sam asked. "Is there where we're supposed to be?"

Glory placed her hands on her knees and remained still, a silhouette in front of the opening she'd made.

"Yes," she said. "Almost. We have to wait for the scream."

Sam crawled up beside her and peered into the opening. She had torn it at two angles. The vertical cut peered across a rooftop and into the deep bowls of a cave lit with scattered torches. There were stairs back there leading up a wide crack. Sam recognized this place. Speck and Cindy did, too, and both snakes slid forward, jerking their heads in Sam's hands.

"This is Manuelito's cave," Sam said. "Where I woke up with the snakes."

"I know," Glory said. "I was there. Or . . . our younger

selves will both be here when that eventually happens."

Sam leaned down over the horizontal opening that was carved in the floor. He was looking into a small native house. A pot sat on a cooking fire. A boy ran in and out of sight. His mother was singing. Sam shifted to the side, trying to see more of the space below him. His eyes locked with a baby—fat, staring straight up at him, gurgling and kicking with curiosity. He was lying on a rug, beside an empty half barrel.

Sam watched while a woman with long white hair entered the house, and then Glory pulled Sam back up.

"Don't watch this part," she whispered. "Just listen."

"Was Peter born here?" Sam whispered back.

Glory shook her head. "Another tribe built this place. Some Navajo hid here when they were being hunted. Peter's people. *My* people. He's my extra-great-uncle. Ghost says my mother came from Tisto and Manuelito."

Sam looked at Glory, her face lit only from below, from the splits she had cut into the world. Her eyes were dark, but far from dim. Her jaw was strong and her will was stronger. Peter was Glory's uncle? Of course he was. They were the two most fearless people Sam had ever met.

The old woman's voice floated up into the air and Sam tried to spy again, but Glory pulled him upright once more.

"Not yet," she said. "Please don't watch." They both sat still, listening, but the words were too faint for Sam to understand.

"Ghost says my mother was taken by the Tzitzimime," Glory said. "Those flying shadows the Vulture sends. She wanted to be strong like they are. She wanted to be one of them—but they made her a lifeless slave."

Sam didn't know what to say. He felt like a fist was pressing into his stomach. And if he felt like that for Glory, then how did *she* feel?

"Glory . . ."

"No," Glory said. "I'm glad. I would rather her be double-crossed and destroyed by those things. I can't stand the thought of her being one."

"Ghost told you all of this?" Sam asked.

Glory nodded. "My brother left me in a bus station. On my birthday. When some cop carried me away twelve hours later, I almost scratched his eye out. I wish I could find him and apologize." Glory exhaled the faint beginning of a laugh. "I guess I can now. I loved my brother more than anything, because he was the only anything I had. And then I hated my brother for a long time after that. Remember how mad I was at the thought of you leaving Millie?" This time Glory did laugh. "Yeah, I have a thing about brothers ditching sisters."

Sam studied Glory's face and said nothing. He

watched the hard shadows on her features and the way she twitched her nose to the side when she sniffed. When she bit her lip and looked away, he noticed the whiteness of her teeth for the first time, and when she sighed and turned her head back, meeting him eye to eye, he didn't see anything else at all.

"Ghost tried to get my brother to do what I do," Glory said. "He wanted Alex to become your friend and live on SADDYR and help Father Tiempo help you. But Alex left me in that bus station and went after our mom instead. Ghost said he's dead. But he also said what's left of him is working for the Vulture's new allies. So you're stuck with the leftover sidekick girl."

"No," Sam said. "I'm not. I could ditch you any time."

Glory smiled. "Yeah, well, I could shake you pretty easy, too."

"Why are you telling me all of this?" Sam asked. "I mean, why right now?" He pointed at the open crack beside them.

"Because I want you to know who I really am," Glory said. "I'm a girl who could become a demon. I could become a total monster. My mother tried. My brother probably is."

Sam smiled. "No. You couldn't."

"Yes," Glory said. "I could. And so could you. Look at us. I'm carrying a scythe the Angel of Death gave me, and you have viper hands. It's all cool, yeah. But it's seriously dangerous. I know I could turn awful, Sam. I know it. And so could you and that's the worst thing that could ever happen to either of us."

"You'd never let me," Sam said. "Even if I tried. And there's no way I would ever let you."

Glory halfway smiled. "You think you could stop me?"

"I know I could," Sam said. "Because you're slow and stupid and have a terrible memory. You daydream, you lose track of things. Speck could beat you by himself."

Glory all the way smiled.

Below them, a woman screamed. Sam lunged forward to see what was happening, but Glory practically tackled him this time.

"Not yet," she said. "You have to make me a promise first. No matter what happens down there, you do exactly what I say, and you only protect this me. Don't try to save the older version, because she's already dead."

"What?" Sam looked down at the opening. The old woman with the white hair. "Glory, that's you? Glory! We can't just let you die!"

"Promise me, Sam!" Glory yelled. "This cave, in this time, this is where I end. We can't change that."

Children were wailing, dogs were barking, and the sounds of total chaos were growing.

Sam nodded.

"Great!" Glory shoved him toward the crack. "Now tell me what you see."

Sam was on his hands and knees above the opening, craning his neck to watch. Cindy and Speck were both trying to writhe forward into the hole, but Sam kept them locked beneath him.

"You're dead," Sam whispered. "But another you came in the door right after. And then another. The Tzitzis are awful. Glory, I have to go in! You're copying Father Tiempo! You're not just dying, you're losing years. Six of you now, Glory, please. You're a bloody pile in front of the doorway."

Shrieking laughter rose up through the crack, and then everything went quiet.

"They're standing above the baby now," Sam whispered. "But they're watching the door in case you come again. Peter is screaming."

And he was. Loudly.

"I can hear," Glory said.

Sam glanced back and saw Glory wiping her wet cheeks.

"Now," Glory said, and she lifted her swirling hourglass. "Aim for the eyes. All four eyes. And then stay out of the way."

Sam nodded, climbed to his feet, checked his bow, placed Cindy in charge of the weapon, took two quick breaths, and he jumped.

He wasn't even all the way through the ceiling when both demons whirled around from the baby's barrel. The feathers around their mouths were caked with blood, their shadowy robes were open, revealing two rib cages packed with human trophies. All eight taloned arms flew at Sam.

Cindy was firing.

Two blue arrows ripped through two black eyes and flew out the back of the skull. Two silver arrows made a messier job of the white eyes, ricocheting in the sockets. None of the arrows slowed the demons down.

Cold, gory forms slammed into Sam before he reached the floor and drove him back against the wall. Shadows wrapped around him, but not fast enough. One final Glory entered the room, falling from above, and her blade was falling faster. Sam had not even had time to yell when Glory split the first Tzitzimitl in two, from skull to hips, and then again from side to side. Razpocoatl the black-eyed fell sightless to the floor in quarters, four portions flapping like dying stingrays. Magyamitl dropped Sam and spun around, sightless and gaping, bent shafts and bloody feathers where her white eyes had just been.

"We *cannot* die!" she hissed. "How many more years

296

do you have left to give us, old woman?"

"Down!" Glory said. "On your face or I will carve you like your sister. Swear peace to me and I will give you peace."

"Fool," Magyamitl muttered. "Who are you to offer me forgiveness?"

"I am Glory Hallelujah," Glory said. "And what I offer is damnation."

Magyamitl snarled. "Your blade is made of time. You can slice me, but I will come together again."

"Not if you can't find the pieces," Glory said.

Sam was on his feet, pressed back into the corner, trying to stay out of the way while frantically reloading his bow. He watched the kneeling demon pull the bent arrows from her eyes and drop them on the floor.

Now. The command came up Sam's left arm from Cindy. *Strike.*

Kill, Speck said.

Sam dropped the crossbow onto his feet. He saw Glory swing her blade and he saw the Tzitzimitl tear a doorway in the air and raise it like a shield. Glory's blow vanished into it, and the demon lashed out with her wings.

Cindy and Speck tugged Sam forward—one step and a leap. Speck slammed his right fist into the monster's ribs. Cindy crunched his knuckles into the side of her feathered head.

Magyamitl spun, sinking her teeth into Sam's left arm, grabbing at his throat with taloned hands.

Glory vanished. Where she had just been, Sam saw only ripples.

While teeth tore into Cindy's scales and claws punctured the skin on his neck, time seemed to slow for Sam, as well. He wondered if he was nothing but an underwater smoke sculpture to Glory right now. He didn't wonder long.

The air in the room throbbed and Magyamitl shrieked. One black wing fluttered freely across and slapped onto the floor.

Glory threw Sam to the ground and vanished into her own accelerated time.

But not for long.

Sam rolled away, rattling as the gaping head and the collapsing remainders of the body rained down around him.

Glory reappeared, breathing hard, her hair mostly torn loose from her ponytail. Bloody claw marks ran down her cheek onto her neck.

She nudged the pieces of still moving Tzitzimime with her toe, and then kicked them away from one another.

Brushing back her hair, she looked down at Sam. "Thanks for that. She surprised me."

Glory refocused on the room. The taller boy was

crouching in terror beside the body of his mother. Five dead old women lay in a heap by the door and one across from the baby's barrel. Fluttering pieces of Tzitzimime carpeted the floor. A pot was boiling on the fire. Glory tiptoed across to young Manuelito, but the boy turned his face away, burying it in his mother's sleeve.

"Now what?" Sam asked.

Glory sighed. "Now we leave."

"But we can't leave them." Sam looked at Manuelito and Peter. "The whole point was a rescue."

"The whole point was prevention." Glory pushed back her hair. "Peter kept his heart. I will return to finish his anointing as a time-walker. And I can't do that yet. I don't know how. It has to be an old me. Then Peter grows up in foster care all over the southwest before assuming his role and authority throughout all the centuries he is meant to tend." Glory looked at Sam. "We have to go. Now that this has happened. I might be here again soon, and then one of me would die."

"Right. Okay." Sam understood. Kind of. But he didn't like it. Crossing the room, he bent over Peter. The dumpling-faced boy smiled at him and kicked, but his cheeks were tear-streaked. Sam carefully reached into the barrel end with Speck, and wiped Peter's soft cheeks with his thumb.

"Hey, Pete," Sam said. And he tried to smile at his

happy friend—a baby unaware that his mother would never sing to him again in this life, unaware that there was nothing in this room or that house or that moment to smile and kick about. Hot sadness boiled up in Sam even though he tried to choke it off. Quickly wiping his own eyes on Speck's back, he sniffed twice and steadied his breathing.

"I'm sorry about your mom," he whispered, and wiped his eyes again, and bit his lip and looked away. "I'm sorry about a lot of things." And then he smiled back at the baby, and he gripped his tiny feet. "But I'm glad you're still here."

Peter kicked. And laughed.

~16~

Island War

WHEN SAM AND GLORY STEPPED OUT ONTO THE BLACK LAVA-rock hilltop and into the cold Seattle air, they both smelled of blood, smoke, and rot beyond rot. Every dripping, fluttering, oozing piece of the Tzitzimime had been collected and mixed up between four blankets. Then—along with a torch—Sam and Glory had lugged the blankets up through the roof and into the darkness. Sam left Glory curled up on the ground, and then he carried each of the blankets as far in each direction as it took to make the snakes nervous in his arms. There he would set his burden down, and there he would set the blanket on fire.

Four great fires. And while the flames rose over Sam's head and smoked enough for a forest, the pile of Tzitzi-pieces that was left when the blankets had burned never seemed to get smaller. All four fires burned bright and tall. When Sam finally helped Glory to her feet and asked if she could take them back, the four fires still towered, showing no signs of dying. Ever.

When Sam and Glory stepped out onto that black lava-rock hilltop and into the cold Seattle air, they both stopped, and they stared at an empty spot where the motorcycle and Samra should have been.

"Great," Sam said. "Now what?"

Glory looked at him, and she smiled. With one big looping motion she swung the hourglass around herself and Sam.

"Once I've done something," she said. "It gets a lot easier. I promise."

A glass cylinder formed quickly around the two of them and a blade remained between Glory's hourglass and the wall. With a tug, she set the cylinder spinning.

"You know what?" Sam asked.

"Probably," said Glory.

"We smell awful," Sam said.

"Agreed," Glory replied. "Perfect for close quarters."

They both watched as time raced backward outside the glass—clouds snapping, blizzard growing and then

shrinking and then growing. Nighttime. Then the sunset reversed and the sun rose and disappeared. Nighttime
again."

"Wow," Sam said. "How long were we gone?"

Glory yawned and leaned her head against Sam's
shoulder.

"Here she is," Sam said. "Feckless girl."

Glory laughed. "What does that even mean?"

Sam didn't answer. He and Glory both watched
Samra and the motorcycle bounce up the hill backward
until it stopped back on its spot.

Glory collapsed the glass, and she and Sam both
stepped into the air beside the bike.

Samra yelped and jumped off the seat. The motorcycle engine was still running.

"Thank God you're back! Where did you come
from?"

"That would take *a lot* of explaining," Sam said, and
he slid onto the seat. "We'll tell you later."

Samra jumped into the sidecar.

Glory looked at the watch on Sam's belt. It was pointing across the water through the blizzard toward Seattle.

"Is he here?" she asked.

"Or he's left a door open to here," Sam said. "You
ready?"

Glory slid onto the seat behind him and hooked her

arm around his waist. She didn't have to say anything more.

Sam pointed the bike down the lava slope straight at the water, and he opened up the throttle.

The Vulture stood at a window with his long arms crossed. Behind him, cold wind flapped tablecloths and tumbled trash through the empty restaurant. A wall of snow was crawling toward the city from across the water. Hundreds of flashing lights crowded the streets by the docks, accompanied by a chorus of screaming sirens.

His plague had begun, but he was restless. Miracle had vanished from his maps.

And since that disappearance, Mrs. Dervish had not stopped poring over both hides. She was hunched over beside the Vulture, whispering worry to herself.

"Dervish," the Vulture said. He saw no sign of the mothers anywhere in the sky. They should have opened more storms by now. They should have been cutting down lives in the streets by the thousands.

More than likely, they were on Miracle's heels, wherever he had gone.

"Here!" Mrs. Dervish gasped in excitement, tapping the map. "He's back! On the water. Moving toward his island. Hit them now, William!"

The Vulture pulled on his beard. "And your mothers?

304

Where have they gotten to?"

"What?" Mrs. Dervish scanned the map and then looked up out of the windows.

"If we want to reopen a doorway to the island, we will need to return to the darkness and do it ourselves."

"They must be here somewhere."

The Vulture turned on his boot heel and began to stride around the restaurant, stepping over bodies and chairs, but keeping his eyes on the windows.

"Bring the maps!" he bellowed.

NEVERLAND WAS AS FULL OF LAUGHTER AND SHOUTING AS IT was of snow. The Lost Boys and their new allies had successfully repelled the first invasion of leviathans. A dozen serpents under twenty feet in length had been killed in the harbor and four over thirty feet had been killed trying to reach the house. There were molten spark ripples from their blasts all over the windows. Tiago and Simon had accounted for the largest beasts themselves.

Despite the initial victory, the island was still on high alert. The truly massive monsters had not yet made any attempts, but they were out there, circling.

Millie was grateful, relieved, and still very disturbed. But she was also refusing to cook any of the beast meat at all. Absolutely not, and the suggestion was not even funny. Which just meant that she was still worried about

Sam and Glory and Peter. The time for laughter would come after their return.

She was peeling carrots when Sam and Glory walked into the kitchen, and she nicked her knuckle with the peeler, but she really didn't care. She would have laughed and cried and thrown her arms around her brother and yelled for all the fools down studying the dead serpents to get up to the house immediately . . . but then she saw the look on his face. She still hugged him.

"Peter's safe," Sam said. "But we're not done, and the boys can't know. I'm not taking them. I'm just here to get my guns."

"Why?" Millie asked. "Sam, does it have to be now?"

"Yes," Sam said. "It does." And he hugged her again. Then Glory hugged her, too, which wasn't normal. Millie didn't say a word about how either of them smelled because it was obvious that both of them weren't sure they would ever be coming back.

There were many things that Millie wanted to say. She wanted to beg Sam to stay. She wanted to ring the dinner cowbell and summon all the boys to stop him. But *wants* were not what controlled Millie Miracle, and they never had been.

"Can you really do it alone?" Millie asked her brother. "Can you stop him?"

Sam didn't answer. He didn't know. He looked down

at the watch and chain pointing into the air off of his belt loop.

"I can reach him, Millie. He's attacking. I have to try."

"Then get your guns," she said. "And then get him." Sam backed out of the kitchen toward his room. But this was one of those moments that Millie knew might be the last of its kind. "Sam," she said. "I'm proud of you. No matter what. Thank you for making that easy."

Sam gave his sister another hug. And he ran.

"Glory," Millie said.

Glory stepped forward. "Yeah?"

"Take some muffins."

"Oh, yes please." Glory laughed. "Take care of these idiots for me while we're gone."

WHEN SAM AND GLORY JOGGED DOWN THE OUTSIDE OF THE island, away from the harbor and toward where they had hidden the motorcycle, Sam had his guns on, and they were both inhaling apple muffins in the fast-falling snow.

And Samra Finn was wedged deep inside the sidecar, ready for a fight. She looked at them both.

"I'm not getting out of this thing."

"Do we really need the bike?" Glory asked.

Sam focused his attention on Samra. "Listen, I'm not playing games. If you get out, I'll give you an apple muffin. If you stay in, I'll give you a muffin anyway, and then

I will take you to a place where you have a very good chance of being torn apart by skin-walkers."

"I'm staying," Samra said.

Sam's watch was floating above his thigh, tugging forward. He checked both guns, and then propped his crossbow across the handlebars.

"Keep your blade ready."

"Okay," Glory said. "Do a loop out there so we can make sure we know where it's pointing."

"Where are we going?" Samra asked. "I know you aren't serious about the skin-walkers."

"I'm dead serious," Sam said. "Have a muffin. We're following this watch."

He handed a muffin to her, popped another one into his mouth, shook the snow off his face, and kick-started the bike, immediately throttling forward to the water's edge.

"Hold on!" Glory yelled. She slid her right hand up in front of Sam's face—fingers spread, glassy black palm flattened. Her hand was trembling. Sand trickled down, streaming over Sam's leg.

"He's messing with time?" Sam asked. He looked back at Glory and then out over the gray water beneath the storm. "And he knows where we are."

Sam's watch suddenly jerked to the side, pointing down the beach.

A blast of warm wind parted the snowstorm, and one hundred yards from the motorcycle, a dark arch opened over the shallow water.

Heavy, snarling animal shapes tumbled out in twos and threes, splashing onto the shore.

From where she was gripping the left handlebar, Cindy knew what she was seeing.

KILL. She threw the thought at Sam as loudly as she knew how, but the boy was stunned. He did nothing.

Pink! Cindy tried to reach the snake in Sam's other hand with her command. *Yee naaldlooshii! KILL.*

Strike, Speck replied. *Die!*

Even before Sam could process what was happening, he felt the hot anger pulse in his arms, and Speck and Cindy were jerking the handlebars toward the dark arch.

"Sam!" Glory yelled.

Cindy let out the clutch. Speck opened the throttle. Flinging rocks from the back tire, the motorcycle launched forward.

The animal shapes all turned—dozens already on the shore.

"Shoot!" Samra yelled. "Shoot them!" Rising up in the sidecar, she grabbed the crossbow off the handlebars.

Glory raised her right hand, and black sand leapt out of it in a snapping, snow-eating tornado. As they approached the snarling animals, Glory swung her enormous whip across the beach, sending the beasts tumbling into the shallows. But all of them rose up again quickly, most in the shapes of men and women, and all of them furious.

Glory focused her storm whip on the arch itself, but as the bike rocketed past the teeming entrance, pulsing darts and sizzling arrows roared out of its mouth in a swarm.

Samra returned fire. "Go behind it!" she yelled. "Flank them!"

Sam heard gunfire from the island above them and he looked up at the house. Tiago and Simon were leaping down rocks. Jude and Barto and Leviathan Finn were all firing. More of Finn's gang were coming into view.

Sam forced the bike out into the water, between two sheets of spray. Glory slammed her storm down in a boiling splash, and leaned over, slowing the surface with her touch.

With gunfire and shouts and roaring behind them, Sam looped the bike out and around behind the dark archway.

Sam blinked away stinging snowflakes. "Can you close it?" he yelled over his shoulder.

"Or open another one!" Samra yelled. "Right in front of that one. Send them all back into the heat!"

"That I can do!" Glory laughed. "Get in there closer."

Sam accelerated. Glory lifted her hand from the surface, and with a long skipping blast of sand the surface of

310

the water slowed in a straight and narrow path in front of them.

"It worked!" Glory shouted. "Stay on that!" Grabbing Sam's shoulders, she stood up on the foot pegs, and leaning forward over him, she raised her right hand.

The black sand leapt up into an enormous, seething cloud, shaped like a reaper's blade, high above Sam's head.

"Look out!" Samra screamed.

Most of the invaders were hurling darts of fire up at the Lost Boys on the island, but a huge, scabby bear had waded out into the water. With a roar like thunder, he swung his paw.

Cindy and Speck both let go of the handlebars.

Five burning yellow claws hissed across the water as fast as fired lightning. Two bolts hissed off the waves, skipping away. One exploded in the bike's gauges, between the handlebars, spraying glass and sparks and metal into Sam's face.

Speck snatched the fourth as it hit Sam in the chest.

Cindy struck the fifth just in front of Glory's face. The bolt punched through Sam's palm and tore out the back of his hand and Cindy's head before kissing Glory with a burn between the eyebrows.

Sam's left arm dropped to his side, limp and flapping, speared with the burning claw. Sam slumped forward, and began to fall off the bike.

The bear raised his other paw.

"No!" Samra emptied her crossbow into the bear's chest.

Glory grabbed onto Sam, holding him up with her left hand.

Speck grabbed the throttle and began to steer.

But the snake drifted off the path Glory had made.

The motorcycle skipped across the liquid. And then wallowed.

And then sank.

GLORY SHUT HER EYES AND EXHALED. IN ANY MOMENT, SHE had as much time as she needed. And in this moment, she needed a lot of time.

As the chaotic world around her slowed, a single heartbeat slammed through her veins and into her eardrums in a long painful crash—like a piano falling down stairs. And during that one beat, her mind raced for miles . . .

Cindy had just saved her life. And she had died because of it. She had to be dead. The bolt went through her head right in front of Glory's eyes. Sam would lose his left arm. Or maybe Glory could take him back in time and Manuelito could get him a new one. A nicer one.

Sam was hit in the chest. Maybe badly. Maybe he wouldn't

be using any arms at all anymore.

The motorcycle was sinking. Even though Sam was limp, Speck was steering. But not well.

Samra was alive. And fighting. Well. She wasn't always a princess.

Glory was angry. That's what the crashing in her ears was all about. Anger. Rage. Werebeasts were attacking her people. Her Sam. They might be undead, but she had a blade for that.

Glory brought down her right arm, and her Reaper's scythe of black sand came with it, stretching out like a long beach of death above the water, hissing and seething and flickering to the slow time of Glory's sight.

Anything that existed in time could be parted by time....

As her heartbeat ended, Glory Hallelujah swung her blade.

Too fast for any bear.

Thunder shook the bones of space and time.

The water's surface leapt with the shock.

Samra's eardrums burst. Windows exploded on top of the island.

Glory's blade parted stones all the way into the heart of the island. And every man and beast in the water or standing on the shore, fell into two halves.

The motorcycle hit the shallow bottom with hissing

pipes and engine, and then kicked forward, bouncing to a stop on the now perfectly silent shore.

Glory reached around Sam and turned off the key. The bike sputtered and died. Steam was coming off it around her. Speck still clutched the throttle.

The Lost Boys stood in silence above her. Samra rose slowly in the sidecar. The mouth of the dark arch was crowded with disfigured beasts and men and women in rotting furs. The water was full of floating, spasming parts of the same. The leviathans wouldn't mind.

"There's nothing for you here!" Glory yelled. "Go back to your darkness!"

The crowd did not retreat.

Sam stirred in Glory's grip, and then sat up, breathing hard. Coughing. His left arm and Cindy were still limp, dangling at his side.

Samra began to thump around in the sidecar, trying to reload her bow.

Twin pale-skinned men with yellowing beards pushed to the front of the crowded arch. They wore only loincloths and their skin matched the snow falling in front of them. The dark furs of great wolves were grown into their backs, and thick tails swayed between their legs.

"He lives?" one of them asked.

"And the bear who struck him does not," Glory replied. She raised her blade again. "I will do the same to you if you do not go back into your darkness."

The other wolf-man spoke. "We must take him to the Vulture. We have sworn. But he did not say the boy was *yee naaldlooshii*."

"You won't be taking him anywhere," Glory said. "Ever."

"Did you not see what just happened?" Samra laughed. Her voice was too loud, like someone shouting under headphones. "She just split at least fifty of you at once!"

"I'm ready," Sam said. "Lead me to him, and I'll come."

"Sam, no!" Glory leaned her mouth up to his ear. "You can't," she whispered. "You're hurt."

"Glory, yes." Sam smiled faintly. "This is what I'm for." Then he looked down at the blood on his chest. Opening his right hand, he winced at the wound on the palm that Speck had earned him.

Realizing that his left arm wouldn't move, he looked down at Cindy. The bear claw was no longer burning, but it was still sticking through Sam's hand and out Cindy's left eye.

"Lift my arm up," Sam said.

"Sam . . . ," Glory whispered. "Please. I can make them leave."

"Just lift her."

The two wolf-men splashed out of the doorway into the water.

"No!" Samra bellowed. "Back!"

Glory twitched her right hand, and both men leapt back up into the doorway, wet tails lashing. Then Glory reached around Sam and raised Cindy and his drooping left arm in front of his chest.

Sam stared at the huge bloody claw sticking out of Cindy's head and his hand. It looked like one of her horns had sprouted into a tusk.

"Do you know how big a rattlesnake's brain is?" Sam asked.

"No," Glory said, glancing up at the watching crowd. "I don't."

"The size of a pea," said Sam. "Easy to miss." Grabbing the claw with his right hand, he jerked it down out of his palm and tossed it into the water.

Cindy's remaining eyelid fluttered. She blinked and her slit pupil focused on Sam.

"Wake up," Sam said. "I know it hurts, but I'm going to need you."

"Sam!" Jude yelled from up beside the house behind them. "We're coming down!"

"No!" Sam yelled back. "You're not! Stay right where you are!"

Speck turned the key. Sam kicked the bike back to life and swung his limp left arm up onto the handlebars. His fingers closed slowly. Looking down at Samra in the sidecar, he smiled.

"You ready for more?" he asked.

"No," she said. "Not really."

"Good," he said. "Neither are we."

Revving the motorcycle engine, Sam tried to blink his head clear. Cindy was feeling a little bit less like dead weight.

"Tell the Vulture we're coming!" he yelled. "Now give us some space. I'm not riding into a crowd."

Sam waited until all the shapes had backed away and the dark arch above the water was completely empty. Then he throttled the bike slowly forward across the water and bumped it up and in, out of the snow and into the darkness.

~17~

Dark March

Two hundred yards in, Sam stopped the bike, and the engine kicked and sputtered into a low idle. Glory could feel his heart beating beneath her palm and his ribs rising and falling with his surprised breaths. But there was no light at all. And they seemed to be completely alone. She couldn't even see the rattle that brushed her jaw as Cindy grew nervous. She was glad Cindy was conscious enough to do anything.

"What just happened?" Samra asked. "Where did they all go?"

"We . . . ," Glory started, but she didn't really know.

"None of this is in the comic," Samra said.

"Enough about the comic," Sam said. "You were cool there for a while." A switch clicked as he turned on the old motorcycle's headlight. "Come on," he said.

"Is the watch moving?" Glory asked. "Maybe just drive a bit and keep your eye on it."

"Pointing forward," Sam said. "I'm on track."

"Gaaaw," Samra moaned. "I feel sick. It's awful in here."

A pale mangy shape crossed through the headlight. It was one of the wolf-men, but on all fours now, huge and gray, with pale human skin for its belly.

"There we go." Sam clicked the bike into gear and throttled it forward. "We follow the *yee naaldlooshii*."

The bike bounced and wandered up and down dark slopes, just barely keeping the wolf's outline visible.

"Sam!" Glory squeezed him from behind and whispered in his ear. "To your right!"

A man was running beside them, with what at first looked like a deer on his back. But his face snarled at them from inside the deer's chest, and then he dropped down onto all fours and raced away, passing the wolf. And more shapes were creeping in on every side, all moving in the same direction, all barely visible on the perimeter of the light, and some quickly dashing across it. Hundreds. Thousands. It wasn't hard to imagine what would have happened if they had all managed to reach the island.

"The watch is pointing this way, too," Sam said. Glory could see it floating in the air above his thigh, and it was tugging in the same direction as the monstrous herd.

"Even if they didn't tell him," she whispered, "he has to know I'm coming."

A tall woman with short white hair stepped in front of the bike and Sam locked his brakes just in time. Her eyes were hidden behind a blindfold of shadow. Her body was wrapped in mummy strips of the same darkness, all but her pale hands and feet.

On each side of the woman, stretching away beyond the reach of the headlight, men and women dressed all in ragged skins stood shoulder to shoulder, facing inward like human fences containing a road. None of them were armed, but all were wild, misshapen, animalian. Some had blood caked down their jaws and chests, and scabbed and blackened all over their hands.

The blindfolded, shadow-bound woman raised a pale hand to her chest. When she spoke, her voice was cold and lifeless.

"I am called Laila," she said. "I will guide you to the Vulture."

"Perfect," Sam said.

But as they moved, Glory's face pressed into the back of his shoulder. He could feel her whole body shaking, and the heat of tears found his skin. Glory was undone.

"Sam," she whispered. "She was my mom."

SAM DROVE THE MOTORCYCLE SLOWLY, KEEPING A LITTLE distance from their shadowy guide. As they rode, the rows of male and female skin-walkers and shifters and werepeople closed behind them like a zipper, and lumbered behind them in silence, lit only occasionally with the red of Sam's brake light.

Dark foul-smelling air pressed in all around them, fogging his brain. Sam was alert only through hunger and pain. And because Cindy was fully alive and very, very angry, boiling with threats of violence and vengeance against those who had taken her eye. Samra slumped over, asleep in the sidecar, and Glory leaned against Sam's back in complete stillness. She may have been awake. She may not have been. He wasn't going to ask. Not after what she had told him. His back and shoulders ached from Glory's weight, but aches could be ignored. He had worse pains.

When Laila stopped, there didn't seem to be any marker that Sam could see. No doorway. No gate.

The motorcycle idled. The army in the darkness behind them continued, stopping just one stride behind the bike. He rolled the bike forward a few feet. The army moved forward a few feet—without so much as a footfall. Sam couldn't even hear them breathing.

"Well, that's unnerving," Glory whispered into Sam's shoulder.

"Matches the rest, I guess," Sam said, and immediately wished he hadn't. "Sorry. I mean . . ."

"I know," Glory said, and she sat up, sliding back on the seat. "Should I talk to her?"

Sam straightened his back and rolled his shoulders. "Maybe," he said. "But you know what side she's on."

"Does it matter?" Glory asked.

"Yes," said Sam. "Or no."

A tall crack of pale light appeared in the darkness. The sound of rattling chains echoed through it, and the crack widened, revealing wide sandstone steps that rose into a massive cavern with a roof so high, it at first looked like stormy sky.

"Come," Laila said. Turning, she began to climb.

"Well," Glory said. "I guess we walk from here."

"No," said Sam. "We ride. I'm not leaving the bike." Sam rose on his foot pegs, and attacked the steps.

Samra jerked, kicking and flailing with each bounce. Glory rose on her own foot pegs, with her hands on Sam's scaled shoulders, just below the rattles.

Sam passed Laila, and the blindfolded woman seemed unsurprised. He rode up until he was blinking in the red light of the underworld city, and damp cool air filled his lungs.

At the top of the steps, the bike surged and bounced out into a cobbled city square bigger than a California stadium. The square was lined with columned buildings and spires, all of sandstone, and enormous yellow banners bearing a black two-headed vulture slowly floated from the buildings, pushed by a slow breeze.

The square was filled completely with men and women in ragged skins, organized in rough phalanxes, but there were no children anywhere. The wild sea parted, opening a path to the center of the square.

Sam drove forward, aware of how strange they must look, aware of how visible Cindy and Speck were to every pair of eyes they passed. He was known here. Completely.

With wet clothes and wet skin, Sam shivered and flexed his jaw to keep it from chattering. Glory's arm tightened around him, and he was grateful.

"Where are we?" Samra asked. "What is this?"

"Somewhere I'd rather not be," Sam said. "And that's all I know."

And then he saw the Vulture.

El Buitre was wearing a billowing buffalo coat that merged with his long black hair below his ears, and he had his arms crossed behind him. His beard had been freshly waxed to a point and he was smirking with obvious pleasure. Six golden watches floated above him and a seventh broken chain pointed at Sam from the outlaw's vest as the motorcycle approached. Sam could feel the seventh watch tugging on his belt with the gentle insistence of a magnet.

"That's really him," Samra hissed, scooting back in the sidecar. "Turn around, Sam. Turn around!"

But Sam's eyes were locked onto the Vulture's. Speck and Cindy were both seething in his arms, rippling scales, tensing muscles, desperate to strike.

"Don't look back," Glory said. "The crowd is closing behind us."

The Vulture was accompanied by Mrs. Dervish, dressed all in black with a golden vulture clasped at her throat, and two men stood together off to the side, both in black—one older and bald with a thick white beard, the other young and tall, with the sides of his head shaved, and his hair combed straight back in a slab on top. On the ground between them, there was a heavy block of pale bleached wood with a neck notch on top. A long-handled ax with a black blade leaned against it.

Glory's arm clamped so tight around Sam's ribs that he gasped in surprise.

"Alex," she whispered into the air. "Sam, my brother. Alex."

El Buitre spread his arms wide, grinning.

"Sam Miracle!" he said, and his voice echoed off the buildings and over the crowd. "Gloria Spalding!

Welcome, daughter of Leviathan! This is my City of Refuge, although many call it the City of Wrath. To what do I owe the pleasure?"

Sam turned off the motorcycle. "Vulture," Sam said. "I am here to kill you."

Samra sank herself as low in the sidecar as she could go. Glory slid off the back. Sam swung his leg over the handlebars and dropped onto the cobblestones. El Buitre eyed the guns on his hips, and his lips twitched a smile.

Glory stood beside Sam, flexing her right hand around the glass burned into her palm. But her focus was on the tall boy with water for eyes.

"Skin-changers!" El Buitre shouted, and his watches danced above his head. "Gentlemen and ladies, werefriends one and all. We are here to witness the execution of a monster! A creature who should never have been created!"

"Yes," Sam said. "We are!" Cindy's mind was hot, her eye socket stinging. She began to rattle harder than she ever had. Speck wasn't far behind.

"He is not worthy to stand in the presence of *yee naaldlooshii*! He has not passed through death, nor can he change his skin, nor has he slain a kinsman. He chooses to stand against us and all who dwell in the darkness! What shall I do with him?"

"KILL!"

325

The crowd stomped and groaned and snarled and wailed, and the Vulture basked in the echo. As it died, Sam spoke.

"I have passed through death!" Sam yelled. "How many times, Vulture, have you killed me but I have risen again to face you? How many times did my soul move in and out of shadow?"

Sam looked around at the mob and raised his twisting arms high. Blood trickled down his scales. "Is this human skin?" he asked. "How many men have vipers for arms? Viper minds sharing their thoughts?"

The spirit of the crowd dwindled to a moan.

"Kinsman!" a voice shouted. "Kinsman or you're false!"

"All right," Sam said. "If the *yee naaldlooshii* must have slain a kinsman, ask the Vulture how many of my sisters are buried in the garden he lost. How many, Vulture? And how many of those deaths did you blame on me?"

The crowd went silent.

"I am Sam Miracle, and I have come to kill the Vulture!"

El Buitre laughed, but the crowd was silent. He spread his arms and beckoned the crowd to join him.

"Blood!" he shouted again. "Slay them and take them. There are three here for you to feed upon! Blood!"

"Yes, please," said Sam.

"Your blood, boy!" El Buitre snarled. "I will drain you. And this time, there is no priest to sweep you away." Throwing back his huge coat, the Vulture drew both of his guns. "This time, Miracle, I will cut out your heart and give it to my dark birds for their necklaces."

"Dark birds?" Sam asked. "You mean those awful women? They've gone to pieces. I wouldn't expect them back for quite a while."

Sam dropped his bow and focused on his guns. He could feel the gold watch pointing, and he watched six others rise up around his foe.

The crowd was silent.

Glory put her hand on Sam.

A strange and powerful stillness poured through him. Black fire burned behind his eyes and behind the three eyes in his hands.

"Are you going to run, Vulture?" Sam asked. "Are you afraid?"

The Vulture's eyes hardened. "Today you die, Miracle. Forever."

Sam smiled. "After you . . ."

In a flash, El Buitre's watches warped the time around him, and he had drawn both of his guns. Alternating blasts flashed light across his snarling face. But Glory's touch was on Sam, slowing the world and quickening his always quick hands. Speck was firing, not at the Vulture, but at his bullets. Lead collided with lead and ricocheted away across the cave. Cindy was firing, too, not at the Vulture, but at his golden watches.

Watch after watch exploded in bursts of glass and springs, while Speck defended Sam and Glory.

Sam's hands were too fast. Loose gold-and-pearl chains rattled down around the Vulture's legs and he staggered sideways, gasping.

El Buitre had fired five times.

Sam had fired eleven.

Five bullets blocked. Six watches shattered.

Speck had one round left.

William Sharon had lost his wings. Time whistled past him as it whistles past any normal man. The Vulture was no arch-outlaw. He was just a killer with the guiltiest of souls.

"Miracle!" he snarled, and he raised both of his guns one last time.

"William, no!" Mrs. Dervish yelled.

Speck loosed his final round, and the bullet flew, tinged with black fire that only Glory saw and understood—Ghost was in the cave, and the Vulture would not escape.

The bullet punched through the outlaw's beard and

into his throat, exploding out the back of his buffalo collar in a cloud of black sand.

The Vulture's eyes widened and he slumped onto his knees. Mrs. Dervish rushed forward, dropping down beside him, sobbing as she examined his wound.

The two generals stepped forward. The bearded man spoke first.

"Scipio the Scarred, general to the Furious Magyamitl, greets his brother, Samuel the Miracle, general to the Furious Gloria. You have thrown down our general. Honor us and take his place."

El Buitre coughed and gargled dying rage.

Glory's brother raised his voice.

"Alexander the Young, general to the Furious Razpocoatl, greets his brother, Samuel the Miracle, general to the Furious Gloria. You have thrown down our general. It is your right to take his place."

While Mrs. Dervish wept, Scipio and Alexander ripped the buffalo robe off the Vulture's back and lifted him to his feet. The arch-outlaw, destroyer of nations, gargled and wept as they dragged him to the block. His booted heels kicked against the cobblestones.

Alexander bundled the broken pearl-and-gold watch chains across the wood. With one swing of the ax, all seven chains were severed and the Vulture slumped onto his face, lifeless.

The crowd laughed and cheered and moaned with hunger.

Scipio and Alexander each grabbed an arm and lifted him up again, resting his neck in the notch, his black hair draped forward, hiding his face.

"Come and take your trophy!" Alexander shouted.

The crowd snarled, and every foot stomped. They wanted Sam to take the ax.

Glory looked at Sam. Sam's face was pale, his eyes worried. He shook his head almost imperceptibly. She took his hand in hers and stepped up onto the motorcycle seat, raising her hourglass palm high.

Sam waited, wondering, but already knowing. When Glory spoke, her voice filled his blood with fire and joy.

"I am Glory Hallelujah. This is my general, Samuel the Miracle, who has slain the Vulture. I am a voice in the Song." She smiled. "I am Mother Tiempo, but some will call me Death because I carry the Reaper's scythe." She swung her glass and a towering black blade erupted out of it, hooking just below the cavern mouth. "*Yee naald-looshii*, with this blade I cut down Razpocoatl Tzitzimitl. I cut down Magyamitl Tzitzimitl. If any of you should enter my world and harm the living, I will unmake you."

The mob grumbled and moaned, but Sam was starting the motorcycle. Only Samra's pom-pom ponytail was visible in the sidecar.

"Alex," Glory said, climbing on the bike behind Sam. Her brother was already staring at her. "If there's any of you left in there, come with me. Please!"

Alex shook his head. "You're a fool. You've angered them. The mothers will return."

Glory smiled. "I love you, Alex. If you change your mind, I'll be at the bus station a long time ago."

Sam spun the rear tire on the stone floor, and whipped the bike around.

The groaning crowd parted.

Millie was doing her best to sing in the kitchen, but the songs were deteriorating to wishes and worries and a few broken prayers she was too worried to finish.

She still had soup on the fire. But she had started another pot. With all of Levi's men, she would need it. After hunting sea monsters in a blizzard and fighting off a monster invasion, everyone would be hungry. Everyone. Even those who had ridden off through that horrible doorway after those horrible creatures. She knew they had survived. And they would be back. She convinced herself by cooking for them.

She was making noodles when the beautiful old woman with the bright eyes and the perfectly white hair stepped out of the pantry and smiled at her back. So she didn't see anything at all. But she felt something new, something strong, something as firm and fixed as the stars.

She felt hope. And it was certain.

Millie's songs returned.

Upstairs, that woman with the white hair waved away layers of glass, and dismissed storms of sand until she was standing above a Navajo boy drained of spirit. Then, quietly joining her voice to the song that Millie was singing below, she cupped her hands above the boy's chest and they filled to overflowing with what looked like water.

"Peter," she said. "It has been a long time, and no time at all. Wake. The one who speaks time speaks of you in it. Take up the life that is yours. Walk the lonely winding roads to the deaths that are yours. Live with open hands."

Peter sneezed suddenly. Then he yawned, stretching on the strangely crooked bed. When his eyes opened, he blinked and then smiled in surprise.

"Glory?" he asked.

By the time Peter Atsa Tiempo walked downstairs, Millie was chopping carrots and seasoning chicken. When he said her name, Millie spun around, and almost burst into tears, she was so happy to see him. He looked more alive than she remembered, stronger, brighter, like his dark eyes had seen mysteries and had laughed at them.

Even better . . . he was hungry.

And if Peter had looked out the window, beyond the tangle of leviathans feeding on strange carcasses and the Lost Boys watching them from the shore, he would have seen a motorcycle, crossing the water.

The Vulture is dead. We are alive. If that isn't peace on earth, goodwill toward men, I don't know what is.

For Christmas, I drew comics for everyone. I even made Samra pretty cool.

Millie made each of us our own pie. Mine was peach and I ate the whole thing for lunch.

Glory has promised us the best gift. At least everyone thought so at first. Every Lost Boy has been offered his choice of time and place. Anyone who wants to leave and go back to their own time and place can. But I don't even remember mine, and I don't think many of the others do, either.

We took a vote and decided to stay in Neverland for a few months. It's nice here, even if we did have to put boards over the broken windows. Barto finally got the generators going, so we have electricity whenever we scavenge gas, but firelight and lanterns are nice once we get used to them.

Peter will be the first one to leave. There are things he needs to learn and things he needs to do and places and times where he needs to be. The more he has learned to navigate time with Glory, the quieter he has become. At night, I sometimes catch him writing notes to his older self. And he says his older self writes back. I don't try to understand.

Sam says we can't stay here forever, but I don't see him in any rush to leave. Of course, I know he's right. We all do. But we're enjoying the peacefulness of this blown-up world for now.

I've never seen anything more beautiful than snow falling in smooth silver water.

Glory and Sam act like they're going to go off and have adventures without us. They're needed, apparently. But we've all made it pretty clear how we feel about that. We've been together this long, whenever she says it's time to go, every last one of us will be loading up, no matter where it is she says we're going.

The way Sam and Glory whisper now, the move is bound to be pretty soon. But I'll hold out for spring.

I didn't think it was possible for Cindy to get any meaner. But with just one eye now, she's crankier than ever.

I had plans to try talking to the snakes while Sam slept. Ask them questions. Give them little yes-or-no cards to touch to answer and see what they understood. Might be a while before that can happen.

Barto made Sam a special belt where he could cinch Cindy up safe at night, but she raged so hard in it, she tore scales off. Maybe she was having her own nightmares. The next night, she broke right through it while Sam was asleep, but then she just curled up with Speck on Sam's belly, and didn't misbehave at all. Turns out, Speck calms her. Only time you can stand close and trust her not to try anything is if they've got their scales touching, and she knows she's not alone.

I can understand that. Especially with the things they've seen . . .

Gratitude

Claudia
Rebecca
Katherine
Sam
Glory
Heather Linn

Don't miss these books by
N. D. WILSON

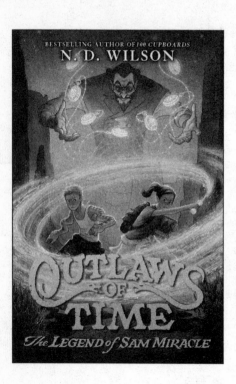

In this race against time, no one is safe